A Novel

HER
LYING
EYES

SUSAN MILLS WILSON

ISBN: 978-0-9911691-1-5

To my twin, Donna, who has been with me since Day One on this journey called Life.

CHAPTER ONE

"Let's do this."

U.S. Marshal Justin Mallard's order was all it took for his partners and four members of the Charlotte-Mecklenburg Police to get into position to execute their plan. It was simple really. They were looking for Lanelle Jones, a.k.a. Misty Knight, who was wanted for her participation in an armed robbery in Richmond, Virginia that resulted in the death of a Minute Market store clerk. They would try to catch her inside a strip-club called The Playground where she worked as a dancer.

From his office in Virginia, Mallard called Homicide Detective Chris Lagoni to ask for his help since Misty was now in the Charlotte area, Chris's domain. When the marshal mentioned the club, Chris said, "Sure, I know it. It's off Wilkinson Boulevard. I worked a case where a guy was gunned down in their parking lot. Rough area."

Around four that afternoon, Chris met Mallard two blocks from the strip club where Mallard's confidential informant said Misty worked. It had been a year since Chris had met Mallard at the Homeland Security conference where they shared classes, training exercises, and drinks at a nearby sports bar. Chris had forgotten that the deputy was built like a linebacker, but he was reminded when Mallard stepped out of a silver SUV with tinted windows. His black polo shirt was stretched tight over a broad chest and huge biceps. He greeted Chris with a firm handshake and a crooked smile on a face that reeked former military.

The plan called for Mallard and his partner to park their vehicle across the street from the club and watch the girls come in for their shifts, hoping to spot Misty. Chris and his partner would take the back side of the club. And to be thorough, Mallard stationed two marshals at the residence of her boyfriend's mother, where she was believed to be staying. If she wasn't at work, they hoped to find her there.

"Like we talked about, I'll send two of our guys inside as customers," Chris said to Mallard. "The employees know me, so I'm no good." He motioned for two detectives from his squad to come over. "Casey and Harris don't work this area, so no one should recognize them. Besides, they look like guys that might patronize a joint like this," he joked, looking at Harris in faded jeans and scuffed boots. "You guys good?" They nodded. "Great. Then just text me if you spot her, and the marshals will move in."

Mallard passed out copies of Misty's mug shot from a previous arrest. "Female suspect is white, five-six, a hundred and thirty pounds, age twenty-eight, distinguishing marks — a rose tattoo on her right thigh and a butterfly on her shoulder, left side. Last seen with long black hair with red streaks. Any questions?"

Police and marshals took their assigned positions. Chris watched Casey and Harris walk toward the entrance with smiles on their faces like they had just hit the lottery. Beer on the city's tab and an eyeful of girls wearing almost nothing was not a bad gig. Chris parked his unmarked sedan in the gravel lot around back facing an ugly door with peeling paint. His partner of five years, Nick Pulaski, who was once mistaken for actor Daniel Craig as James Bond and then ribbed about it by the whole squad, sat in the passenger seat. He tapped a ballpoint pen on his knee as if it was a drumstick keeping beat to rock music. No matter how many times Chris told him to cut it out, he still did it.

"Sorry. Can't help it, " Nick said. "I hate the waiting. We're wasting our time. Mallard didn't spot her going in."

"Won't be long. We should get something quick. Real quick. If our guys don't see her, they'll chat it up with one of the girls and find out where she is. Have you ever seen Harris with the ladies? Smooth operator, real smooth. Could teach us a thing or two." Just then, there was a sound like gurgling or rumbling.

"What was that?" Nick asked.

"My stomach's growling. I missed lunch." Chris reached behind him and pulled over a tote bag onto his lap. "Here," he handed his phone to Nick. "I've gotta eat something. Watch my phone for messages."

At the bottom of the bag, he found a pack of crackers, the cheesy kind with peanut butter in the middle. While he kept his eyes on the view outside the windshield, he used his teeth to open the cellophane package. Chris heard the beep of his phone, indicating an incoming text.

"She's not there," Nick said as he read the display. "One of the girls said she called in sick."

"Okay, lemme give Mallard a buzz." Chris took the phone back and called him. A chunk of cracker dangled from his lips as he waited for the agent to pick up. "Mallard, the guys just sent a text. She's not there. Called in sick. Whaddya want to do?" Chris listened as he chewed. After he swallowed, he said, "Okay, sounds like a plan."

Chris looked over at Nick. "They're going to move in at the mom's house. Mallard is going to join the team already there. They spotted movement inside the house, two cars parked out front. I guess I can tell our guys to finish their beers and come on out. You know they're going to take their sweet ol' time."

After he sent a text to Harris, he got a text back. He slammed his fist onto the steering wheel and yelled, "Shit!"

"What the hell, Lagoni?"

Chris pressed his lips together and shook his head. "They said my ex-girlfriend is in there!"

"Which one?"

"The troublemaker. Jamie."

"The newspaper reporter? What's she doing in there?"

"They said she's sitting at a table like she's waiting for someone to show up."

Nick frowned. "She shouldn't be in a place like this."

"No kidding. I'm going in."

He drove the car around to the front of the club. As he got out, he glanced up at the club's sign that featured a curvy woman in silhouette. Chris opened the back seat door and reached for his gray suit jacket from his "spring collection," as he often joked since his salary gave him few options to be fashionably in style. Although the weather and the establishment did not require a coat, he needed it to conceal his holstered gun.

Minus a window or sign, the heavy black door gave no hint of the activities on the other side. Until his eyes adjusted to the darkness inside the club, he stood with his back to a wall and looked around. He spotted his former girlfriend at a corner table. She sat with her legs crossed, looking like a sweet morsel for the tasting, a temptation for any man with a weakness for brunettes with luscious lips and doe-like eyes. Chris noted that Casey and Harris enjoyed the view staring at her over the rims of their beer mugs. When they looked his way, he jerked his chin to let them know they could skedaddle at any time. Their frowns told him they got the hint. He didn't want them around when he confronted her. And he sure as hell didn't want to be the target of any more bullshit trash talk back at the precinct. He'd already had his share of that a few years back, and all because of her.

Her mouth fell open when she looked up and saw him standing at her table.

"Jamie, what the hell are you doing here?" He sat down across from her.

"I could ask you the same question."

"I'm working a case. This is no place for you, girl. It's not safe."

"I'm fine." She shrugged and took a sip of wine.

"Answer my question. Why are you here?"

"I'm working too. I'm meeting someone, but it looks like he's a no-show."

"Who? Who are you meeting?"

"Just like old times," she said. "You asking me a lot of nosy questions."

"And I see you haven't changed one bit. Still flirting with danger. Who is it, Jamie?"

"Relax, Chris. He's not a criminal. He's a whistleblower." She shrugged again. "But I guess he got cold feet."

"Maybe he values his life. What are you mixed up in, Jamie?"

"I'm working on a story about corporate corruption. There's a lot of that going around. Seems to be catching. Wish they'd find a vaccine against it. Greed. They need to eradicate greed just like they're looking for a cure for cancer."

"Still trying to fix the world I see." Back when they were together, Chris got an ear-full of her opinionated rants. He'd tune her out, just let her blow off steam. "C'mon, Jamie, let me walk you out. Those assholes over there are watching you as much as the girls without clothes. Why did you pick this dump anyway? Couldn't you have gone somewhere else?"

"Not my first choice. My source picked it. He wanted to go somewhere no one would look for him. He thinks people are watching him."

"Are they?"

"Maybe."

"Well, if they're watching him, they're watching you too, Jamie. Whatever you're involved in, it's not worth it."

Her eyes went soft. Her smile turned deliciously sexy. *Damn her.* She used her best assets like a weapon against his anger. It made him relent with a smile of his own. "C'mon, Jamie, let's get out of here."

As they walked out, he placed his hand on the small of her back. It felt good to have her close again. He remembered the looks he got from his brothers in blue the first time he showed up with her at his side. It was at the chief's retirement party. The guys didn't come right out and say it, but he knew what they were thinking: *Damn, Lagoni! How did you win that trophy?* They seemed as captivated by her dazzling smile and luscious pouty lips as he was. And damned if her big brown eyes didn't make grown men go weak at the knees. Yeah, he was one lucky dude until the awful day he felt betrayed by her. Then it all went to hell.

The last time he saw her was when she brought over a box of his "stuff" from her apartment. She shoved it into his chest and turned on her heels, sashaying back to her car without so much as a goodbye. He didn't beg or grovel, just kept his eyes focused on her ass in tight jeans as she walked back to her car. But when she scratched off in her little Honda, he felt like his heart had been ripped in half.

"Where's your car, Jamie?"

She pointed. "Over there."

"A new one, huh? Nice. The Honda had a lot of miles." He started to say more, but paused. "Actually, darlin', you're going to need —" He walked around the vehicle, frowning at what he discovered. "You need new tires. Someone punctured all four."

"Oh, crap! I can't believe it! Damn!"

Chris studied the damage. The rims touched asphalt. "I'll call a wrecker. They'll take care of it." He led Jamie over to his sedan, where Nick looked on with curiosity. "Nick, you remember Jamie." Before he could respond, Chris said, "Looks like someone has messed with her car. Did you see anything?"

"Nope, I was watching the door, not the parking lot. Good to see you again, Jamie." Nick turned away from her to survey the damage. "Damn, that's messed up. People are into all kinds of meanness these days."

"I'm calling a wrecker," Chris said. "And I'm calling it in. Get a patrol car over here, see if they find anyone suspicious."

Jamie reached out so that her hand touched his coat sleeve. "Wait, Chris. I know who did it." With a raised brow and lips set tight, he waited for an explanation, and to his satisfaction, she seemed uncomfortable with his silent stare. Finally, she said,

"I think some guys are trying to send me a message. Telling me to back off the story."

"THEN, BACK OFF!" He stepped closer. "Jamie, let it go. Whatever the story is, it can't be worth it. Putting yourself at risk is fucking crazy!"

He caught the pout on her lips even though she bowed her head. "You're right. It's not worth it. I'll talk to my editor tomorrow."

"No you won't. You're just saying that. Damn, Jamie, you're just as stubborn as ever." He shook his head and walked over to Nick, out of Jamie's earshot. "Nick, can you get a ride back to the precinct with the unit on their way? I'm taking Jamie home. Gotta talk some sense into her. She's going to get herself killed."

"You sure this is just about her safety? I saw the way you looked at her. Reminded me of my dog slobbering over a new rawhide bone."

Chris cocked his head to one side and stared Nick down. "I just wanna have a talk with her, that's all. See ya later."

Nick pressed his lips together, but said nothing. *A good thing,* Chris thought, because he was getting pissed. He didn't need advice from anyone on how to handle his ex-girlfriend. He turned his back to Nick and called a wrecker service. When he ended the call, he walked over to Jamie to wait.

She said to him, "You don't have to do this."

"What should I do, Jamie? Leave you stranded here?"

Twenty minutes later, the wrecker hauled her car off on a flat bed. As Chris and Jamie drove off, an extended silence made for an awkward passing of time until Chris cleared his throat and looked over at Jamie. He said, "You know, I could show you what it looks like to have your body shot up or cut up. I don't want to be called to a scene one day and find you the victim of some crime. No chance to marry, have kids—, your life cut short."

She scoffed at his remark with a little chuckle. "You trying to scare the bejesus out of me or is this a marriage proposal?" After a pause, she added, "Okay, Chris, I'm sorry. I know you care. I'll be more careful. Promise."

"That's not good enough, Jamie."

"Okay, you're right. About this story — I'm going to drop it. Maybe someone else will do it, but it's too hot. Another project interests me more anyway. You happy?"

He didn't answer. She reached over and touched his arm. And that scared the bejesus out of him.

CHAPTER TWO

Jamison Jackson, also known to her readers as Jamie Jacks, investigative reporter for *The Charlotte Chronicle*, was a pain in the ass. In Chris's opinion, she always was and always would be. Yet, he had to admit he still had lingering feelings for her. Damn it.

He had met her at the precinct when she interviewed him for a story she'd worked on concerning the decline of homicides in Charlotte. For him, it was lust at first sight. She had made him chase her, pretended she wasn't interested. A flirt and tease, she had let him drool like a sick puppy for the entire week she had spent at police headquarters. Finally, she agreed to dinner. She met him at a restaurant downtown. Dinner, nothing more. He didn't even get a goodnight kiss. But two weeks later, she invited him over for dinner. He had *her* for dessert *and* stayed for breakfast.

From the strip joint to her apartment, Chris battled his inner demons that urged him to once again have carnal knowledge of the beauty in his passenger seat. For that reason only, he hesitated when she invited him inside. But in the end, he surrendered to a desire too strong to resist. As soon as he stepped inside, memories kicked in. Some good and some not so good.

They'd been together for two years. When they split, it was because he let his pride get in the way. Although she begged him to forgive her, he couldn't — a mistake he had always regretted.

"Want something to drink, Chris? I don't have much. Wine, orange juice, water, tea."

"Water's fine."

He followed her into the kitchen. While she reached up into the cabinet for a glass, he checked out her butt. It always puzzled him how she could walk around in five-inch heels, but damned if they didn't look nice with her long shapely legs. He noted that she let her hair grow longer, halfway down her back. Like her eyes, her thick locks were dark brown. He redirected his stare to the window when she turned around with his glass of water. She handed it to him and in the transfer, their fingers touched, sending a tingle to his most erotic zone. With embarrassment, he wondered if she'd noticed.

He leaned against the counter while he drank, avoiding her stare. She had him completely discombobulated, tongue-tied. He fumbled around for something to say.

"How's Snickers?"

Jamie tilted her head back and laughed. "We haven't seen each other in two years and you ask about my neighbor's cat?"

He managed a weak smile as he scratched his cheek. "I don't know what to say, Jamie, except that I've missed you. Think maybe we could start over?"

She folded her arms over her chest and took a position across from him, her back against the dishwasher. "You never forgave me. I don't think you ever will."

"That's where you're wrong. I do forgive you. Now that I've had time to reflect on it, I know that you didn't take advantage of our relationship for your story."

"You wouldn't even listen, wouldn't let me explain. You were never my source, Chris. Other cops had already told me about tensions between the prosecutor's office and the police. I had permission to quote them if necessary, just not to use their names. Your frustration was the same as theirs."

"But, sweetie —"

"No, let me finish. I thought someone should tell the story of how you guys risked your lives going after suspects and then the prosecutor would plead them out or drop charges. But I also gave the DA's side of the story. His office was understaffed, he couldn't hold on to good ADA's, and the court docket was always full. Took years to try a case. It was a good piece, fair to both sides."

"Yeah, right."

He was being sarcastic, but either she chose to ignore it or didn't catch it. She said, "It's regrettable that it made the atmosphere more toxic between the two departments and the police chief was upset with me. I was just doing my job, Chris."

"I understand, sweetie, but do you understand where *I* was coming from? I kept getting these looks at the precinct. Like *I* was the reason you ran with the story. Like I put you up to it. If only you had told me the story was going to run; I found out after it went to press."

"I didn't go looking for the story, Chris. It came to *me*. Someone on the force approached *me* and I thought, why not? The DA was up for re-election and I thought I was helping the police."

"I get it, Jamie. C'mon, let's put this behind us and move on." Chris set his glass down on the counter and reached out to take her hand in his. He pulled her close, wrapped his arms around her waist. "Can we start over?"

Her eyes locked with his. He liked that their close proximity meant her hands were on his arms. But his optimism waned with her next words. "We were never good together, Chris. We fought more than we made love. Remember?"

"I work crazy hours, Jamie. I can't do anything about that."

"The problem was you'd work the case even when you were off-duty. You know it's true, so don't give me that look. You thought I didn't notice, but I did. I mean, I could walk into the room naked with a blond wig and look like Lady Gaga and you wouldn't even notice. Your mind would be a million miles away, thinking you missed something."

He smiled. "Not true. Honey, if you walked into the room naked, you'd have my undivided attention. Lady Gaga?" He screwed up his face like he bit something sour.

"I'm just saying —"

Chris placed his finger under her chin and kissed her square on the mouth. It caught her off guard. She stepped backwards with wide eyes, pulling herself out of his reach. He knew he was blowing his chances with her, moving too fast, not taking a more calculated approach, but hell, he didn't have all day. He started to say something, but his cell phone interrupted with an incessant annoying, croaking sound like frogs. That damn Polaski has messed with his ringtone again. For the hell of it. He immediately started thinking of ways to get even.

Chris cursed under his breath and then said, "I gotta take this."

He walked away with the phone to his ear. After a few minutes, he came back and said to her, "I just picked up a case. Gotta go. We'll finish this conversation later, Jamie."

"It confirms what I was saying, Chris."

He kissed her forehead and dug in his pockets for his keys. "I know. Maybe we can work it out."

"By the way, I never answered your question."

His brows knitted with puzzlement. "What question?"

"You asked about Snickers," she said. "He died."

"Damn. I hate to hear that." His half-smile exposed his lie.

CHAPTER THREE

As soon as Garrett Reynolds returned from the bar with her second Cosmopolitan, Jamie planned to ask him the favor she had debated for days. It took the first two drinks just to build up her courage. And she hoped he was feeling enough of a buzz from his straight bourbon that he wouldn't laugh in her face or tell her she was out of her mind.

She watched him weave through the partygoers with a glass in each hand. To say he walked toward her was too mild of a word. He *glided* with his chin held high and his square shoulders back. Garrett Reynolds reminded Jamie of a character out of a F. Scott Fitzgerald novel. Wealthy, charming and devilishly handsome. He smiled at her in a way that seemed to transmit a secret message: *I can't wait to take you in my arms.* She wished that were true. It would make the favor she was about to ask of him so much easier.

"Your drink, Miss Jackson," he said as he handed it to her. He took a sip of his own drink and said, "So Jamie, what is it you wanted to ask me?"

"Wait until I finish my drink."

She looked around at the partygoers, all wealthy, the crème de la crème of Charlotte society. They gathered on the lawn of the magnificent estate to celebrate the fortieth wedding anniversary of Gar and Catherine Reynolds. Their only child and heir to the family fortune, Garrett, had invited Jamie to be his date. Although, they had known each other since childhood, Garrett and Jamie had let their busy lives keep them from seeing each other frequently. The last time she'd seen him was at Christmas, six months earlier. His recent phone call came out of the blue and surprised her. They'd never even dated, so she straight out asked him why he chose her out of all the women he could have asked out.

"For a number of reasons," he had said over the phone. "First, we haven't seen each other in ages and secondly, I'm not seeing anyone right now, and your name popped into my head."

That was two weeks ago. Time enough for her to find the right words to make her request sound less crazy, less bizarre than it was. He wouldn't see it coming, that much was certain. She studied him over the rim of her glass, trying to determine the best time to spring her desperate appeal.

"I'm glad you asked me to come," Jamie said. "I've missed you. Last time we talked, you were madly in love with some mystery woman. So what happened?"

He hesitated as though it brought up painful memories. Jamie took his silence to mean it was none of her business. Just as she started to apologize for asking, he said, "What can I say? She plucked my heart out, stomped on it, and left me devastated. Said there was someone else."

"You say that like you don't believe it."

"Because I don't. What we had was *real*. I mean, I can't imagine her seeing someone behind my back." His crystal blue eyes, full of mischief, squinted at her. He smiled and said, "You know her, Jamie."

"I do?"

"Yes, it's Erica. She was at some of my parents' parties. Dark hair, brown eyes, fabulous body, petite."

"Doesn't ring a bell."

"You know, Sophia's daughter."

Jamie's eyes widened. "Sophia? Your parents' housekeeper? I heard her father is in prison. You can't possibly mean *that* Erica."

"Yes."

"Damn! What did you do, Garrett? Sneak away from the rest of us to make out with the hired help in the broom closet?" His hard stare made her say, "I shouldn't have said that. Sorry."

"That's okay. It was nicer than my father's reaction."

"I imagine he had a coronary."

Garrett laughed. "Not exactly. When I brought Erica over for dinner, my father took one look at her and then turned to me and said, 'You can't be serious.'"

"Ouch. That had to hurt. What about your mother?"

"She was a little nicer. She didn't say anything, just looked to my father to do something, make me see the error in my judgment. Anyway, Erica handled it well. She is so strong, Jamie. Incredibly strong. Gutsy. Anyway, she told them she did not want to be with people who considered her inferior and made her feel unwelcomed. She asked me to take her home. I expected her to cry, but she didn't. My parents are snobs, Jamie, as if you didn't know. I was born into the wrong family. Stuff like that drives me crazy. I mean, in my opinion, there's only one race — the human race. We're all equal." He smiled and added, "You should have seen their expressions when she told them that with all their money, they should buy some manners."

Jamie laughed. "Oh, I would've loved to have seen that. It's crazy, none of us knew you had a thing for Erica."

"I didn't! Not then anyway. I admit I thought she was a knockout, but I kept my distance. I knew the rules: one does not fraternize with the help." He said it with a snooty tone that mocked his parents. "We only fell in love years later when Uncle Scott was sick in the hospital. Remember Scott Michaels? I called him my uncle, but he wasn't. He was just always around when I grew up. Chief Financial Officer for Reynolds Industries. My dad's go-to guy. Anyway, Erica was his nurse. I was shocked and delighted to see her again. During his illness, Erica and I got to spend a lot of time together and we started dating on the sly. Uncle Scott knew about it, but not my parents. He encouraged us to come out in the open, so when I did bring her over for dinner, it didn't go over so well, like I said."

The band came back from their break to play "I'll Take the Night," a song requested by the Reynolds. She took Garrett's hand in hers and led him over to the dance floor. "C'mon, let's dance just like old times. Remember that night we all ended up in the pool in our formal wear?"

He smiled. "Yeah, I remember. That was a crazy night. I got wasted, felt like crap the next day." As he drew her into his arms, he said, "When are you going to ask me for the favor, Jamie? Don't keep me in suspense. You know I'll say yes. Can't ever remember saying no to you."

She cast her eyes down and stared mindlessly at his silk tie. "Not yet. I'm not sure you'll say yes this time. Maybe I should get you drunk first."

"Tell me, Jamie."

"Guess who I ran into yesterday?"

"Ah, so you're changing the subject on me. Okay, I'll take the bait. Who?"

"My ex-boyfriend. Do you remember Chris Lagoni?"

"RoboCop?"

She grimaced to show her displeasure. "The gorgeous Italian guy."

"He looks like he's waiting to kick someone's butt. Scary dude."

"Be nice, Garrett. He's actually very sweet when he's not lecturing me, like he did yesterday. And I think he's sexy. Great in bed."

"Like me?"

"How should I know? You and I were never an item. We could have been, but you always had eyes for someone else."

He gave her a perplexed look. "What does that mean?"

"I was always a little in love with you."

"Jamie, c'mon. Don't tease."

"I'm serious. I told you once that I loved you, remember?"

"Yes, but you were drunk and besides, I was seeing your college roommate."

"I thought you only dated her to piss off your parents. Simone is black, not socially acceptable to the Reynolds dynasty."

"Do you really think I'm that shallow? I cared about Simone. And as for you, I always considered you like the sister I never had."

She dropped her arms to her side. As though the music had stopped, her feet stayed in place. Her body went rigid. "Let's sit down, please."

As she walked away, Garrett caught up to her and placed his hand on her arm. "Jamie, did I say something wrong?"

She found a seat at a patio table and sat down. Garrett pulled over a chair that scraped noisily across the brick pavers. Once he settled in, he put his hand on her knee. "Jamie, did I say the wrong thing?"

She refused to answer him. "Why don't you get me another drink?"

"Two's not enough?"

"One more, that's all. Okay?"

"Sure. Be right back."

On his walk from their table to the bar, he spoke to four women, kissed two on the cheek. Who was she kidding? Garrett would never have the same feelings for her as she had for him. She didn't care about his money, never had and never would. She liked his charm, his wit. They had oodles of things in common. Both liked sailing and tennis. They liked the same music, the same food, and the same social causes. Since teenagers, they thumbed their noses at the self-absorbed gluttony and greed of their parents. They wanted to save the world, save the planet. The fact that Garrett was drawn to Erica was no surprise. She was a nurse and like them, she was devoted to helping others. It all made sense to her now. The way she saw it, if he couldn't have Erica, then he could have the next best thing — her. Or maybe not. After all, he made the stupid comment about her being like a sister.

Jamie heard her name and looked up to see Garrett's father with a big smile.

"Mr. Reynolds, how good to see you," she said, recovering quickly from her thoughts.

His good looks and physical fitness belied his age, an unknown number somewhere between sixty and seventy. She liked to think of him as a clone of James Brolin and George Clooney, rolled up into one dashing, debonair man.

Garrett's father stepped around the corner of the table and planted a kiss on her cheek. "I'm delighted to see you, sweetheart. My, my, young lady, you're just as pretty as ever. I'm so glad Garrett brought you."

"Please, join me. Garrett went to get me a drink," she said. "I'm glad he invited me. Nice party, and by the way, happy anniversary."

"Thanks. Catherine and I wanted to celebrate with all our friends."

"I've seen so many people I haven't seen in years."

He sat down in the seat his son had vacated. "Well, it's the same crowd, just older and grayer. How are your parents?"

"They're fine. They love living in Virginia where they can see their grandchildren any time they want. Don't know if you've heard. My sister had another baby. A boy this time. He's four months old. Cute as he can be."

Gar smiled. "I can't wait until the day I have grandchildren to spoil. Of course, at the rate Garrett is going, that may be a very long time."

"He just has to find the right girl."

"Of course," he said. "I'm so glad he got over that little Mexican gal he was so fond of. It would have been a disaster. On the other hand," he said with a devilish glint in his eye, "you and Garrett make a handsome couple. You could make great babies together. With your good looks and his intellect, we'd have awesome heirs to carry on the Reynolds name. Catherine and I were just saying —"

He didn't get to finish. From behind him, Garrett cleared his throat to make his presence known. His father turned with a look of surprise. "There you are, son. I stole your date and your seat. Hope you don't mind."

"No, Dad. But I want her back." He set their drinks on the table. "C'mon, Jamie, let's dance."

Garrett pulled her out of her chair. Gar was left to sit alone at the table.

"Don't you think you were a little rude to your father?" she asked.

"No, I don't. He and my mother are plotting my future as we speak."

"What makes you say that?"

"I just had a little chat with Mommy Dearest. They are thrilled that you are here with me. I can almost hear my mother calling the club to reserve the grand hall for our wedding reception."

"That's crazy, Garrett. One date after not seeing each other in months? Besides, I'm like a *sister* to you."

He tried to draw her into his arms for a dance, but she kept hers at her side.

"About what I said — I didn't mean it, Jamie, I swear. I should have explained myself better. At one time, I felt like you were a substitute sister, but not anymore. You are a beautiful, sexy woman and I'm attracted to you."

"Is that the truth or are you just saying that to make me feel better?"

"I mean it," he said. "Are we going to dance or not?"

"Not," she said. "No longer in the mood. You know, your father said the same thing to me that your mother said to you. He said we would make great babies together. Did Mama Reynolds say that to you? No? Well, hold that thought. It might come up soon."

"Huh? I'm not following you."

Since Gar was no longer sitting down where they had left him, she walked back to the table and downed the remainder of her drink. When she turned, she found that Garrett had followed her over.

"Jamie, what were you saying?"

"Never mind," she said, and knew that Garrett was not satisfied with dismissing her random remark. She set the empty glass back on the table. "Hey, your father is a cad. He couldn't take his eyes off my breasts."

"They are magnificent."

"Garrett Andrew Reynolds! Don't be like other men. Like me for my intelligence, not my body. Please."

He chuckled. "I do like you for your smarts. The good looks are an added bonus." After he scanned their surroundings, he put his arm around her shoulders and led her away. "Okay, Jamie, tell me the favor you want from me. I'm tired of waiting. We'll sit down over here. Away from the others."

After they sat side by side on a wrought-iron bench in the flower garden, she twisted her body to face him. She took both his hands in hers. "Okay, Garrett. Here goes. Have you ever thought of being a sperm donor?" She paused to swallow hard. "Oh, hell, I'll just come right out and say it. I want you to be the father of my baby. Your dad was right about that — we would make great babies together."

Garrett's silence frightened her more than words ever could. It seemed like time froze solid, the music faded away, and the world went dark. Her bold question seemed to stay suspended in the air as she awaited some kind of response.

"Garrett, say something. Please. I'll die if you keep staring at me like that."

CHAPTER FOUR

Garrett's crystal blue eyes stayed on Jamie with the intensity of a laser beam. She waited for his response, but he remained silent. After he withdrew his hands from hers, he stood up and walked away, intentionally keeping his back to her. Agonizing minutes dragged by before he spun around to face her.

"Are you out of your mind?" were the first words out of his mouth, and then, "You want me to father a baby? What the hell, Jamie? What brought this on?"

She sprung up from the bench and walked over to him. Words already rehearsed spewed from her lips with a fierce resolve. "I'm thirty-six and not getting any younger. My sister told me that if I'm going to have kids, I'd better get busy while I still have the energy. I've seen her with her two and she's right. I've always wanted children, more than I want a high-pressure job with the paper. In fact, I'm thinking of going it alone, doing free lance work from home. Besides, I have no one in my life and it looks like I may never marry, but I want to have a baby, Garrett. Is that so crazy? I just want your sperm. Just go with me to a fertility clinic. They'll explain everything. It's no big deal, really."

"You'll marry, Jamie. *Then,* you can have a child. Thirty-six is nothing."

She shook her head. "The good guys are all taken — except you." *And although I'd marry you in a New York minute, you'd never ask me.* "Look, Garrett, I've never had a long term relationship. Well, okay, Chris, but that's it. I can't really explain why I've always found it hard to stay with someone." *Yes I can. No one touched my heart like you have.* "But I just feel like it's never going to happen for me. It's now or never, Garrett. A simple favor between friends."

"Simple? No it's not! We're talking about a human life here! It's one thing to be your friend, another to be the father of your child."

He looked down at a rose bush, one of dozens that his mother's gardener had planted. He cupped his hand under one pink bloom and yanked it up, severing the flower from its stem. As he closed his fist, the petals fell away to the ground. Jamie stayed silent, left him alone in his private thoughts.

Finally, she said, "So your answer is no?"

Garrett raised his chin, looked into her eyes. "I didn't say that. Why me? Why not Top Cop?"

"Lagoni? If I asked him, he'd get the wrong idea. He'd want to do the whole marriage thing, and I'm over him." She paused to take a deep breath and then continued, "I've known you practically by whole life, Garrett. And I know your family. The Reynolds bloodline is a sure thing. Good looks, intelligence, physically fit, long life. We'd make a beautiful baby," she said with a smile. "Look, I'm not asking you to have a relationship with the child. Just help me make a baby, that's all." His mischievous grin silenced her. She gave him a hard stare, then snapped, "It's not a joke, Garrett. I'm serious."

"I know you are. It's just that I didn't see this coming. I mean, when you said you wanted a favor, I imagined you asking for a loan, something like that. But this? You never cease to amaze me, Jamie."

"Don't think for one minute it has anything to do with money. I'm capable of supporting a child. You will have no legal obligation, no ties. Think like a friend helping a friend, Garrett. Don't think like a member of the Reynolds family conducting a business transaction."

"You confuse me with my father," he said tersely.

"Sorry. I didn't mean to offend you. Will you think about it?"

"Yeah. Just give me some time to let this sink in."

"Fine. Just don't take too long. Remember, my biological clock is ticking."

§

The next morning Jamie had regret *and* a throbbing headache. Once she and Garrett left the rose garden and headed back to the house, they split up, mingled with different people. When he finally drove her home, they said little to one another. Who was she kidding? Garrett thought she was nuts. He didn't say it, but she was sure he was thinking it.

If life was fair then Garrett would have the deep feelings for her that she'd always had for him, but instead he thought of her as a kid sister. Although he tried to back away from that analysis, she believed it. And she had been in love with him for — how long? Since she was eighteen. Hell, she could remember the moment it hit her. Their high school graduation party when they walked down to the lake and he caught her when she slipped and almost fell into the water. Their eyes locked. She kissed him. He kissed her back. When she wrapped her arms around his neck and pressed against him, he pulled back. She never forgot his words: "What are we doing? Trying to mess up our friendship?"

If there was a vaccine that would eradicate the outbreak of old memories, then she'd take it. She wanted to be immune to crazy feelings that stirred whenever Garrett was in her presence. Damn him. Damn the whole interlude of courtship that was supposed to lead to marriage, then children. Sometimes romance was out of kilter. Lopsided. One-sided. Screw that.

As if the morning could not get any worse, she spilled coffee on her skirt as she headed out the door on her way to work. She had to go back inside to change. As she drove in rush hour traffic, she got a phone call that stopped her cold. It was her anonymous source, the no-show at the strip joint where she was escorted out by Chris.

"Steve, what happened? I waited an hour."

"I was followed, so I just kept driving. Didn't stop. I can't do this. I just want to go on with my life. Forget about all of it."

Jamie pressed her lips together and stared out the side window at the traffic now at a standstill.

"So you're going to let the bastards get away with it?"

"I'm not going to put myself or my family at risk. You'll have to find another way."

"Steve, listen to me. Without you, there *is* no story. You worked for the company for fifteen years, and I need your file, your documents. I need direct quotes. You told me that their chemicals contaminated the lake, the ground, the drinking water. Forced the camp for underprivileged children to close down. The company bigwigs did all they could to cover their asses. Falsified the water and soil testing. Changed reports. Paid off the inspectors. Some bad stuff, Steve. They need to be held accountable. Don't you agree?"

"Please leave me alone, Miss Jackson. I won't take any more of your calls. I just want to live in peace. I gotta go now. Sorry I couldn't help you."

"Steve, listen to me —"

The phone clicked. Silence.

"Damn it!"

She hit the steering wheel with her hand and broke a nail.

"What next?" she yelled.

§

The curse of being born the only child of Gar and Catherine Reynolds was living up to their expectations. For Garrett, it felt like an albatross around his neck. He waited on the terrace for his father to finish a call with a business associate.

What was it this time, Garrett wondered. Why had the old man summoned him to the family estate? What was so damn important that he couldn't have approached him at work? Hell, his office was only two doors down from his father's executive suite.

He stared out at the rose garden and reflected on being there with Jamie. Her outrageous request had blindsided him. He didn't know what he would tell her, but he did owe her some kind of response. And knowing her, if he didn't act soon, she'd call him and demand an answer. If he knew one thing about Jamie, she was persistent.

Do I or do I not honor her request? he debated. If he said no, would she be angry? Would she ask someone else she knew to be the sperm donor? Or would she go with a total stranger? Maybe she would change her mind and do the sensible thing: wait for the right guy to marry, and *then* have a baby. His thoughts came to an abrupt halt when his father ended his call and made his way over to him, his tall physique silhouetted against the sky painted in majestic hues of peach and rose from the setting sun.

"Sorry about that, son." Gar Reynolds picked up a brandy from a tray that the butler had set out on a table. "That was Mitchell calling about his meeting tomorrow at the Pentagon. The military brass is calling for more concessions. Boeing is going to hang tough, and so are we. I'll have another go-round with the senator if I have to, but we'll get this deal done, I assure you."

"Sure, Dad," Garrett said. "Now what did you want to discuss with me?"

Gar's smile showed creases on a very tanned face. He combed his hand through his thick crop of white hair and then took a sip of brandy.

"Your mother and I were thrilled that you were with Jamie at our party," he began. "She's from a great family line, but I don't need to tell you that. Her father, a retired colonel in the Air Force, and a Greek beauty for a mother, a distant cousin of Maria Callas. And Jamie's just as beautiful."

"What are you getting at, Dad?"

Gar delayed his reply while the butler walked toward them, holding open a wooden humidor. "Your cigars, sir," he said.

"Thanks, Spencer." Gar withdrew one and looked to Garrett. "Go ahead, son. Have one. They're the best. Flown in from Cuba via Canada." He shot Garrett a knowing wink.

Garrett took one even though he didn't want it — his father would have insisted. Using an engraved lighter passed down from his father, Gar lit his son's cigar. After he exhaled a cloud of smoke, Garrett said, "Back to Jamie. What's your point?"

Gar smiled at his son's question. "Your mother and I are hoping that this blossoms into a full blown romance. She's perfect for you. I'm surprised that you haven't snatched her up already. But of course, you had your little distraction."

"Are you talking about Erica? She was more than a distraction, Dad. I loved her."

"Did I ever tell you about that hot little gal down in Panama that I had a thing for? Man, I couldn't even think straight. I was head over heels in lust. But I came to my senses and I'm glad I did. I met your mother after that."

If Garrett could will his hard stare to be lethal, his father would have keeled over. Finally Garrett said, "Maybe I'd better go. Can't stand listening to you berate the love of my life like she's trash."

After he crushed the cigar in an ashtray, Garrett set his shot glass on the table with a bang. He turned to leave, but stopped when he heard his father call out to him.

"You are going to want to hear what I have to say, son, so come back. It concerns your future."

With reluctance, Garrett walked over to his father. With hands on hips, he shifted from one foot to the other. "Go ahead, I'm listening."

"Sit down." Gar barked the words like a drill sergeant, his brows knitted with annoyance. Gar pulled out a chair from the table, picked it up a few inches off the terrace stones, and pounded it back down, making as much noise as possible. Garrett plopped down in it and crossed his arms over his chest, his long legs stretched out in front.

"That's better," Gar said as he took a seat, facing his son. "It's time that you stopped chasing tail and settled down, son.

You're thirty-eight. Should have been married long before now. If you were to marry someone wonderful — socially equal to you, like Jamie — then I'd retire and let you have full control of the company."

Garrett sat up straight. "You'll step down? Transfer ownership?"

"Yes, that's what I said. It's what you've been waiting for, right? You will own the majority of shares. With my urging, the board will vote you in as my successor. I made this decision even before you were born, Garrett. It's been the plan all along. My father started Reynolds Industries before the second World War, and I envisioned the company staying in the family's hands for many generations to come. Hell, I'm sixty-nine and not getting any younger. I want to be fully retired by the time I'm seventy. So make it happen."

"What do you mean by that? Are you saying that you'll be there until I marry?"

"*And* give me an heir. The fourth generation to run the family business."

"That's crazy."

"Maybe to you, but not to me. We must keep our legacy strong. I owe it to my father. The Reynolds family has always been a moving force in this community. Our name means something around here." Gar tilted his chin up to blow smoke into the air. He looked out at a sky no longer pink as darkness set in. "I'm running out of patience, son. I expect you to do the right thing."

Oh, you're so romantic, Dad. "You make marriage sound like a business proposition."

"Historically it has been in our family," Gar said as if reflecting on his own marriage. Garrett knew it to be a merger of two powerful families.

"Let me see if I've got this straight. You won't step down until I marry and give you a grandchild. Is that the gist of it?"

"Precisely. If you can't grasp that, I can have the lawyers put it in writing, make it official. I know you want to make changes and you feel I'm holding you back. Maybe you thought I wasn't paying attention, but I was. You can have your damn upgraded programming with 3-D imaging, and all the other technological crap your heart desires. Like you said, I'm a dinosaur. I used to make deals on a handshake. Now we have to have a slew of lawyers to put it all down in writing."

"Dad—"

Gar cut him off by adding, "I expect you to give this serious consideration. Don't wait too long. If you do, well hell, I just might sell the whole damn business to Landon Aeronautics. They've made a decent offer. One worth considering."

"You wouldn't do that."

"Oh, no? Don't bet against it, son."

CHAPTER FIVE

No new case, paperwork caught up and email correspondence completed. Chris grabbed his cell phone and keys and headed for the elevator. His partner, Nick, beat him to the nearest exit by five minutes. Now if he could just get past the sergeant's glassed-in office without being sighted, he too could be on his way out.

Too late. Sergeant Sam Holden, leader of Chris's squad in the homicide unit, stuck his head out his door and called him over. His barrel chest pressed against the doorjamb as he stood half in and half out of his proprietary domain. He rubbed the top of his bald head and snorted.

"Lasagna, got something. Come in."

Holden had nicknames for all the guys in his squad, mostly related to food. The sergeant's expanding waistline explained his obsession with good eats and his renaming of the detectives. As a recent transplant from the north, the guys introduced him to the Southern cuisine that he blamed for his ten-pound weight gain.

Chris cringed at the sound of his boss's Jersey accent that never failed to get his attention. He walked into the office and plopped down in a chair facing the sergeant's desk. Holden's dark eyes stayed on him a few seconds before he said, "Where's your sidekick, — Kielbasa?"

"Polaski already left."

Holden shrugged. "Well, I just got a call from the DA's office. After two days in jail, our girl, Cassandra, is ready to talk. I knew she'd come around. Just had to get her head straight and realize protecting 'her man' wasn't worth spending extra time in prison."

"We've already got video of her in the parking lot in the getaway car while her boyfriend was inside the pharmacy.

What's she going to add?"

"The video is grainy and it doesn't show the license plate number. Of course, she doesn't know all that. Her lawyer called and wants to work a deal. Wants to plea to a lesser charge. She can lead us to the weapon. DA wants that bad, real bad. She was driving when her Casanova told her to pull over so he could dump it in an open field of weeds. She can lead us right to the spot — hopefully the gun's still there. Maybe we can lift prints, but if not, it'll still match up to the bullet recovered from the victim's body.

"Here's the thing, Lasagna. She'll only talk with you. They're bringing her from jail as we speak."

"I was on my way out, sir."

"Whaddya want me to do? Put her in a holding cell until you can get around to interviewing her? We gotta strike now before she changes her mind."

Chris nodded. "Right, right. Okay. Is her lawyer on his way?"

"You'd better believe it. And the ADA will be watching on the monitor, so mind your Ps and Qs, detective."

He slapped Chris on the back and walked him down the corridor. Chris resigned himself to putting in a few more hours. With luck, Cassandra would spill her guts and he could be on his way. They'd send a patrol unit to retrieve the weapon, and he could then go straight to Jamie's apartment to finish the conversation they started three days ago. He hoped she'd be glad to see him, flash her big smile and invite him inside. Over a glass of wine, he could explain to her how he had changed. He could go off duty and put whatever case he was working on out of his mind, just chill and give her his full attention. No problem. She just needed to give him a chance to prove it.

Chris ran his hand over his face and exhaled a deep breath. He muttered to the empty interview room, "Come on, Cassandra. Don't keep me waiting. I've got to see another woman, one with more class than you, sweetheart."

§

Jamie almost collided head-on with Chris on her way out the door. Her car keys jabbed his arm as her breasts pressed into his chest. He made a reflexive move to brace her with his hands on her arms.

"Whoa, girl. Where's the fire?"

"Chris! I was on my way out. I'm late."

He let his eyes take in a long drink of lust as if to quench his thirst from an unusually long dry spell. When was the last time he'd been out with a woman? Certainly no one that excited him the way Jamie did. Her tight red dress dipped low to show the swells of her breasts and definitely advertised amorous intentions, but with whom? His hands rested a long time on her soft skin until she backed away. He was forced to drop his arms to his sides like a dope. He had made her uncomfortable. He sensed it when she cast her eyes down and pushed back a strand of hair from her cheek.

"This isn't a good time, Chris. I have a date."

Another once-over, and then he said, "I can see that. I just happened to be in the neighborhood and thought we could finish our discussion."

"There's nothing more to discuss. I've moved on. I suggest you do the same."

"Here's the thing, Jamie. I'm stuck. Can't go forward."

"Find a way."

He stepped closer, again put his hands on her arms to rub her soft dewy skin. "I've changed. Give me another chance, Jamie. Give *us* another chance. Please."

"I can't, Chris. Sure everything would be fine at first, but then, we'd be at each other's throats."

"Sweetie, if only—"

She cut him off. "It's the job, Chris. I can't handle it. The interruptions, the long hours. Okay, I'm selfish. I didn't want to share you with the police department. We'd have plans and then you'd get a call. I — I, well, I never liked it. And every time you left, I worried that something terrible would happen to you."

"Baby, I'm careful. You know I am. It's *you* that take risks. Like the other day."

"And here we go again. See what I mean, Chris?" She hugged her purse to her chest and licked her lips. "I really have to go. You know that in my heart, there will always be a special place for you." She went up on tiptoes to kiss his cheek. It left a lipstick print that she wiped off with her thumb.

"Whoever you're going to see is damn lucky," he said. "The dude better treat you right or he'll have to answer to me."

She laughed. "Maybe he was right about you," she said softly.

"What does that mean?"

"Oh, nothing. I was just thinking about what he said about you."

Chris's brows knitted. "Is this someone I know?"

"Yes. Garrett Reynolds."

"Thought you two were just friends."

"We are. Friends having dinner."

"But you said you had a date."

"A little white lie."

"Then why are you dressed like that?"

"What do you mean?"

"That dress says you want to take your friendship to the next level."

"Are you jealous?"

"No, I'm not jealous." After a pause, he added, "So you don't deny that what I said is true?"

She stared down at her strappy heels and refused to answer him.

"Sweetie, I don't think you realize the message you're sending. That dress says 'Go ahead and fuck me.'"

She put her hand on her hip and glared at him. "How dare you! You'd better leave now, Chris, before I throw the f-bomb back at you."

Chris blinked away the threat, his lips pressed tight. He turned to leave and cursed to himself all the way to his car.

CHAPTER SIX

Garrett lived in a downtown condo built and designed for the affluent. Business executives with stock options and obscenely lucrative bonuses. Professional athletes like those with the Carolina Panthers or Charlotte NBA team, or maybe even its owner, Michael Jordan. And of course, retirees rich enough to buy the high-rise or the entire block. As Jamie entered the lobby, she admired the plush surroundings. Soft leather settees the color of cream. Mahogany-paneled walls with original oil paintings. A scattering of imported hand-tied area rugs on a custom tile floor.

She asked the concierge to call Garrett and announce her arrival. After she was escorted to the private elevator for residents and guests, she took it up to the tenth floor. Garrett greeted her at his door. The aroma of spices hit her nose as she hugged him.

"Something smells good," she said.

"I hope you like it. Pasta with Italian sausages, my special homemade pesto, a little garlic, some basil. Marlena's recipe."

"Ah, yes, Marlena. Your family's cook. I think your mom was jealous that you spent more time back in the kitchen with Marlena than you did with her."

"She kept me entertained."

"I remember. Do you think the stories of her childhood were true? Especially the one about the ghost visiting her bedroom. When she told us that one, I slept with a light on for weeks."

Garrett laughed as though he remembered it with fondness. He put his arm around Jamie's shoulders and led her inside. He looked down at her and said, "I'll get a glass of wine for you. Why don't you enjoy it on the balcony and I'll join you in a minute. Got to check on the food first."

"Need any help?"

"Nah. Stay out of the kitchen, Jamie. I'm afraid you'll

distract me and I'll burn the whole dinner. Damn, that dress is something else. You look stunning."

"Thanks." She regarded Garrett's casual attire: khaki shorts, navy polo shirt and boat shoes. "I think I'm overdressed."

"And I'm glad you are. You look sexy as hell, girl." He gave her a wink and sent her to the balcony with a glass of Cabernet Sauvignon.

After dinner, she let Garrett pour her a third glass of wine. She reflected on the efforts he had taken to impress her. He had served dinner on the table on the balcony, using a linen tablecloth and his set of hand-painted ceramic plates that she guessed had never been taken down from their shelf until now. She stared at the flicker of the candle flame that put her in a trance-like state. She had the sudden sensation as if she could dance on clouds. She figured it was the buzz she felt from too much wine.

"Oops, my sandal just came off," she said with light laughter.

Garrett ducked under the tablecloth to scoop up the shoe. Letting it dangle by the back strap, he came around and knelt at Jamie's side. Like the handsome prince in Cinderella, he slipped it on her foot. For what seemed like minutes, he stayed on his knee, stroking her calf. His smile hinted at salacious thoughts.

"While you're down there, you can propose marriage," she said with a chuckle. *Dreams might come true for Cinderella, but I'm not living a damn fairy tale.*

He rolled his eyes and smiled. As he stood up, he reached for her hand. "Let's go inside and listen to music."

"I'll help with the dishes," she said.

"Leave them. I'll get it later."

Garrett pulled her up and led her to the doorway. Inside, he walked over to the custom-built entertainment center and punched a button on his audio system. As though he had made his selection in advance, based on her taste, Bryan Adams crooned a love song, "Please Forgive Me," on surround-sound speakers. She mouthed the lyrics: *Please forgive me, I can't stop loving you.* She reflected on how the song expressed her feelings for him.

"May I have this dance?"

He gathered her in his arms and held her close. His chin pressed against the side of her head and she caught the subtle hint of his aftershave, a light scent of sandalwood. Clasping her right hand, he pulled it in close so that it was against his chest. His thumb stroked her fingers softly. She closed her eyes and imagined her fantasy dream come true: Garrett had the same feelings for her that she had for him. *If only.*

As though conflicted and confused about what he should do next, Garrett kept her in his arms, mindlessly taking the lead in one slow dance after another until Jamie pulled away. She looked up to find that his eyes were closed, his lips set tight.

"Can we sit down now, Garrett?"

He nodded and led the way over to his sectional leather sofa. She playfully pushed him down and then plopped down at his side laughing, her bare leg rubbing against his. His laughter stopped the minute he turned to face her. He pressed his lips lightly over hers and then used his fingers to brush back a strand of hair that had fallen onto her cheek. She was taken aback, but also pleased.

In a voice more sobering than his actions, he said, "You've tormented me all night, Jamie. That dress. That provocative smile. You just being you."

And you have tormented me since I was eighteen. "Are you going to do anything about it, Garrett Reynolds?"

"I want you."

She tempered her delight by biting down on her lower lip. "I've waited a long time to hear you say that."

He paused as though she had spoken a language he did not understand, but then comprehension translated into a slow smile. "So you and I are on the same page. If I did this," he said as he unzipped her dress, "you wouldn't mind. And if I did this," he said as he pulled it off her shoulders, "you wouldn't stop me from taking the whole thing off, would you?"

"No," she whispered, her breathing heavier.

As he tugged it down, she stood up and let it drop to the floor. While she stood before him in a black lace demi-bra and bikini panties, he gave her a once-over and judging by his smile, he seemed pleased by the view. He pressed his lips to her midsection and then rubbed his hand over her abdomen.

"And I would not get a protest from you if I got this other stuff outta the way?" He reached behind her and unhooked her bra, then took one breasts in his mouth. She fell forward over him as he leaned far back on the sofa. "Oh, Jamie," he moaned, kissing and sucking both breasts.

His hand found its way inside her panties and he managed to pull them down her thighs. They fell around her ankles and she kicked them aside.

For a time, she allowed him to grope her, rub his hands over her body, and trail kisses everywhere, but then she pulled away. Without saying a word, she got up and tugged on his arm until he also stood up. With a jerk of her head, she indicated his bedroom, and to her delight, he took the hint, lifting her up into his arms.

As he carried her down the short hallway, he said, "This is the correct way to make a baby, Jamie. No damn clinical method."

After their lovemaking, they lay on their backs in a room that had become dark and silent in the hours past sunset. Jamie hoped his semen found a fertile egg to begin the makings of a Reynolds-Jackson baby. She turned her head to the side to study Garrett. With his eyes closed and his hands folded over his chest, he was as still as the uncirculated air in the room.

"That was something," she said softly.

He opened his eyes and said, "What was?"

"The sex, silly. It was better than I imagined."

"You've thought about it? I mean — *us* having sex?"

Jamie covered her face with both hands. "Did I say that out loud?" She giggled, then added, "I hope this doesn't ruin our friendship."

Again, Garrett closed his eyes. "Of course not."

"Garrett, why are you so quiet? What are you thinking?"

The question went unanswered until he finally opened his eyes and turned to face her. "I'm not thinking anything. Well, maybe what you said — that the sex was great."

"Why did you keep your eyes closed the whole time? You never looked at me."

"I didn't realize that. Sorry if that bothered you."

"No, that's okay." She laughed and drew the sheet up over her breasts. "I'm sorry about the miscommunication."

His laughter indicated he understood her comment. "When you first started moaning, I thought you had already climaxed. And I thought, wow! That didn't take long."

After a giggle, she said, "The sheet got twisted around my foot and it hurt!" She moved closer so that she felt the warmth of his body. Her hand stroked his bare chest. "This takes us past friendship, wouldn't you say?"

He raised his head enough to kiss her forehead. "Yep, you could say that."

§

Jamie did not know when Garrett came back to bed to sleep. He insisted she stay put while he went into the kitchen to clean up from their dinner. She went to sleep without him and again, found his side of the bed vacant when she awoke in the morning.

She put on one of his dress shirts and followed the scent of fresh brewed coffee into the kitchen. In boxers and a T-shirt, he stood at the stove frying strips of bacon. She wrapped her arms around him to kiss his back. He placed his hand over hers and turned his head to one side to plant a kiss on her head.

"Hope you're hungry, Jamie."

"Hmm, it smells wonderful." She found that he had set out a cup for her next to the coffeemaker. As she filled it, she said, "Got any cream?"

"Sure. In the fridge."

It amused her that Garrett had a humongous stainless steel, double-door refrigerator often found in commercial kitchens, but it made sense. Anything smaller would have looked silly in the massive kitchen. The focal point of the room was the granite-top island with cabinets made of hand-crafted dark wood and carved designs on each corner posts.

The few items inside the fridge looked lonely. She found a small carton of half-and-half creamer next to a six-pack of beer. Leftovers of their meal were covered in plastic wrap. She closed the door with a bump of her hip. While she stirred her coffee, she caught Garrett flipping an egg over with a shake of the frying pan, a feat she had never mastered.

They ate in the breakfast area where a window lent a pleasant view of downtown Charlotte. The sight of people walking briskly below reminded her that it was a workday and she should be on her way to her office instead of enjoying a leisurely breakfast with Garrett.

"I'm keeping you from work, Garrett."

"It's okay. I've already called in and told them I'll be late. Nothing pressing today."

"Jeez, I don't know what I'll tell Stu," she said. "My boss has mood swings. One day he might be totally fine with it and the next day blow a gasket. Hope this is one of his good days. Guess it's time to find out." She retrieved her phone from her purse and called Stuart Blackmon's direct number.

At first, he sounded irritated, but then mellowed. "Okay, JJ," he said in his gruff voice. "When you do get here, come see me first thing. We need to talk."

She smiled every time he called her by her initials. To her it was a form of endearment. After all, he was like a father to her, always giving her unsolicited advice that she warmly received but didn't always take.

As she enjoyed a second cup of coffee, Jamie noted that Garrett had grown pensive, staring out the window, maybe to avoid any eye contact. She cleared her throat. "Garrett, are you having buyer's remorse?"

He turned to lock eyes with hers. "What?"

"About last night. About what we did."

"No. Hell no. How can you ask me that, Jamie?"

"You're so quiet. I just thought maybe—"

"Don't you feel just a little awkward? I mean, we were friends — well, still friends, but now — at least for one night — lovers."

"One night?" Jamie's antenna went up. Her heart dropped.

"Oh, shit, I didn't mean it that way. Jamie, our relationship is different now. Don't you see? We can't go back."

"I was hoping we could go forward."

"Me, too."

"Then what's got you so scared?"

"Scared? Hell, I'm not scared. Except that I have feelings for you, different than before."

"That's a good thing." She smiled and took a sip of coffee.

"Marry me."

Jolted by his words, she sprayed her sip of coffee onto the table like projectile vomit. She pressed a napkin to her lips. "What?" Her voice went up two octaves. "Are you out of your freaking mind?"

She grabbed another napkin to mop up the mess she'd made.

"I'm serious," he said. "I care for you more than I realized. Maybe I've cared all along, Jamie, but because you were parent-approved, I denied it. You once accused me of only wanting forbidden love. Remember? In college, it was Simone, and more recently Erica. It was gratifying to piss off my parents, but I'm more mature now. Rebellion has lost its thrill. Look we have the same goal. I absolutely want you to be the mother of my baby, and as you've said, you want me to father your child. It's a win-win, don't you see?"

"That's all very nice, Garrett, but you didn't say the one thing I needed to hear."

"What? That I love you? Is that what you're waiting for?" He reached for her hand and brought it up to his lips for a kiss. "Of course, I love you."

CHAPTER SEVEN

Because Jamie had to go home to shower and change out of her sexy dress, she didn't get to the office until after eleven. She went straight into Stuart Blackmon's office. As editor of the news department, he juggled work demands like he had caffeine intravenously infused into his bloodstream. He jumped up out of his chair and rushed over to her side. With his arm around her, he ushered her over to a seat across from his desk.

"Okay, okay, 'kay, gimme the scoop. Whaddya mean goin' to that stink hole by yourself, young lady? Cudda got hurt. Y'know damn well I wouldn't have allowed it. We're shelvin' the story. Not worth it. I know they're doing some bad stuff. It's hurting kids. But most people don't give a crap if it's not in their backyard, not their kids. Sad fact, but that's the way it is. You sneaked off to meet your whistleblower without checking with me first. Didn't check 'cause you know I wudda stopped ya. Zeke told me all about it 'cause he can't keep a secret. Damn glad he can't. Heard about your car, the tire thing. That's bad, Jamie, real bad. What am I 'pose to do? Okay an expense for new tires? Can't and won't. Talk to your insurance company, darlin'. Don't care why you're late 'cept that you have this silly grin on your face while I'm trying to talk some sense into you. What gives, JJ?"

"Can I take two weeks' vacation back to back?"

"Whaddya talkin' 'bout? Hell, you don't take the vacation you're entitled to and now you want two full weeks together, like bam, bam? What the hell, JJ?"

"I need one week to get ready for my wedding and one week for a honeymoon."

She wished that Zeke Parker, the paper's photographer, was there to take Stu's picture. He put his hands on his protruding belly like an overdue pregnant woman whose water just broke. With bugged-out eyes, he stared at her, too dumbfounded to speak. He mumbled, stuttered and shot out spittle until he finally got the words out. "Married? You gettin' married? I didn't even know you were datin'! Do I know the guy? Better not be anyone around here, JJ. Y'know I hate office romance. Please don't say it's Zeke. No, couldn't be. That would be a downgrade. Well, don't just sit there. Who is the son of a bitch?"

"Garrett Reynolds."

"*The* Garrett Reynolds of the Reynolds family? Reynolds Industries that make the freaking aircraft parts for the military, that have government contracts out the wazoo, that have buildings named for them, that donated the money for the new hospital wing, that own that big-ass mansion on Lake Norman? *That* Garrett Reynolds?"

"Yes, Stu, *that* Garrett Reynolds."

"Holy shit! This calls for a drink even if it *is* still morning."

§

Nick and Chris drove out of the parking garage at police headquarters to work a case that had gone cold until a new witness stepped forward. She refused to come to them but agreed to meet at her mother's home in the projects. The further west they drove, the more run down the neighborhoods became: row after row of deteriorating brick apartment buildings with whitish corrosion stains running down from window A/C units and peeling paint on wooden trim. They had worked two cases in the area recently, both the result of a drug deal gone bad. The view out the car window would have put Chris in a bad mood if he wasn't already in a bad mood, and Nick wasn't helping any with his unsolicited advice.

From the passenger seat, Chris said, "So Pulaski, let me get this straight. You say I owe Jamie an apology, is that right? I said what I said because — because — Hell, I don't know why I said what I said."

"Because you're an asshole, that's why. At least, you are around her. Don't you get it? You insulted her, Chris. You treat her like she doesn't have good judgment, like she's naive and stupid and she'll let men take advantage of her. That's not Jamie, and she's not yours to boss around."

"So I should call her? Tell her I didn't mean it, even though I really did? I've seen how guys look at her. You shudda seen the way she was dressed, Nick. To be honest, *I* wanted her right then and there." Nick's silence and hard stare said more to Chris than words ever could. He conceded with a shrug. "Okay. When we park, give me five and I'll call her."

Nick pulled in at the edge of the parking lot, under the shade of an oak tree, and got out. Chris appreciated that he walked away to give him some privacy. Still in the passenger seat, he pulled out his cell phone and found Jamie's number, pressed the call button, and put the phone to his ear. She answered on the second ring.

"Hi, Jamie." He heard laughter in the background and paused. "Is this a good time to talk? I can call back."

"No, this is fine. We're just having a little celebratory drink, that's all."

"Oh," he said with no interest in finding out what she and whoever were celebrating. "Look, I just wanted to call and apologize for what I said last night. I was a total jerk and I'm sorry. I shouldn't have said those things to you."

"It's okay, Chris. I'm not mad. Right now, I'm very, very happy."

"Oh, really." He heard what sounded like her boss's boisterous voice. He remembered Blackmon as a guy who ran his mouth whether anyone was listening or not. "Jamie, what's going on? Kind of early for a party, isn't it?"

"Chris, you'll never believe this. I'm getting married!"

Chris dropped the phone. It fell onto his lap. When he picked it up, he accidentally pressed something that made the phone beep twice. He heard a faint *hello, hello,* and again Blackmon's voice in the background, followed by more laughter.

"Chris? Are you still there?"

"Yeah, I'm here. I dropped my phone, that's all."

"Did you hear me? I'm getting married!"

"Huh, well, I gotta go. Nick and I have to question a witness."

After he ended the call, he stared hard at the cell phone like it had betrayed him. He was dazed and in a state of shock when Nick finally waltzed over.

"Chris? You okay? How did it go?"

"How did it go? She said that she's fucking getting married! That's how it went!"

"Wow! No shit? What did you say when she told you?"

"I told her I had to go."

"You didn't congratulate her?"

"No. Why should I?"

"So you pretty much just hung up on her?"

Chris had a sour look when he nodded and said, "Guess now I should call back and tell her I'm sorry I hung up like that and forgot to say congrats."

"Then you'll say more stupid shit and you'll have to call back and apologize for *that,* and this could go on and on. Let's just go find our witness. I'll buy you a drink after work. That should cheer you up."

"No, I wanna go to the firing range. I think I can improve my score today. Feel like shooting something. *That* should cheer me up."

§

With Jamie at his side, Garrett rang the doorbell to his parents's home. Although he grew up in the eight-thousand-square-foot English Tudor on the shores of Lake Norman, he didn't feel right just walking in. Formality and manners drilled into him since childhood dictated that he wait for the housekeeper or one of his parents to greet them.

"Are you sure I look okay?" Jamie asked.

Garrett surveyed her pastel pink sundress with a light cotton sweater and smiled his approval. "You look fine. Relax. Believe me, when I tell them our news, it's going to put a big smile on their faces. We'll tell them first thing. They'll want to start with cocktails on the terrace, so I'll bring it up then. We'll discuss details over dinner. Sound like a plan?"

Jamie nodded. "This is happening so fast."

"It is what you want, isn't it?"

"Of course. It's what you want too, right?"

"You know it is, Jamie." He heard movement on the other side of the door. "Ah, here they come."

It was Catherine Reynolds who came to the door, offering a cordial smile. Her Charleston-born-and-bred upbringing made her soft voice come out as sweet and thick as molasses on a buttermilk biscuit. "Why, hey there. Y'all come on in. My, my, Jamie don't you look sweet. So glad Garrett extended our invitation to you. Y'all head on back to the terrace and we'll have cocktails before dinner. Isn't this a fine evening? My kind of weather, not too humid and just an occasional breeze to cool the air."

Her beauty defied her sixty-six years although there were subtle hints of aging; her golden hair had now paled to platinum blond and in the corners of her green eyes were new creases. Garrett thought of his mother as a delicate flower, pampered and spoiled. She always gave the impression of a woman who just walked out of a salon, face and hair fussed over with meticulous detail.

She kissed him and rubbed her pink lipstick print from his cheek. Jamie got an air-kiss on both cheeks as Catherine gave her a hug. With her hand in Garrett's, Catherine led them to the terrace where Gar awaited their arrival. He nodded a greeting to his son and then made his way over to Jamie.

After a kiss to her cheek, he said, "You look beautiful, Jamie." He turned to his wife. "Catherine, doesn't she look wonderful? Like a breath of spring. Come sit down, sweetheart. Spencer is getting some drinks for us."

After Jamie and Garrett settled into a cushioned love seat, Gar took the chair beside them. He tapped his son's arm with the back of his hand. "Today was a good day. Right, Garrett?" He turned to Jamie and explained, "Our tax accountant found a way to save us thirty thousand dollars in taxes. Just do our reporting a little differently. But enough about business. Tell me, Jamie, how are your parents?"

"They're fine. Dad had a little health scare. He had a growth removed from his neck, but it turned out to be benign. Nothing to worry about. And Mom is as busy as ever, mostly being a grandmother to Caitlyn and Madison. She watches them twice a week while my sister works part-time at a greenhouse nursery."

"That's great. Can't wait until we have grandchildren." Gar gave his son a pointed look that he abandoned as soon as Spencer made his entrance with a tray of drinks. The ladies were served first. It was Marlena's special concoction of peach schnapps with lemon-lime soda and a touch of cranberry juice. A slice of lime hung over the rim of each glass.

While glasses were suspended in mid-air, Gar offered a toast. "Here's to family and friendship."

Glasses clinked together. Everyone took a sip except Garrett. He stared down at the brick pavers and then set his sights on the lake where a small fishing boat puttered along toward the main channel. The water shimmered white in the last remains of daylight. "Mom, — Dad, Jamie and I have an announcement to make." All eyes were directed at him. He kept them hanging until he finally blurted out, "We're getting married!"

Catherine's fingertips went to her mouth, covering her broad smile. Tears pooled in her eyes. Gar popped up from his chair to give his son a back-slapping bear hug and then, a tight squeeze for Jamie. With his hands resting on the shoulders of his son and future daughter-in-law, Gar said, "Well, well, isn't this a happy day. Another toast?"

As he had promised, Garrett did most of the talking. His mother's surprise at the rapid progression of their courtship led him to believe that she was not privy to the conversation he had with his dad recently. And when he mentioned the expediency of their wedding, his mother poked her lower lip out in a pout.

"Why so soon, Garrett?" she asked. "We don't have time to plan a wedding in one month! My goodness! We need to reserve the club six months in advance for the reception. And the church, too. And then there's the caterers, the band, the flowers. Surely, you kids can wait until you can have a proper wedding."

"Here's the thing, Mom. Jamie and I want to have a baby as soon as possible."

In stunned silence, Catherine looked first at Garrett, then Jamie. She licked her lips as her gaze stayed on her future daughter-in-law. "Jamie, I know you want to save yourself for your husband. I understand, I truly do. I insisted on it when I married Gar. Of course, he wanted to move up the wedding date," she said with a blush coming to her cheeks. "There'll be plenty of time for children, dear, unless you run into problems like I did. I had trouble conceiving and then when I did, I had to spend the last month in bed under a doctor's supervision." She looked over at Garrett and gave him a big smile. "Of course, he was worth everything I went through. What I'm saying, Jamie, is that you're still young and there's no point rushing things. Don't you want a big wedding? I'm sure your parents will agree with me."

"Actually, Mrs. Reynolds, I have spoken to my parents and they're okay with it. What Garrett and I want is just a small ceremony in a chapel. Then, we would like it if you and Mr. Reynolds could host the reception at your lovely home. We only want a few of our closest friends and family to attend. Both of us want it to be simple and sweet."

One brow arched high as Catherine turned to her son. "Darling, is this what you want?"

"Yes, Mom. We don't want a big fuss."

"But all of our friends, dear. If they think we snubbed them, excluded them—"

"I don't give a shit!"

"Enough!" Gar barked. "Don't talk to your mother that way."

Catherine gave her husband an appreciative look. "Gar, do something. Can't you talk any sense into these kids?"

"I think they should have the kind of wedding they want, darling. If they want a small ceremony, then so be it."

Resigned to being overruled, Catherine exhaled a long breath. "Well, I guess that settles that. Garrett, I wish Uncle Scott had lived to see you get married. He was so fond of you."

Over dinner, the young couple shared ideas of what they had in mind for the ceremony and reception. Garrett could tell that his mother, on several occasions, pressed her lips together to suppress her objections.

While the women enjoyed coffee and dessert on the terrace to discuss the bridal gown Jamie wanted to keep secret from Garrett, the men had cigars and brandy in the study.

Gar exhaled a plume of smoke into the air as he clasped both cigar and shot glass in one hand. He looked over at his son. "I don't like to have this discussion, but it's necessary. I'll have Ramsey draw up the prenuptial agreement right away."

"Dad, Jamie doesn't care about my money."

"I know, I know, but we must protect the family assets. Things can get messy if ever there were a divorce, and I hope to God there never is. And of course, a child or children will complicate things. It's just a formality, Garrett. Everyone does it nowadays."

Garrett stared down at the carpet and nodded. "Okay, Dad. Whatever you say."

The men soon joined the ladies on the terrace for a few final words before Garrett said he needed to drive Jamie home. On the way to his car, Jamie jabbed Garrett in the ribs and smiled. "Your mother thinks I'm a thirty-six year old virgin."

"Let's not spoil that fairytale, princess," he said with a chuckle and a wink.

CHAPTER EIGHT

The wedding reception for Garrett Reynolds and Jamison Jackson was held on the plush lawn of the Reynolds's estate. Tables, tents and a dance floor were set up so that everyone had a panoramic view of the lake as well as Catherine's pride and joy, the rose garden. The deck and dock, stretching out over the water, were also decorated with ribbons, lanterns and flowers galore.

Guests mingled with drinks in hand and looked at Chris like he was a wedding crasher, or so he thought. So what if he wasn't a part of the country club set? He wore his best gray suit with a new fifty-dollar silk tie. He took sips of an imported beer, a label he'd never heard of, and studied the bride from a safe distance. He felt certain Jamie didn't know he took her up on the invite. She'd be surprised to see him, no doubt.

In his biased opinion, she made a beautiful bride. He liked her floor-length dress that looked to him more like a slip than a gown. Simple but sexy. He'd heard one of the female guests say it was a Vera Wang, whatever the hell that meant. Her hair was half up and half down, resting on her bare shoulders in soft curls. He remembered she sometimes wore it styled that way when they were a couple. Fondly, he replayed in his mind the times he had pulled out the pins that kept the whole damn thing in place. Then, he'd run his fingers through the chestnut tresses that had a heady, sweet fragrance when his lips were pressed against her head. Just a fond memory, never to happen again.

At last, Chris saw a table of people he knew. Jamie's co-workers from *The Charlotte Chronicle*. He recognized the shaggy-haired photographer, Zeke Parker, and stepped over to say hello. But it was Stu Blackmon who offered him a seat. He eased down into a chair and took a phyllo-wrapped hors d'oeuvre from the server who passed them around the table.

Stu said Jamie's mom called it spanakopita. Chris bit into it and tasted spinach and feta cheese. Not bad, he thought, and wished he had taken two.

Stu slapped him on the back. "Yes, I remember you, detective. You and JJ were an item for a long time. Three years, wasn't it?" Chris had his mouth full; he held up two fingers. Stu said, "Oh, I thought it was longer. Seemed like three. Anyway, she's a beautiful bride, isn't she? No wonder. Did you see her mother? Gorgeous lady. My wife caught me gawking at her. Busted," he said with a chuckle. "She pinched me on my arm hard enough to leave a bruise, I'm sure." He chuckled again. "And her dad. Doesn't he look like someone famous? I'm thinkin' the former prime minister, Tony Blair, minus the British accent. Her dad is a former fly boy, but I guess you know that. Flew missions over the Gulf during that first ordeal, got a chest full of medals to prove it. 'Course now he's retired and makes big bucks as a military consultant. Gets paid for what he knows. Jamie and I get paid for what we *learn,* what we discover. She's a helluva reporter, that girl. Glad she's still gonna keep her job. Thought she might just live off the Reynolds money, but you know her. Gotta keep her nose to the grindstone, get her hands dirty. What a gal. Like a daughter to me. I got teary-eyed during the ceremony."

Finally, Blackmon took a breath. Chris noted that the well-wishers had thinned out around Jamie, and he jumped at the chance to have her all to himself. He set his empty glass on the table. Although he hadn't uttered a word during Stu's monologue, he said, "Good to talk with you, Stu. Think I'll go over and say hello to Jamie."

When he walked over, his eyes stayed engaged with hers long enough to cause a stirring of emotions. It pained him to see her wed to another man. But he'd had his chance, and he blew it. He wondered if she was aware of the hurt he hid behind his fake smile.

"Chris, I didn't think you'd come."

He leaned forward and kissed her cheek. "I didn't go to the ceremony. Just thought I'd drop by to give you my best wishes and say something to the groom." He took both her hands in his and stepped back to admire her. "You look beautiful, Jamie. Spectacular, in fact."

"Thanks, Chris. You're sweet. You clean up nice yourself."

He dropped his hands to his side and felt as awkward as a schoolboy. He cleared his throat before he spoke. "Look, I just want you to know that I'm always here for you. I mean, if you ever need me, you know you can count on me. Understand what I'm saying?"

"Yes, I know. I'm glad we can still be friends."

"Always, darlin'." He smiled and gave her a quick wink. From the corner of his eye, he saw her new husband waltz over to take a proprietary stance at her side. Chris masked his annoyance with a smile.

Jamie turned to him. "Garrett, you remember Chris Lagoni, don't you?"

"Of course," he said and extended his hand. "Nice of you to come, Chris."

"Congratulations. This young lady is the best, but I guess you already know that."

Garrett draped his arm around her waist and smiled. "Yes, I know. That's why I couldn't let her get away."

After he cleared his throat, Chris locked eyes with the groom. "Let this be a warning. If you ever hurt her, I will—"

"Beat my ass?"

"No. Kill you."

"I consider myself duly warned," Garrett said haughtily, trying to make light of it. "I will never hurt Jamie, so you have nothing to worry about, detective."

"Good. Glad to hear that." He leaned forward to plant a kiss on her cheek. "Bye, Jamie. Gotta go. Have a happy life, sweetie."

§

Their honeymoon on the island of St. Bart's was over too soon. Jamie and Garrett stayed in a villa overlooking the azure bay, the hilly emerald terrain off in the distance and a private beach with sand as white as talcum powder. They had their own pool and Jacuzzi on a sundeck complete with outdoor shower and total privacy. When they weren't lying on the beach or lounging on the deck, they were just inside the French doors making love while a gentle breeze drifted in. As much time as they spent trying to make a baby, Jamie thought it did the trick. The timing looked good.

After a week-long honeymoon, it was time for them to return home to their daily routine. As Jamie dressed for her first day back at work, she turned to Garrett and said, "Want to eat in tonight? First home-cooked meal prepared by your new wife."

He took his time to respond. While she waited, he turned up his shirt collar and slipped on his tie. Finally, he said, "I forgot to tell you. I'm meeting with some business associates tonight. Sorry, Jamie. We'll do dinner tomorrow night."

As she stepped into high heels, she frowned and made sure he saw. "We've just got back and you already have a business meeting?"

"My dad set it up. Wants me to meet some guys. If I'm going to take over the business, I have to play ball. That's just the way it is."

"When Daddy snaps his fingers, you come running," she mumbled to herself.

"Don't start that again, Jamie."

Surprised that he had heard her, she said, "It's true, and you know it."

"We're not going to have this conversation."

"Okay, sure. Just know that tomorrow night, you're all mine."

Garrett smiled and reached for his keys. Before he left, he brushed his lips lightly over hers. "I won't be too late. I'll call you later. Have a good day, Jamie."

She grabbed his arm and pulled him close. "You call that a kiss? C'mere, you." She gave him a long, crushing kiss and stepped back. "Now, that's more like it."

He smiled. "Definitely."

§

"Why lookie here. If it ain't the blushing bride! All tanned, rested up and glowing," Stu said when Jamie walked into the office. "Glad you're back, JJ. It wasn't the same without you. No one can handle Zeke like you can. He's just like a big kid. Went to the wrong location to take his damn pictures twice. Said you always write out directions, can't figure out his GPS. Why is this guy on my payroll?"

"Maybe it's because he takes award-winning photos that make you look good."

Stu scratched his bald head and nodded. "Yeah, maybe that's it. I've gotta see you in my office, JJ. That story you want to do about the illegal dumping of chemicals and the cover-up? We got the green light from legal to proceed, but they see everything before it goes to print, understand?"

"Absolutely." She gave him an appreciative smile. "Thank you, thank you. It's going to be a great piece, sir, I promise."

"JJ, I'm warning you. Go slow, follow the rules. None of that shit like sneaking off to meet a whistleblower without my knowledge. Promise me?"

She held up her hand as though taking an oath. "I swear on my grandmother's grave."

"I hate when you say that. Every time you do, the shit hits the fan."

CHAPTER NINE

Jamie wished they could give back the wedding present from Garrett's parents. But how do you return or exchange a freaking house? Three months to the day of their wedding, they moved in. Fully furnished more to Catherine's taste than Jamie's, it was a four-thousand-square-foot brick home in an upscale development, only five miles from the Reynolds's estate. Although it wasn't on a waterfront lot, in the wintertime when the trees were bare, a person could stand on the second-floor balcony off the master suite and see a sliver of the lake from a mile away. At least, that is what the real estate agent told them.

Although Jamie thought the house was beautiful, she *loved* Garrett's downtown condo. From her office, it was a five-minute drive, or ten minutes by trolley, fifteen minutes by foot. However, the new home was close to an hour commute by interstate.

In her opinion, the condo was all they needed. In the three months they had lived there, she had enjoyed adding her special touches to turn it from Garrett's bachelor pad to a cozy couple's home. She had envisioned the corner bedroom as a nursery for their future baby. She had it all planned out. Then the Reynolds had handed her a tiny box wrapped in metallic silver wrapping paper. When she opened it, she found a key to the house they had purchased as a surprise. *Surprise, my ass,* she thought. *I hate surprises!* She had wanted to scream at them instead of doing what she did — wrapping her arms around them for a group hug to say thanks.

However, Garrett was fine with it. He wanted to rent out the condo and move in even before the furniture arrived. She had managed to hold off the moving date until everything was in place, which gave her more time to enjoy the condo. On their first night in their new home, Jamie said to him, "I know why you like the house. Now you have room to set up a man-cave complete with weights, pool table and Xbox, you big kid."

He laughed. "Oh, yeah? Okay. Busted."

Their bed in their condo was a queen-size. However, the new one in the house was king, which meant Garrett had to turn on his stomach in order to grab her and pull her over to his side. He pinched her butt and then tickled her sides. "I'd rather play with you, Jamie." When she giggled and tried to squirm out of his hold, he got a firmer grip on her and pulled her closer. He pinned her down on her back and rubbed her abdomen with soft, sensual strokes.

"I'll bet you're already pregnant, Jamie."

A week later, she agreed with his prediction. While he shaved, she stepped out of the shower and wrapped a towel around herself. She turned sideways, opened the towel in front, and ran her hand over her abdomen. Finally, she turned to Garrett and said, "I'm a week late. I'm going to stop by the drugstore on my way home and buy an EPT test. You might get some good news tonight, Garrett."

He gave her a prolonged stare as if he needed time to process her words. With one corner of his face still covered in lather, he broke into a broad smile. He stepped over to gather her in his arms. Despite the lather, he kissed the top of her head.

"I hope you're right," he said.

She wiped white foam from her hair with her towel. "I have this feeling. This is it. I just know it."

She had tears in her eyes when she said this, feeling silly. Damn, she was supposed to be this hard-nose, take-no-prisoners reporter, and yet she wanted to burst into tears. Not just today, but every day this week. Stu had said she was hormonal. Women get that way, he explained. Zeke said women stayed on an emotional roller coaster just to drive men crazy.

The waterworks started up again soon after she arrived at work. Stu called her into his office to tell her that her investigative report on the cover-up toxic spill was put on hold. Lawyers were reviewing the merit of the report, which actually meant they were trying to cover their asses.

"Don't give me that sad-sack look like you're gonna cry, JJ. Be patient. You'll get to do your damn story. Just hold tight. Look, I need you on another story. Somebody's gotta cover it, so guess that's you. Take Zeke with ya. It's not as boring as it sounds. A cabinet member with the White House is in town to make an appearance at the Education Summit for North Carolina schools. Well, not actually the Secretary of Education, but one of his assistants. There'll be some big-wigs from Raleigh there, too. This guy — what's his name? Krooner, maybe. No, that's not it. Clooney? No, he's an actor. Okay, got it. George Conner. That's it. Anyway, he'll be touring some local schools after the big powwow. It's a two-day assignment. Just follow him around and ask a few questions. Find out what the hell they're gonna do to budget education. In my opinion, if they don't budget for education, they might as well budget for more prisons. Without education and no hope for a job, these kids will turn to crime. Tell the dude I said so."

"Stu, education is not my beat."

"Do I look like I care, JJ? 'Cause I don't. I need troops on the ground. Right now, you're it. So wake Zeke from his morning nap and get outta here. Bring me something with zing. Makes readers think. Makes advertisers happy. Know what I mean?"

The assistant to the secretary of education avoided Jamie and Zeke like they had the plague. Whenever he saw them coming, he ducked. She learned he was being investigated by the ethics committee in Washington for a questionable relationship with a lobbyist. She wished Stu had told her that. Readers would be more interested in reading about scandal than education reform. Although he dodged her for fear she'd bring it up, a State House member up for re-election wanted to be in their faces, on the record, telling the world that he had a wonderful bill coming to vote that would revolutionize the funding of education. Similar to vouchers, it would help parents get a tax break for private education.

"Zeke, this is a drag. I don't have a story. You don't have any photos. Let's just pack it in, start fresh tomorrow."

"Sounds good to me. Wanna stop by O'Malley's for a drink before we head back?"

"Can't," she answered, a little too quick for Zeke. He gave her a puzzled look. She wasn't going to tell him she thought she was pregnant and didn't want to drink, or that she was anxious to buy the home pregnancy kit to find out if she really was. "I promised to fix a nice dinner for Garrett. So I need to head home. See you tomorrow."

She stopped at the drugstore and dashed home. It was good timing for the test because she needed to pee so badly, it felt like her bladder would burst. As soon as she pulled her panties down, she found there was no need for the test after all. Although one week late, her period had started. She cursed and then she cried.

Any minute, she hoped Garrett would be home. He'd gather her in his arms and kiss away her tears. If only he would hurry home. "Please, come home, Garrett," she whispered as she choked back tears.

§

If Garret had remembered to bring a deposit slip, he would never have seen her. But because he left it in his desk drawer, he was forced to go inside the bank instead of his usual habit of using the drive-through window. He chose the branch close to the hospital because it was only a few blocks from the office building where he had just left a meeting.

Seeing her again made his heart pound. She was two people ahead of him in line. He recognized her shiny raven hair contained in a ponytail. Dressed in hospital scrubs, he assumed she had just left work. He noted her slender waist. The roundness of her hips. Her narrow shoulders. The birthmark on her neck that his lips had kissed many times. Although he could not see her face, he would know her anywhere.

Erica, *his* Erica. The woman who sent him away months ago, even though his heart stayed stubbornly behind.

She did not see him until he placed his hand on her arm just as she stepped back from the teller's counter. Her dark eyes widened as if stunned by his presence. He expected her to be as thrilled as he was, but she gave no hint of a smile.

"Erica, wait for me. Outside. I'll be right there."

"No. I can't."

She brushed past him and headed for the door. He relinquished his place in line and followed her out. Although she took brisk steps, he caught up to her and grabbed her arm.

"Erica! Stop! We need to talk. Please!"

In surrender, she stood still and lowered her head so that she stared down at the asphalt. He noticed that she stiffened and looked as if she wanted to break into a run. When he placed his hand under her chin, she looked up. He saw that her eyes had filled with tears.

"We can't see each other, Garrett."

"Why?"

"You're married. I saw it in the papers."

"Erica, please. You don't understand. Let's go somewhere and talk. I can explain."

"No. Forget me, Garrett. I can't be with you. Go home to your wife."

Hurt by her words, he felt as though he had been publicly flogged. No visible wounds, but an ache in his heart. He removed his hand and stepped back. She took the opportunity to walk away. But as soon as she backed her Toyota sedan out of her parking space, he cranked up his car and followed her through traffic. At her apartment building, she stayed glued to her seat as if she needed time to compose herself. Finally, she opened her car door and stepped out. As if he wasn't there watching her every move, she walked up to her door and turned the key. When he saw that she left her door open, Garrett followed her inside.

CHAPTER TEN

By eight o'clock, Jamie was panicked because Garrett was not yet home. He hadn't called and he wasn't answering his phone. She had left two messages for him that went unanswered. She expected him home two hours earlier. She needed to hear his comforting words. Garrett the Optimist would say, so what if she wasn't pregnant this time; next time it would happen.

Although she called around, none of his friends had heard from him. She waited until the late news came on TV before she felt desperate enough to call his father. He said that he and Garrett had left a meeting at a client's office hours ago. Gar said Garrett had told him he was going to the bank and then head home. Jamie let her imagination go wild. It wasn't like Garrett not to call. If he didn't answer his phone or call her, then he was injured, assaulted, left for dead. There was no other explanation. Near hysteria, she called Chris.

"Chris, it's me. Jamie."

"Jamie —what's wrong?"

"Something's happened to Garrett. He's missing. He should have been home hours ago. He doesn't answer his phone. No one knows where he is. Something's happened, Chris. I just know it. I thought of calling the police, but then I thought of calling you."

"Calm down, Jamie. I'm sure there's a simple explanation."

She couldn't keep the tremor out of her voice when she said, "Can you check for me? Put out an APB or something? Please."

"I can't do that. Someone has to be missing for twenty-four hours before we do anything. Do you want me to come over? Stay with you?"

"Forget it. Sorry I called."

"Jamie, wait a minute. Maybe—"

She hung up. With no help from him, she turned to alcohol. She poured a glass of wine and propped the pillows up in the king-size bed in the big-ass house miles from the city and waited for her husband to come home. When he walked in around one o'clock, she had already succumbed to sleep while hugging an empty bottle of Merlot. When he dropped his keys on the dresser, she awoke and propped herself up on her elbows.

Standing in the doorway silhouetted by the hall light behind him, she noted that he had foregone his usual dapper appearance. His shirt collar was open, his tie removed, and his hair hastily finger-combed in place. When he approached her, she noted that he smelled of perfume, scotch, and sex. While he sat on the edge of the bed to pull off his loafers, he avoided any eye contact.

Before she had a chance to ask, he said almost mechanically, "I got tied up at work and then I met a business associate. We went to dinner and we were talking business the whole time and then I realized how late it was. We ended up talking longer out in the parking lot. There was an accident on the interstate. Traffic was backed up for miles. I couldn't call you because my phone went dead. Sorry if I worried you."

"You're lying!"

"It's the truth!"

"I needed you, Garrett. Who were you with? No lies!"

He twisted his body around and reached for her, but she scooted away. "I told you, I'm sorry." He stood up with his hands on his hips and studied her. "You've been drinking. This isn't like you, Jamie. Has something happened?"

"If you'd been here, then you'd know. I don't feel like getting into it right now. It's been a rough night, and I have to get some sleep. I've got an early start in the morning."

She got out of bed and padded across the carpet to the master bath. Garrett followed and watched as she opened the medicine cabinet.

He grabbed a bottle of pills from her hand. "What are you doing? You can't take this! Not after all the wine you just had."

She snatched it back. "Give that to me!" She took a pill out and popped it into her mouth, then washed it down with water. She watched Garrett's reflection as he stood behind her, his jaw clenched. She intentionally bumped up against him and then stumbled back to bed.

"My God, Jamie. Booze? Sleeping pills?" She stared icily. "Okay, okay. Have it your way," he said, hands up in surrender.

§

Jamie and Garrett slept as far apart as the mattress would allow, each facing outwards. By morning, they had not come any closer together. Already dressed for work, Garrett sat at the table in the breakfast area when Jamie walked in, her high heels tapping noisily on the hardwood floor. His face was hidden from her by the morning paper. She poured coffee into the mug he had set out for her, walked over to where he sat, and then slammed the mug down on the table. Coffee sloshed out all around. As intended, it got his attention.

He looked up, one brow raised, as she yelled, "I'm not pregnant! False alarm! Of course, you would have learned that last night if you'd come home after work. Do you realize how much I needed you?"

"Sorry." Garrett's attention stayed on the local news, which she knew he only pretended to read.

"Whatever you were doing last night has to stop," she said. "We need to concentrate all of our efforts on the baby-making project."

She saw the spread of anger in his face. "Jamie, what's wrong with you? Why are you saying this?"

"I'm not stupid, Garrett. You were with someone. Was she worth it? I think that you got with your friend Justin and the two of you went looking for action, just like old times. Why didn't I think to call him? I called everyone else!"

"Jamie, that's not—"

"Save it, Garrett! It'll only be more lies." She watched him mop up the spilled coffee with a napkin. She cleared her throat and said, "Maybe it's you. Maybe you're the reason I'm not pregnant. You should get tested. Maybe a venereal disease from sex with too many women has made you sterile."

"Stop it! You're the problem, Jamie, not me. You need to chill out. You're too uptight about conceiving, like it's one of your projects with a set deadline."

"I'm the problem? My *age* is the problem. I'm thirty-six. Did you know that by the time a woman is thirty, her odds of getting pregnant are down to fifteen per cent? By forty, it's five. Women between thirty-five and forty have up to a thirty-five percent chance of having a miscarriage. Time is of the essence."

Garrett finished his coffee, folded the paper, and stood up. He raked his fingers through his hair and looked at her. "What do you want from me, Jamie?"

"Right now, nothing. I want nothing."

"I'll see you this evening. Let me know if you want me to pick up anything for dinner."

With car keys in hand, he went out the side door past the laundry room. To her relief, he skipped his routine of kissing her goodbye. She would have pushed him away. She listened for the car engine as his BMW sedan backed out of the garage and then the drone of the automatic door closing. At last, she could let the tears spill freely down her cheeks.

§

Garrett leaned into the doorway of his father's office as if he could get by with a quick in and out. "Dad, you wanted to see me?"

Gar looked up from his paperwork and waved him in. "Garrett, come in. Have a seat."

He hesitated, noting the tight muscles in his father's face. From past experience, he knew that was never a good sign. Garrett stood behind a chair facing his father's desk, his hand gripping its back. He looked on as his father straightened a stack of papers and set them aside. With elbows propped up on the desk, Gar made a steeple with his fingers and pressed them against his chin.

"Jamie called last night looking for you. Where were you?"

"That's between Jamie and me. Don't see how that's any of your business."

"I make it my business when you are a partner in this company. What you do reflects on all of us. If you can't tell me, then you've must have been up to no good."

"Like I said, Dad, it's none of your business."

"You've been married what? Three months? Are you already looking for some action on the side?"

Garrett took a few steps toward the door. "I'm done here."

"Wait, there's something I want to know. You're not getting mixed up with that Mexican girl again, are you?"

"That Mexican girl has a name. It's Erica. I'm married to Jamie. I go home to her every night. Think whatever you want, Dad."

When Garrett turned to leave, he heard his father say, "Don't fuck it up, Garrett."

Garrett spun around and lunged for his father. Only the separation of the desk stopped him from grabbing him by the throat. "You're one to talk. You think you can pay people off or buy their loyalty. You use power and money to make people dance to the beat of your music. It sickens me, Dad. So in my opinion, you're the one fucking things up, not me!"

"Get out! Don't come back until you've had time to cool down. I wanted you to join me and Mitchell for lunch at the Executive Club, but I've changed my mind."

"Good. I wouldn't go anyway." Garrett lowered his voice, fighting to hold back his anger. "Y'know, I've tried to be a good son, do what I was told. I've tried to show respect, but I don't think I can anymore. You've crossed a line, Dad, and I can never feel the same about you ever again."

"What in God's name are your talking about?"

"Maybe you've been manipulating people so long that you

don't know the difference between right and wrong."

When Garrett walked out of the room, Gar swept his arm furiously over the desktop, sending a stack of reports sailing through the air and onto the carpet.

CHAPTER ELEVEN

"JJ, what's wrong, honey? You look like your best friend just died."

Stu asked the question as he held a coffee carafe in mid-air. He filled her cup first and then his own. Two co-workers slipped into the break room behind them with cheery good morning greetings. With his arm around Jamie's shoulder, Stu steered her away from their curious stares. At a small corner table, he pulled out a chair for her.

"Thanks," she said. "I guess it's obvious that I'm upset. Garrett and I had our first fight."

"Oh, I'm sorry. Well, you went three months, that's gotta be a record." He chuckled in an effort to cheer her up. "Look, JJ, marriage has its ups and downs. Why, Gloria and I fight over the dumbest things, like whose turn it is to load the dishwasher. Or who left the cap off the toothpaste. Crazy, huh? Personally, I like the kiss and makeup part. We never stay mad. Never harbor a grudge. You and Garrett are just adjusting to the whole marriage bit, that's all."

"I don't think it's quite that simple, Stu. But I'm not ready to talk about it. Maybe if I just get buried in work, I can take my mind off my troubles."

"Sure. Go back to that Education Summit and this time, pin that guy to the wall. Make him talk. I gave you the list of questions, didn't I? Doesn't make a damn bit of sense. Usually a politician likes to hear himself talk and this guy clams up? What the hell? He should be using this opportunity to crow about what the administration is doing or wants to do."

"I told you, Stu. I got word from a source in Washington that he's being investigated. He thinks I'll blindside him with questions about that."

"Then, tell him point blank, that's not what you want."

"And if I don't mention it in the article, some will say I'm giving him a free pass."

"Listen, JJ. When I gave you the assignment, didn't I tell ya I wanted to hear about education reform? I don't care about anything else. I don't care if the guy got caught for a hit-and-run while drunk after leaving his pregnant mistress on his way home to his wife. Not relevant. I'm not going to let anyone dictate to me what our stories are about. You got that?"

"Yes, sir."

"Times have changed," Stu mumbled more to himself than Jamie. When he realized she was still staring at him, he added, "When I majored in journalism at Carolina, we were told to be informative. Cover the who, what, where, when, and why. No sensationalism. As Jack Webb used to say, 'Just the facts, ma'am.'"

"Was he a famous journalist, or one of your professors?"

"Good God, you *are* young. Just Google him, JJ, you'll see."

Stu stood up. He hitched up his pants with a tug on his belt, but still his belly hung over. His stubby fingers went around his mug as he picked it up. Together they walked out and headed for their work area.

"Don't worry about the fight with Garrett, JJ. My daddy used to say, 'If you wanna make the missus happy, just nod a lot before you nod off to sleep.' Me? By gosh, I stand my ground. I let Gloria know what I'm thinking and she lets me know what's churning around in her brain. We go at it a while, nothing physical mind you, just respectful words of disagreement. And then, like I said, we kiss and make up. The best part," he said with a wink.

Jamie managed a weak smile. "Thanks, that helps."

"Good. Feel free to come to Uncle Stu for advice any time."

§

As soon as Garrett left his office, Gar picked up the phone and dialed a number he got from his private list of contacts, tucked away inside a locked drawer. He canceled his lunch plans and arranged to meet the man identified only as "Carlson" at the Greenway Park courtyard downtown. Both knew that the lunch crowd and mommies with preschoolers would pay little attention to them, two business men talking in low voices over a light fare of turkey subs and iced tea.

Carlson kept Gar waiting fifteen minutes, but he figured the surveillance and security consultant was close by even before he announced his presence. He would have covertly made sure there was no unforeseen threat. The guy was a former intelligence officer, maybe CIA. Gar wasn't sure. Whatever he was in his past or present life, he seemed mistrustful of everyone. Gar knew that included him. He showed skepticism when Gar had called and requested his services.

As he took a seat across from Gar, he wasted no time. "So Mr. Reynolds, you want me to run surveillance on a young lady named Erica Romero, age thirty-two, of Mexican descent. What possible threat could this young lady be to you?"

"That, I'm not at leisure to disclose. What difference should it make to you? All you need to worry about is getting paid, and like I said, I will make it worth your time. So please make arrangements to plant a tracking device on her vehicle, cameras and mic in her apartment, photos of her and whoever she has contact with. She works the first shift from six to three. She's an RN on the critical care floor at the main hospital downtown, CMC." He withdrew a piece of paper from his coat pocket. "Here's her address."

"Do you have a recent photo?"

"No, I don't. But I can describe her. She's petite, maybe five-two, around one hundred and fifteen pounds, dark features. Her hair is black, usually tied back. Beautiful woman."

"A femme fatale?" Carlson said, allowing a smile to crack his stone face.

"Yes, I'm afraid so. A threat to my family. That's why I require your services."

"Can you give me any background on her?"

"She is the daughter of a woman who worked for my family for over twenty years, Sophia Romero. She was our housekeeper until poor health forced her to leave our employment. Her father is Ramon Romero, serving time in some prison in North Carolina for murder. Erica apparently worked her way through school or got a scholarship of some kind. She graduated from Carolina with a degree in nursing. She has no siblings, but I think she has an aunt and some cousins. Not sure where they live."

"And her father, does he have known associates outside of prison?"

"How should I know? The man is a convicted felon, which in my opinion makes his daughter that much more dangerous."

"Mr. Reynolds, with all due respect, nothing you have said makes me think she is any threat to you or your family. There's more you're not telling me."

Gar gave him a hard look. "A man in my position has enemies all around. My money and power can attract someone who wants to exploit my family for their own personal gain. It's a curse I've learned to live with, but it has made me cautious. Selective."

"I take it Miss Romero fits into that category. How soon do you want me to start?"

"As soon as possible. Like yesterday." Gar's eyes landed on children at play under a fountain. Their laughter brought a smile to his face. "I should have a grandchild over there playing with the other children. Do you have children, Carlson?"

He shrugged and eased into a smile. "Not that I'm aware of."

"Family is everything. You are what? Forty-five? Fifty? You still have time to carry your seed to the next generation. My ancestors have been in this country since the 1600's. Two signed the Declaration of Independence. My great, great grandfather fought in the Civil War, on the Confederate side, of course. I have his battle sword, his letters home. I like to go back and read them from time to time. I hope future generations of

Reynolds will appreciate their legacy."

"Whatever floats your boat." Carlson dabbed at his mouth with his napkin and made a ball of his sandwich wrappings. He glanced at his watch. "Anything else, Mr. Reynolds?"

"I may need the name of someone who can terminate the threat, if, of course, you find out that my suspicions have merit."

Carlson raised one brow, paused to ruminate over the gravity of the older man's statement. "Now, that will cost you some serious money, my friend."

"Money I am willing to pay."

CHAPTER TWELVE

Garrett waited two endless days before he returned to her apartment. Now that his liaison with Erica was set into motion there would be no turning back. Out of caution, he regarded his surroundings before he knocked on her door. As he waited, he saw a couple going to their car, a young mother pushing a baby stroller, and a car parked across the street with a man seated behind the wheel. What did he expect? Jamie to blindside him? His father to call and ask how his seminar was going?

He bailed on that. He'd signed up to attend two sessions on the future of aluminum honeycomb panels in aviation components. The subject didn't thrill him as much as being with Erica. They had one hour together, no more. She was on her lunch break from the hospital.

As she leaned against the doorjamb, she greeted him with a sexy smile. He did not gather her into his arms until he went inside. His hands found their way underneath her hospital scrubs and pressed her tightly against him. He made no apology for his lack of self-control, groping and kissing with a savage hunger. Finally, she pulled back. Her fingertips touched her lips where he had given her a crushing kiss.

"Wow, that was an intense greeting. Slow down, Garrett, and let me catch my breath."

He smiled sweetly. "Sorry, I can't help it. It's all I have thought about all morning—holding you in my arms—making up for lost time."

"I can't believe I'm allowing you back in my life," she said. With her hands in his, she kept him at arm's length. "I'm not sure about this, Garrett."

"It's fine, baby. Call it destiny or serendipity, but for whatever reason, we happened to be in the bank at the same time. The minute I laid eyes on you, that spark was rekindled. Actually, for me, it never fizzled out."

"It must have fizzled somehow because you got married. And to Jamie of all people."

"So you remember her?"

"Yes, of course. I remember the time she didn't like the hors d'oeuvres I served. When she thought no one was watching, she fed them to your mother's poodle." When Erica smiled, the tip of her tongue slipped between her front teeth. Her mannerisms, quirky and cute, endeared her further to him. "Jamie knew I saw her and she winked at me. Our little secret." After a beat, Erica became more somber. "She's a good person, Garrett. What we're doing will hurt her."

"Of course, I don't want to hurt her. But for once, I want to have what *I* want. Is that so wrong? Hey, baby, let's not talk about her, okay? We've got what?" Garrett glanced at his Rolex watch. "C'mere, you. Don't play hard to get."

Garrett understood Erica's hesitation, but he did not want to waste another minute on talk. He couldn't wait to have her, to come inside her. Maybe too forcibly, he pulled her against his chest, then boosted her up in his arms. His hands cradled her ass as he carried her to bed. If he'd had his way, he would have ripped her clothing from her body. She coaxed him to take his time and guided his hand as he pulled her panties down and unhooked her bra. He took a minute to gaze at her lying naked, thinking she was so beautiful, so vulnerable to his strong desires. His eyes locked with hers and he wondered if she could read his thoughts. Like a few days ago, they would again reaffirm their love for one another. The heat and the passion would smolder long after they had left each other's arms.

She responded to his urgency, wrapping her hand around his hardness, smiling when he moaned and cursed, knowing he wanted to last longer but couldn't. She was already wet when he slipped inside her and climaxed. Then, he pleasured her until she too came in an explosion of ecstasy, whispering his name.

On his bare chest, Erica rested her head while he stroked her hair. Then, as though the magic spell had been broken, she looked at the clock that he cursed, thinking of it as their enemy. She rolled off the bed and covered her nakedness with a short silk robe. Garrett slipped his boxers back on and followed her into the kitchen. She opened the refrigerator and pulled out two clear plastic boxes that contained turkey croissants and fruit salads.

"I picked up lunch for us at the cafeteria," Erica said to him. "We don't have much time, so let's eat."

Across the small table in the breakfast area, he enjoyed watching her take tiny bites of her sandwich, like a little girl at a pretend tea party. Everything about her was dainty, sweet, which made him love her even more. Her hair was now free from the ponytail, an ebony swirl that rested on one shoulder. Her doe-like eyes locked onto his. She smiled and then dropped her gaze. With her legs crossed, she made circles under the table with her bare foot.

"Is something bothering you, honey?" he asked.

"Yes. You. Us. Two people that have no business being together. We're like a strong magnet that can't be pulled apart. Damn you, Garrett. I'm too weak to resist. You know, my mother wouldn't like this any more than your parents."

"I always got along fine with your mother. I thought she liked me."

"She does. It's just that — well, she wanted me to marry a good Catholic boy, someone from a similar background. And you were supposed to end up with a sophisticated, wealthy woman with an influential family. Like Jamie."

He shook his head, set his napkin on the table. "I'm too much in love with you. The whole time I've been with Jamie, I couldn't shake you from my mind. Although my father tried, he couldn't keep us apart. I will hate him for the rest of my life. If I didn't want to expose our relationship, I'd go to him right now and beat the living shit out of him for what he did."

"Don't talk like that, Garrett. He's your father. He was only looking out for you."

"Bullshit. He was looking out for himself, his reputation. Can't have his son marrying a woman not up to the family's standards. What an embarrassment. I still can't believe he bribed you to make you get out of my life."

"I accepted the bribe — don't forget that. I'm so sorry, Garrett. I feel so bad about that. I'm surprised you forgave me so easily."

"I know how persuasive my father can be. Besides, you were desperate to help your mother. No insurance, nothing to live on. Sick with cancer. Damn, Erica, I wished you'd have come to me. I would've helped. You know I would have."

She shook her head. "I couldn't ask and I didn't want you to get the wrong idea — that I was after your money. I thought I could manage, but then the bank wanted to take her house. I panicked. Then your father came along with a solution to my problem, albeit a difficult decision." Erica placed her hand over his. "I thought I was doing what was best for you, too. For your family. I was a fool to think I could snuff you out of my life."

She stood up and carried their empty lunch boxes to the garbage can. As she turned to face him, she said, "I've got to freshen up before I go back to work. You should go, Garrett. We shouldn't be seen leaving together."

He laughed. "Do you think my father is spying on me?"

"Maybe. I don't know. Truthfully, I don't know what your father is capable of." She paused to study a change in his expression. "Did I say something wrong?"

"No, it's just that I was remembering that Jamie once made a similar statement. Weird, huh?"

"Life is weird. Full of surprises."

"Amen to that."

§

Because of him, Erica would be late returning to work. Garrett had to hold her one more time, give her a slow, passionate kiss that made him want to carry her back to bed for a repeat of their earlier lovemaking session. He resisted the urge with difficulty.

As he walked back to his car, he still felt the sweetness of her lips, imagined her arms around him. The rest of his day would be shot because his mind, heart and soul were held captive by continuous thoughts of her. He'd have to avoid his father. One look and the old man might see through his facade.

On his drive back to his office, he thought about how his Uncle Scott would applaud their union. He remembered how the man had teased them even while he lay dying in his hospital bed. One day out of the blue and before they were dating, he said to them, "Well, kids, how long is this flirting back and forth going to continue before you two act on it? I'm running out of time here. Dying, in fact."

Erica was so embarrassed she dropped the IV tube in her hand. But Scott's quick wink put her at ease. Garrett remembered how he gave Scott a hard stare, but then eased into a smile.

"Well, Erica, what do you say we make a dying man happy? Want to have dinner with me?" Garrett had asked.

"Now you're talking," Scott said. With his head pressed back into the folds of his pillow, he closed his eyes. "Get outta here. It's my nap time. Erica, play hard to get. Tell 'im you'll have to think about it. Make 'im sweat."

When Erica did agree to go to dinner with Garrett, she made it clear that it was to make her patient happy. But they both knew their feelings for one another had been building for weeks, reaching a crescendo that could only be satisfied by acting on them. Garrett waited a month to tell her that he loved her. She had cried when he first spoke the L-word. He reflected on that dramatic scene, her admitting she felt the same but was reluctant to continue their relationship.

"You don't want to pursue this because of my family," he had stated. "Their prejudices and snobbery. Is that it?" He had demanded her admission.

"Garret, please. I don't want to cause trouble for you."

"If you end this, Erica, you might as well rip my heart out. I want you. I need you, and to hell with my family. This is not about them. It's about us."

But in the end, she did end it. Thanks to good ol' Daddy and his money and influence. Garrett was still angry about that and it gave him another reason to avoid seeing his father at the office.

He skipped a conference call with a military contractor because what was the point anyway? His father and his entourage of yes-men would say whatever the contractor wanted to hear in order to get the work. His input would mean nothing.

At a quarter to five, he left the office and headed for his condo downtown. As yet, he didn't have the heart to rent it out or sell it. Jamie still lamented over the move, reminding him repeatedly that the condo was close to her work, to their friends, and to their favorite haunts. All he could do was listen and remind her how important his parents's gift of a new home was to them.

When he arrived, he found that Jamie was already there. That morning, they had agreed to meet after work to change into evening wear for their obligatory attendance at a cocktail party and fundraiser for the hospital foundation that his mother chaired. Instead of driving back to their lake home to dress and then make the long drive back downtown, they'd decided a quick change at the condo would save time.

When he walked into the bathroom to shave, she emerged from the shower with a towel wrapped around her. A tinge of guilt soared through him when he thought of seeing Erica in the same state of undress earlier that day. He blinked away any telltale signs of his secret thoughts. He kissed her lightly on the lips. "How was your day?" he asked.

"Good."

He felt a chill from her terse response. "How long are you going to punish me, Jamie?"

At her vanity sink, separate from his, she stared into the mirror and combed through her wet hair with her fingers. "I'll have to wear my hair curly. I don't have time to straighten it."

"I like it curly. Answer me, damn it."

"I know when I'm being lied to, Garrett. But we won't discuss it now. I'm not going to this party with tears in my eyes and mascara running down my cheeks." She fussed with her hair as she gazed into the mirror. "So you like it curly. I thought you liked it straight."

Garrett exhaled an exasperated breath. "I like it both ways. You're a beautiful woman, Jamie. You can't go wrong either way." She stayed silent. While he lathered his face, he cut a sidelong glance to find her leaning into the mirror to apply fresh makeup. "Jamie, I'm sorry about your disappointment — the negative results of the pregnancy test. I didn't mean what I said about you being the problem."

"Maybe I am, but we'll soon find out. I made an appointment to get checked to see if I can't have children for some reason. Maybe we should have checked under the hood before we married. Since it's a deal breaker."

She slammed her lipstick tube onto the hard surface of the vanity sink, and in her anger, yanked out more tissues than she needed to press against her lips.

"What are you talking about?"

As she continued to fuss over her hair and makeup, she glared at his image in the mirror, staring back at her and waiting for a response. She smacked her lips together and added a final touch of lip gloss. Finally, she said, "It's why we rushed into this marriage, isn't it?"

"We married because we were in love and didn't want to wait."

She turned her whole body to face him. "Note how you said *were in love.* The fact is I came into this marriage thinking your love for me would eventually equal the love I have for you. I'm an idiot."

"Jamie, don't say that. And you're wrong. You're my wife. I love you."

She looked down at the diamond watch he gave her as a wedding present. "Shit! Look at the time. We'd better hurry or your parents will send out a posse looking for us."

"Can you pretend not to be mad at me tonight?"

"Well, you're the pro at pretending," she said through clenched teeth. "But I guess I've picked up a pointer or two from you. I'll do my best not to let on how angry I am."

Mocking her, he said, "Very kind of you, *sweetheart.*"

On their way out, Garrett grabbed her arm and brought her hand up. He stared down at her left hand that was missing her wedding ring. "You forgot something."

Her eyes met his and without missing a beat, she said, "No, I didn't. Shall we go?"

CHAPTER THIRTEEN

The gala was called "A Night Under the Stars," although there wasn't a constellation in sight. The Reynolds Foundation rented the rooftop of The Carlyle, a four-star hotel in the heart of downtown Charlotte for their fundraiser. Money from a silent auction of original artwork would help fund the new hospital wing to be completed in eighteen months.

As if the auction itself was inadequate to generate enough funding, Catherine Reynolds came up with an innovative idea to add more to the coffers. Long before guests arrived in their glitzy evening wear, they had the opportunity to have a candle lit in honor of or in memory of a loved one for a measly donation of five hundred dollars. Across the expanse of the pool, decorative objects resembling lily pads provided the base for the candles that floated on the water's surface. Once the sky blackened, the effect was spectacular as the flames flickered and reflected off the dark water. And to add to the ambiance, a band that consisted of a piano, bass, and drums played soft jazz from one corner while the opposite corner was occupied by the open bar.

Jamie wore a black dress that exposed a cutout teardrop of skin across her chest, showing cleavage, and a wide oval in the back down to the waistline. The jersey material clung to her figure and stopped two inches above the knee. From the stares of the men in attendance and the disparaging look from her mother-in-law, she feared she had dressed far sexier than she had intended.

Despite Garrett's plea that they put on a good show for his parents, she quickly distanced herself from him. She walked the perimeter of the patio alone, feeling a little self-conscious because of the male gawkers that followed her every move.

She had tried unsuccessfully to reach Bert Castleman, CEO of KleenBrite, all week, and she had not expected to see him just a few feet away. Only his profile was visible, but she would recognize him anywhere. Tall, barrel-chested, and in his signature Western boots, even though it had been years since he had lived in Texas. He swirled an ice cube in his glass of scotch and looked up when she blocked his passage.

"Mr. Castleman, hi. I'm Jamie Jacks with *The Charlotte Chronicle*. You're a hard man to reach."

"I know who you are, Miss Jacks."

"I would really appreciate a comment from you about the article I'm writing for the paper."

"The one that will end up in a flurry of lawsuits against my firm. Is that the article you're referring to?"

"There are two sides to every story. I've heard one, but I'd like to hear yours. That's only fair."

"Fair? You've been listening to a bunch of whackos with no merit to their claims." Castleman stepped closer to Jamie, who had no room to put distance between them. Her back hit the edge of the bar. She got a whiff of the alcohol on his breath. Without warning, he grabbed her wrist, clamped his hand tight around it. "You have no idea who you're dealing with, missy. You're in way over your head."

"Let go of my arm!"

"You wanna play hardball. Okay, I'll play hardball with you."

"Just answer my questions. Why did your company do nothing to clean up the toxic spill? Why did you cover it up? Why did you allow the runoff from the containment tank to overflow into the lake? Am I wrong? Maybe you did something to stop it. That's what I want to know."

Castleman tightened his grip. "Like I said, you don't want to stick your nose where it doesn't belong, missy. Drop it now before you get in too deep."

"Let go. You're hurting me."

From her right, a man walked over and put his hand firmly on Castleman's shoulder. At first, Jamie feared Castleman would slug the guy, but to her relief, he stepped back and released his grip on her. With eyes only for Castleman, the stranger said, "Is there a problem here?"

"Who are you?" Castleman looked him up and down with abhorrence.

"Doesn't matter who I am. I think you need to leave the lady alone."

"She got herself into this situation."

"And I will get her out of it." He kept his determined eyes engaged with Castleman's. Then he dropped his gaze to take in Jamie. He looped his arm through hers. "Let's go inside and get some fresh air."

She noted right away that he resembled Garrett with similar dark hair, blue eyes, and good looks. But he had at least two inches in height over Garrett. With her arm threaded through his, she felt his rock hard bicep. By the time they reached the French doors that led inside to a lobby, she was still too dumbfounded to speak. His eyes and his smile stayed on her as he held the door open.

"Who *are* you?" she asked.

"Brennan McKeever."

She was too angry to return his smile, and she wanted the man to know she didn't appreciate his interference. "Well, Mr. McKeever, I didn't need your help," she said with a tilt of her chin. "I had more questions for that guy. Now I won't have the chance. You blew it for me."

"Well, excuse me for coming to your rescue." He looked on as she rubbed her wrist. "Shall I get some ice for that?"

"It's fine," she said, allowing her annoyance to soften. She gave him a weak smile. "Look, I'm not exactly a damsel in distress. I'm perfectly capable of taking care of myself."

"Guess I should have stayed on the sidelines and watched the show."

"I know you meant well, but I've been trying to make contact with that guy all week."

"Shall I call him back? Maybe you two could arm wrestle or something."

She rolled her eyes. "Look, I'm not mad or anything. It's just that I'm frustrated, Mr. McKeever. But don't worry, Castleman has not seen the last of me. I'm as tenacious as a bulldog."

"I don't doubt it. Please, call me Bren. And you are?"

"Jamison Jackson. You may know me as Jamie Jacks, reporter for *The Charlotte Chronicle.*"

"The Charlotte what?"

"Do you read the paper, Mr. McKeever?"

"Please. It's Bren. Let's forget the formality, okay? And no, I don't read the paper. Too depressing."

"Information is the key to change." She smiled at him. "How come I've never seen you at one of these fundraisers before?"

"I'm new to Charlotte. I moved here several months ago from Boston. If you assumed I was one of the benefactors, well, I'm not. I'm here in Mr. Miller's place. He couldn't make it."

"Miller?"

"As in Beck and Miller. I was hired on a contract basis to help with the design of the new hospital wing."

"So you're an architect working with Beck and Miller."

"Yes, I'm the detail guy. I do construction drawings for bidding."

"And when your work is done, you go back to Boston?"

He shrugged. "I have a couple of months left on my contract, so we'll see. I don't have roots anywhere yet. I'm still sampling different places. Charlotte looks interesting." Bren looked her up and down, giving her a devilish half-smile. Undeterred when she stepped back, he added, "I could use a tour guide."

"Don't look at me."

"I was hoping that maybe you—"

"No. Not possible." She looked past him and saw Zeke Parker making his way to her. "I'd better go."

With his camera bag hanging off his shoulder, Zeke stopped in front of Jamie. Ignoring Bren, he said, "There you are. I got your text. You want a ride home?"

"Yes, if you don't mind."

"No problem. I've taken all the shots I need. Getting ready to wrap it up."

"Okay. I'll be right there." When Zeke walked away, she turned to Bren, "Well, good luck with your work. Can't wait to see the finished hospital wing."

"Are you with him?"

"Not in the way you think. Zeke and I work together. For the paper."

Bren scratched his cheek and looked down. "This may be presumptuous of me, but let me get you another drink. We got off to a rough start. Sorry I broke up your little meeting with Al Capone. Let me make it up to you. It would be my pleasure to give you a ride home. My car's just across the street."

"No. Thanks anyway. I'd better go."

"One drink."

"I have to go."

"I get it. You have a deadline to make."

She was puzzled at first, and then it occurred to her that he assumed she was there covering the event for the paper. She didn't bother to set him straight.

"C'mon, Jamie. I'm double parked," Zeke said.

For a split second, she debated telling Zeke to go on without her, but in the end, she turned to Bren and checked to see if Garrett was watching them from a distance. Assured that he was, she stretched up on tiptoes and kissed Bren's cheek. Then she pirouetted in her spike heels and followed Zeke outside, where partygoers milled around the pool area with drinks in hand.

Near the glass doors that led out to the elevator lobby, she felt a hand on her arm. She turned to see Catherine Reynolds in a shimmering dress of cobalt blue accessorized by a diamond and sapphire necklace.

Her red lips barely moved as she said, "Jamie, are you leaving?"

"Yes. Zeke is going to drop me off at the condo. Thought I'd stay there tonight."

"What about Garrett?"

"He looks like he's still having a good time." She noted that Catherine's gaze had found Garrett on the opposite side of the pool. Oblivious to their stares, he held his cell phone with both hands and seemed to be texting.

"So you've met Brennan," Catherine said, a disapproving tone to her voice. "Nice young man. I assume he knows that you are my daughter-in-law."

She shrugged. "The subject never came up."

"Does he know you're married?"

"Hmm, I don't know."

Catherine grimaced. "He seemed to be flirting with you. Maybe you should have let him know that you're spoken for."

Jamie felt the heat rise to her cheeks. She looked around for Zeke and found him impatiently tapping his hand on the side of his pants. "Well, I'd better go, Catherine. Zeke is waiting for me."

Catherine smiled. "A Southern lady always keeps a gentleman waiting. My goodness, women today rush about so, it just seems wrong. What's this world coming to anyway?"

"Times are a-'changing, Catherine," Jamie said with a sweet smile. "Goodnight. Lovely party, by the way."

CHAPTER FOURTEEN

Jamie would never stoop so low as to spy on her husband. She had Zeke do it for her. On Saturday morning, he followed Garrett from his downtown condo to an apartment building in the Dilworth community, one of the oldest and grandest areas of Charlotte that had fallen by the wayside for a time but had recently been restored to its prosperous past. Now it was home to a diverse group of singles and families, well educated and appreciative of all forms of the arts, including the preservation of architecture of times gone by.

Over the phone, Zeke reported back to Jamie of seeing Garrett leave an apartment with his arm around a beautiful young woman. He said they got into Garrett's BMW sedan and drove away.

"She's small, Jamie," Zeke said. "Petite. You could beat her ass, no problem."

"Is she Hispanic?"

"Maybe. Probably. Yeah, I think so. She has dark features."

"Erica."

"Who?"

"Doesn't matter, Zeke. You can leave now. That's all I need to know."

§

Carlson was pissed that his time had been wasted. He'd done covert extractions in foreign countries, worked as a mercenary against the drug cartels in Central America, and gotten shot up during a failed special ops mission in the Middle East. It was an insult beyond fucking believability that Gar Reynolds hired him to spy on his spoiled son.

He did not wait for Gar Reynolds to finish his golf game to give him a piece of his mind. He found the asshole in the clubhouse enjoying a cold beer with his friends after playing the front nine. The old man did not look happy when he pulled him away for a private discussion.

"Why are you tracking me down here? Can't this wait until Monday?" Gar asked, showing his irritation with a scowl.

"Here's my bill for my services. I'm off the case. I pulled my equipment from Miss Romero's apartment and her car right after she left this morning." He thrust an envelope into Gar's chest and responded to his shock by saying, "You're spying on your son. You could have told me. There is no threat from this woman."

"Would you have taken the job if I told you I wanted to find out if my son is cheating on his wife?"

"No. You know my reputation, Mr. Reynolds. That is not what I do. Leave that to the scumbags who work for divorce lawyers and jealous spouses. I do covert operations where there is a real threat."

"She is after his money. Miss Romero will suck the life out of my son. I told you, her father is a convicted felon."

"Funny you should mention that. His case is being appealed. I think he was railroaded. I saw the transcript of the trial. He claimed self-defense. The other guy started the fight and was about to crack his skull with a tire iron, but Romero shot him before he could deliver the fatal blow. His court appointed lawyer told him to take a plea, not risk a jury verdict that could send him to prison for life. In my opinion, the lawyer didn't do squat for his client."

"Maybe I was wrong to think you would take this seriously. You came highly recommended."

Carlson stepped closer. His chest bumped into Gar's, causing Gar to step back and put distance between them. "How about you look under a rock for the right person to do your dirty work, Mr. Reynolds. If your son wants to get involved with the wrong woman, make a bad choice, that's his business. I don't see how it's yours. Good afternoon. I expect payment soon and that will sever all ties between us. Understood?"

"Wait, what about the other information I needed from you."

"You mean someone to do a contract murder? Can't help you with that."

"You are making a mistake, Carlson. You just don't seem to know it."

CHAPTER FIFTEEN

*Y*ou cannot talk to a live person on the phone anymore, Bren lamented when he dialed the number for *The Charlotte Chronicle*, and it went to an automatic recording. He selected Jamie's direct number from the directory and got her voicemail. It was Saturday, and he figured she wouldn't be in her office until Monday morning.

He held up the diamond earring that had fallen onto the carpet when she hurried away as if she'd turn back into rags at the stroke of midnight, Cinderella-style. As he studied the earring, he came to the conclusion that it was expensive. The stone was maybe a carat with a platinum drop chain from which a smaller diamond hung. Simple but elegant.

When he heard the sound of the beep, he left a message for her: "Hi, Jamie, this is Bren McKeever. You dropped your earring on your way out last night. I have it and would like to bring it to you. Please call me and let me know when I could do that. Thanks."

He smiled at what he didn't say. He didn't say she met his criteria for a dream girl — beautiful, smart, sexy, and independent. When they stood close, he felt a strange sensation, as if an all-systems-go button had been pushed inside of him. He wondered if she felt something too. Probably, because she had kissed his cheek. He hadn't expected it, but it was a nice surprise that he had replayed in his head over and over again.

He had always felt lonely as hell coming to a new place. Hopefully, this time he'd find a connection with a woman. It didn't happen in Boston. Months ago when he had told his friend and co-worker, Toby Thomas, he was headed for Charlotte where he might have better luck, Toby warned that all the pretty Southern women were taken. However, Jamie did not wear a wedding ring, and she was not "with" the guy with the long hair she had called Zeke. As far as Bren could tell, she was unattached.

He pulled out an envelope from a kitchen drawer and dropped the earring inside. While he debated where to put it for safe keeping, he tapped it against the palm of his hand. Finally, he stashed it in a cabinet behind a box of Cheerios.

He felt the familiar wet nose of his golden retriever, Quincy, on his leg. The dog jerked his head up to release a loud bark.

"I get the hint, Quince. Time for your walk."

Bren pulled out a chair and sat down at the kitchen table to put on his running shoes. Just as he finished lacing up, his cell phone rang. He looked at the display and saw that it was his dad calling.

When Bren's voice sounded less than enthusiastic, a gruff voice responded, "What's got your panties in a wad?"

"Hi, Pop. Sorry. I'm in kind of a hurry. Quincy and I were heading out to the park."

"Tell the damn mutt to sit on it," Mac McKeever said. "You've got time to talk to your old man."

"What's up, Pop? You okay?"

"Well, I've got good news, and I've got bad news. Which you wanna hear first?"

"The bad. Go ahead, hit me with it."

"Our fishing trip's off. Denny broke his leg and you know damn well that son-of-a-bitch is not gonna let us use his boat unless he comes along. Just 'cause I bumped into the fucking dock that time."

"No problem. We'll go some other time. What's the good news?"

"Well, the good news is that my colonoscopy is over and done with and my plumbing looks good. I mean, they didn't find shit." He paused to give Bren time to get the joke. "Guess I should rephrase that. I mean, it came back negative. You know, my doctor says I'm in great shape for sixty. I think I over-flirted with the nurses. Does that word exist? Over-flirted? Y'know what I mean. Too bold and brassy for an old coot."

"You're not an old coot, Pop. Can I call you later? Quincy is pitching a fit. I'd better take him out."

"All righty then. Well, call me later. And come up and see me sometime. Y'know I'm just two hours away."

"Sure. Sometime soon. Promise."

Bren had intended to leave work early Friday afternoon and drive up to see his dad, but Miller insisted that he make a command appearance at the hospital fundraiser. And because he had met Jamie, he was glad that he'd conceded to Miller's request.

In his mind, he replayed the shock in her eyes when the man had grabbed her wrist. But he also noted her fierce determination not to let the man intimidate her. Only when he felt she could be physically injured did he intercede. And what kind of thanks did he get? Hell, he got reprimanded instead. She was sexy when she was riled up and even sexier when she softened. Definitely not a pushover, Jamison Jackson seemed to be a strong, independent woman. A challenge. And he loved nothing more than a challenge.

CHAPTER SIXTEEN

Jamie had not left the condo since Zeke drove her home from the fundraiser. After he had called her the next morning to report seeing Garrett with another woman, she had been barely able to function. She missed her Saturday morning ritual of going to the Farmers' Market. That evening she heard the front door open. Either Garrett had come back to the condo or a burglar had gotten pass security and forced entry. Either way, she didn't care. She stayed in the dark, stretched out on her back in the center of their bed. The last time she checked herself in the mirror she saw an image she didn't like. Swollen eyes from crying, cheeks streaked red, hair a tangled mess. Even splashing water on her face did little to help. But she had to admit no woman would look her best on the very day she discovered her husband is a lying, conniving cheater.

So if it was Garrett who entered, he would find a pathetic creature in their bedroom in a ratty T-shirt and panties. She heard a clink as keys were dropped into the ceramic bowl on the credenza. Garrett's voice called out to her. She didn't respond.

The bedroom light flicked on. She opened her eyes to see Garrett leaning against the door jamb. "There you are," he said as he came closer.

She sat up and stared at him with cold eyes. "I know, Garrett." She swallowed, then added, "I know you were with Erica."

His eyes drifted down to stare at the comforter, not really seeing it. He pressed his lips tightly together. It surprised her that he showed no alarm, no sign of remorse.

"For how long, Garrett? Since before we got married?"

He frowned and shook his head. "No, no, no."

"How long?" she screamed.

"Okay, okay, I'll tell you if you'll calm down. It's like this — I ran into Erica at the bank. I wanted to just talk to her. Then one thing led to another and well, you know the rest. It wasn't planned, Jamie. I didn't plan to get back with her. It was going to be you and me forever, I swear."

"Forever, my ass. I'm starting to get the real picture. I was the bride that was acceptable to your parents. Did they have anything to do with why you asked me to marry you?" He stared back at her but refused to answer. "Tell me, damn it! Is that why you married me? To make your daddy happy? Get him off your back?"

"I thought we'd be happy together, Jamie. I intended to make it work."

"I've always loved you more," she said. "What a mess! And it's my own damn fault! I knew it, yet I married you anyway. I am so stupid. Stupid — stupid — stupid!" She pounded the heel of her hand against her head.

"Jamie, don't. I'm so sorry I hurt you. No, really. I wanted to make us work, I swear. It's just that—"

"You still have feelings for Erica."

He shrugged. The silence that brought more distance between them seemed to shred away any threads of her sanity.

With fire in her eyes, she screamed, "Get out! Go back to that big damn house you love so much and leave me alone!"

"Jamie, please don't—"

"I swear, Garrett, if you don't leave in the next minute, I will throw that bronze statue at you and I won't miss. Trust me."

"Jamie, I'm so sorry."

"Too late for sorry."

"Sorry" was a word that she didn't use often and didn't like to hear others say. It was an expression of regret, of the loss of innocence, the annihilation of integrity. There was nothing noble about *sorry* even if it was heartfelt.

§

Sunday morning, Jamie found Garrett on the patio at their house near the lake. He turned in the lounge chair to see her standing behind him in front of the French doors. She made her way over to him and silently fumed over his audacious inspection of her less-than-stellar appearance.

"Did you get any sleep?" he asked.

"A little."

"You don't look so good. You okay?"

"What do you think?"

He frowned, then gestured to a chair. "Sit down, Jamie. We need to talk."

"I'd rather stand."

"Suit yourself."

"Even if I asked you to make a choice between me and Erica, you would choose—"

"Don't!" he yelled. She stiffened from his raised voice, his hard eyes. His tone was softer when he added, "Don't, Jamie. Please don't ask me to choose. I swear I never meant to hurt you."

"So this is it. You're back with Erica." Silence from him, more cruel than words. "Then, we're done. Our marriage is over. I want to stay in the condo. You can have the house."

Instead of a reply Garrett stared out at nothing in particular. A bee that buzzed around seemed to capture more of his attention than she did. She waited, but he stayed silent.

"Well, then," she began. "I'm going inside to get some of my things. I'll take just what I need and I'll come back for the rest later."

"Sit down, Jamie. I told you we need to talk."

"You can't have us both, Garrett." When he tossed a thick envelope onto the glass table near where she stood, she stared down at it and said, "What's that?"

"The prenups that you signed. I mean, we signed."

"I've read it. You think I'd sign my name to something I

haven't looked over? Besides, you said it was meaningless, just a formality to please your father."

"You read and signed the first draft. It's been amended. Changed. *This* is the official legal document bearing your authentic signature."

She had a queasy feeling in her stomach. "Any changes would require my approval."

"True, but if you intend to fight it, you'd need to go to court, file a judgment, go through the whole rigmarole to get it thrown out. I don't think you have the time or the money to do that. However, if you just listen to me—"

"How did you manage to change the document?"

"Not complicated. Just had the paralegal change the margin settings, change the format to a different font, and then reprinted, except for the last page with our original signatures and that of the notary's. Looks legit to me."

"You bastard!"

"Hear me out, Jamie. Basically it says that if you leave me, then you get nothing except what was yours before you entered into this marriage. Not much. However, if I initiate the separation, you get a sizable allowance. You will get half of our jointly owned assets, like the house, plus you'll receive alimony. Of course, you won't have any claim to the trust set up by my grandfather or to any shares in Reynolds Industries, but I assure you that you'll be a very wealthy woman. On the other hand, if you start divorce proceedings, well, I'm sure your lawyer will look out for your best interests, but you will have a fight on your hands that could take years to settle."

His long pause seemed intentional. "Jamie, stay in the marriage for now. A child would of course add thousands of dollars to your monthly stipulation. Although we would have joint custody, I would allow you to raise our son or daughter. So you see, Jamie, it wouldn't be smart for you to walk out on me. I will decide when the time comes to separate and divorce."

"You must be joking if you think I have no say in this!"

"You're a business woman, think like one."

"Marriage is not a business proposition. It's supposed to be based on love and trust."

"Well, I blew the love and trust issue, didn't I? So I guess it's down to business."

Jamie sighed an exasperated breath. "Garrett, do you remember the time we were all admiring Dr. Collins's art collection in his living room and someone asked what he thought it was worth?"

"No, can't say that I do."

"Of course not. Anyway, he estimated it was worth maybe two million and you cursed under your breath and whispered that two million could fund a poor village in Africa. I guess you thought no one heard you, but I did. It occurred to me then that you had the same compassion for others as me. And I loved you for it. I wanted to believe you were different. But it's obvious that you're filled with the same ambition and greed as your father. My mistake."

"Jamie, you're so naive."

"Maybe," she said with a shrug. "But I'll tell you this, if you think I'll stay in this sham of a marriage, you're crazy. As far as I'm concerned, you can go to hell!"

She stormed off and into the bedroom, where she snatched clothes from the closet and flung them onto the bed. Moving at a frantic pace, she did not see Garrett come up behind her. He grabbed her and forced her to turn around and face him. He walked her backwards and pinned her against the wall.

"Jamie, listen to me. Don't do anything rash. Stay with me for now. Please. I want my parents to think we're fine together. Once we have a baby, we can go our separate ways. We'll both get what we want. You'll have a child, and I'll have the business. Don't you see? It's a win-win for both of us."

"If you think I'd let you in my bed now, you're crazy."

"We'll go to that damn fertility clinic you mentioned. Do it that way."

"How can I trust you?"

"I swear, Jamie, I never meant to hurt you." He pressed closer to whisper in her ear, "We've always been there for each other."

"Always, but not now."

When she looked into his eyes, she saw tears. Her gaze stayed on him while her mind waged a battle between love and hate, because she felt both. It would not take much to cross over the line that separated the two. His hand went to her cheek, but she slapped it off. She put her hands on his chest and gently pushed him back.

She whispered, "You've betrayed me, Garrett. Not only with your infidelity, but by not being honest with me. Do you think I would have married you if I'd known you still had feelings for her?"

"Don't you see? I thought I was over her."

"You've been lying to yourself, Garrett, just like you've lied to me."

CHAPTER SEVENTEEN

As if her life couldn't possibly get worse, on Monday morning Jamie was arrested. She sat in a holding cell and reflected on how she got there. She would face the magistrate around three o'clock and learn if the two charges against her would stick. Her co-worker and co-conspirator, Zeke Parker, was detained somewhere else awaiting his fate.

It was all her fault. She'd gotten a call around eight-thirty that morning that prompted a series of actions that landed them both in jail. Bert Castleman had called to say he would meet with her in forty-five minutes at his company, KleenBrite. She barely had time to grab her notebook and recorder before she was out the door. Because he agreed to have his photograph taken, she brought Zeke along.

Castleman had kept them waiting thirty minutes. In the reception area, a mounted marlin over a knotty pine cabinet stared down at them. Framed photos adorned the walls of Castleman in aviator sunglasses and shorts, posing next to game fish as they dangled lifelessly from a giant hook. Zeke fixated on one photo and named the deceased marlin Merlin. He whispered a ridiculous story to Jamie about its capture that sounded a little like the movie "Jaws." To keep a professional persona, Jamie fought hard to suppress her laughter.

Finally, Castleman's secretary ushered them into his office. While Zeke fidgeted with his camera, Jamie played her game. As always, she started out with small talk to gain trust. After ten minutes of mindless chit-chat, she pulled her one-two punch. The hard questions came in rapid succession, relentless, designed to snare.

She locked eyes with him when she said, "Mr. Castleman, why did your company not sound the alarm when the spill occurred? I mean, with the steady downpour of rain that day, you had to know the containment tank would overflow, yet no action was taken. Is that correct? According to EPA rules, you are required to report the spill within twenty-four hours. Why is there no record of a report? I checked."

Castleman squirmed in his leather chair. Its mechanism squeaked in the hushed silence. He cleared his throat before he said, "We were pumping the excess mixture into a secondary tank from the start of the storm so preventive action, in fact, was taken. We averted an overflow, and if the kids' camp says otherwise they're mistaken."

"Are you saying there was no spill?"

"Yes."

"And toxic material did not contaminate the drainage ditch and then the lake?"

"A toxicology report by our testing facility showed no contamination in the lake water. I have the report right here."

He slipped a sheet of paper under her nose. She glanced at it and said, "Is this the original?"

"No. A photocopy. You can have it to keep if you like."

"I'd like to see the original."

"Sorry. It was sent to our home office."

"May I speak with the person who signed the report? Mr. William T. Abbott. Is he here?"

"He's on medical leave."

How convenient. "I see. The problem with this report, Mr. Castleman, is that it contradicts the report from an independent lab that tested the water."

"Abbott is a certified technician with a degree in chemistry. Well qualified. Shall I show you his diplomas? He has a wall full of them in his office. His testing was thorough and accurate. I have no doubts about that."

"Well, we might be comparing apples to oranges, Mr. Castleman. Perhaps he didn't test for the same chemicals. Here is a list of the chemicals used by your company and found in samples from the independent lab."

He glanced at it and grunted. She spent another thirty minutes going around in circles with him. No matter how she posed her questions, he denied any spill, any contamination, any liability. Finally, she saw that he'd had enough. With a frown, he glanced at his watch.

"I'm sorry, Miss Jackson. I'm afraid I'll have to end this. I have a conference call in ten minutes. I'll have Miss Pettijohn walk you out."

Jamie stood up when Castleman did. "Don't bother. Zeke and I will see ourselves out. Thank you for your time."

On their way to Jamie's car, Zeke said, "Well, that was a waste of time."

"Maybe not. Let's go around back and see that tank. I want to see if there's any telltale signs of a spillage."

"Are you crazy, girl? We can't just go back there unescorted. Besides, there's a fence with a sign. For those of us that can read, it says *No Trespassing.*"

She rolled her eyes and blew air through her lips. "Like that's going to stop me."

Zeke thumped his head with the heel of his hand. "What was I thinking?"

"C'mon, Zeke. We'll just take a quick peek." She nudged him with her elbow and added, "No harm in that."

She walked toward the side of the building, glancing back to make sure Zeke was behind her. As they rounded the corner, a sliver of an above-ground tank came into view. Once they cleared the shrubbery, the container was clearly visible. The pungent fumes forced them to cover their noses. A stain of a grainy white substance ran down the sides like tentacles of an octopus, clear evidence of a spill. But the most damning proof was the pooling of the toxic liquid in a low-lying area about the width of a whirlpool tub. The carcass of a bird floated on top.

Jamie tapped Zeke on the arm. "Do you see that? We have got to get pictures. The tank. The bird."

"Can't. The fence is in the way. It'll obstruct the view. Besides, I don't have a zoom lens with me. Gotta get closer, which we can't."

"We can if we climb the fence."

Zeke put his hands on his hips and shook his head. "No way. And get arrested? Or worse, get shot? Let's go, Jamie."

"We need this for proof. A picture says a thousand words. I've gotta have it, Zeke."

"Nope. Ain't gonna happen, girl."

With his middle finger, he pushed his sunglasses up the bridge of his nose and turned in the direction of the parking lot. But he made another 180-degree turn when he heard Jamie exclaim loudly, "Uh-oh!"

She pointed to her purse on the other side of the fence as she shrugged an apology.

CHAPTER EIGHTEEN

Zeke paced alongside the fence, running his fingers through his shaggy hair. "What the hell, Jamie? Why did you go and do that? Damn!"

"My purse has my keys in it. We'll have to climb over the fence."

"*We? We?* You mean *me!* Shit, Jamie!"

"Oh, don't be a baby, Zeke. It's not like it's electrified. Not even alarmed. Piece of cake. Just climb over, take a few click-clicks, get my purse, and then we're outta here."

With hands on his hips, he made a face at her. "You're going to get me killed or fired. If I'm killed, you're paying the burial cost. If I'm fired, you're paying my rent."

"Time's a-'wasting, Zeke. Hurry up before someone comes."

Once over on the other side, Zeke took ten photos of the tank and the standing water from different angles. He made sure he got a close-up of the dead bird. When he heard a door at the loading dock spring open, he spun around. Filling the expanse of the opened doorway was a security guard in a gray uniform. He had apparently let his body go soft and fat, which made Jamie think he would not be a contender if they decided to make a run for it. Staring back at the man, Zeke gulped and slung his camera over his shoulder. He grabbed Jamie's purse and hightailed it for the fence. As soon as his fingers clawed the chain links, a shout called out to him.

"Hey, you! Stay where you are!"

Jamie gasped when the guard drew his gun and pointed it at Zeke. The photographer froze and seemed to debate what he should do, but he finally backed away from the fence. Then, he put his hands up.

The guard walked toward Jamie. He kept the gun pointed at Zeke while his other hand hitched up his belt under his protruding belly. His sagging jowls shook from his quick steps. He kept his hawk-like stare fixed on Zeke although he seemed aware of Jamie's presence on the other side of the fence.

The guard said to Zeke, "You there, come with me." He turned his attention to Jamie, "And you, young lady, walk slowly around to the front of the building. Another guard will meet you. Don't even think of making a run for it. Cops on their way. You won't get far, honey."

§

The hinges of the door to the holding cell squeaked open. Jamie looked up, hoping to see the lawyer that Stu promised to send over. Her mouth hung open when she saw Chris, who looked at her like he wasn't surprised to see her in jail — as if it was just a matter of time.

"Assaulting an officer? Resisting arrest? Are you out of your mind, Jamie? What were you thinking?"

Jamie licked her lips, tried to display remorse with innocent eyes. "Chris, it's not as bad as it sounds. The officer over-reacted."

"No, Jamie. *You* over-reacted!" he retorted. "I talked with him. So don't bullshit me, okay?"

"He was putting handcuffs on Zeke for no good reason. I just tried to push him away, but he wouldn't stop, so I pushed him again. You saw him — twice my size, so to think he felt threatened is crap!"

"Jamieeee—"

"Look, Chris, it was all my fault. I made Zeke go over the fence. He was trespassing because of me. I was just trying to keep him from being taken away."

"And then, when Officer Benton tried to keep you back, you lost it. He said when he cuffed you and asked you to get in the patrol car, you refused. He had to force you inside. You kicked him? Really, Jamie?" Chris grimaced as he stepped back and propped his shoulder against the wall. He folded his arms over his chest and peered down at her. "When Nick told me you were down here, I thought it was a joke. But here you are! Damn, Jamie!"

"We're up soon to talk with the magistrate. Do you think Zeke and I will get released then?"

"Maybe. I'll talk with Benton, see if he and the DA will cut you some slack." Chris stepped away from the wall and hooked his thumb in his belt. When his suit jacket fell open, Jamie was surprised he wasn't wearing his gun. Then she remembered that he would have left it in a locker before he was allowed to enter the processing area. "So Jamie, why didn't you call me back? I was worried about you."

"What are you talking about?"

"You know, when your husband went AWOL. That night you called. Upset. Panicked. I called the next day and left a message. Just wanted to know if everything was okay. Never heard back."

"Well, since I didn't return your call, you should've assumed everything was okay."

"You're lying. I see it written all over your face."

"Maybe it's none of your business, Chris."

"I'm somebody who cares, Jamie."

"Don't worry about me. I'm fine. Really."

"Tell me something. Did you marry him to get back at me?"

"How could you think that? Of course not!"

"I don't think you ever forgave me for being an asshole when we broke up."

"That is ancient history, and yes, I did forgive you."

"You know I'm always here for you, Jamie. If it ever gets—"

"Everything — is — fine," she said with slow, deliberate pronunciation of each word as if he didn't comprehend the English language.

"Well, I gotta go. Try to stay out of trouble, Jamie."

He was disappointed in her, she could tell by the look he gave her as he walked out. In truth, she appreciated his concern. She liked that Chris was someone she could always count on even if there was nothing in it for him.

She heard a commotion in the open area where some suspects waited on long vinyl couches for their time before the magistrate. As he was being led away in handcuffs, a man was screaming obscenities. "I didn't do it!" he said more than once.

The deputy ignored his rant and stayed stone faced. "You can tell it to the judge, sir." Jamie gulped, afraid she might await the same fate.

CHAPTER NINETEEN

Charges against Jamie and Zeke were dropped. Jamie felt she owed some thanks to Chris who she figured had something to do with the dismissal of her resistance and assault charges, although he'd probably deny it. They shook hands with the lawyer that Stu had sent and made their way back to the office. Jamie slipped past Stu's closed door and dropped down in her desk chair with a sense of relief. It was short-lived.

An inter-office call from Stu summoned her to the conference room. There, she faced Stu, the managing editor and some guy she knew worked in Human Resources, but she had forgotten his name. All eyes were on her. Their serious looks forewarned what was ahead.

Stu slid a piece of paper across the table and under her nose. "Jamie, please read the following statement and then sign it."

She read it once, then twice, and looked up with incredulous eyes. "What's this? My resignation? Are you kidding me?"

"Guys," Stu looked at the editor and Mr. H.R. "Lemme speak with Jamie alone. For just a minute. Please."

They hesitated, shrugged, but then agreed to step out. Once the door closed behind them, Stu turned to Jamie. "What did you expect, JJ? A welcoming committee once we sprung you from the joint? This is serious. I can't cover for you this time. You didn't even tell me about the meeting with Castleman. Just grabbed Zeke and left."

"I-I didn't have time! You were in a meeting. I had thirty minutes to get there."

"Trespassing? Resisting arrest? Assaulting an officer? Come on, JJ. What the hell?"

She gasped. He seldom showed the emotion he displayed now. She'd never heard his voice tinged with so much anger and disappointment.

He cleared his throat and lowered his voice. "Gibson hit the ceiling, demanded your firing. He owns the damn paper, he can do whatever he wants, but I refused at first until he told me I could follow you out the door. I've got a daughter in college, bills to pay, and I need medical coverage. I'm not going down with you. Can't and won't.

"I warned you, JJ. This time you went too far. It's over. Damn, I hate it. You're like a daughter to me. We've worked together for how long? My hair wasn't even gray when you came here! I was thin, remember? And you were as green as grass, right out of college. God, I'll miss you."

Stu edged toward the door as if he could not bear any more discussion. Before he motioned the others to come back inside, Jamie said, "Stu, did you ever break the rules to get a story?"

His hand was on the door-knob. "This isn't about me, Jamie."

"I'm just curious. Yes or no?"

"Yes. Once. That was enough."

He took a few steps closer to her, moving away from the door. With hands on his hips, he scowled at her and said, "Just sign the damn paper, Jamie. You'll get severance that way, medical coverage for three more months. Please don't make a fuss, okay?"

She did as Stu suggested. Although she would have liked a hug from him, she did not make the gesture — nor did he. He hung his head low and walked out with his hands in his pockets. She had never seen him so quiet, at such a loss for words.

In the end, her time at the paper, all fifteen years, amounted to one cardboard box filled with miscellaneous items including her nameplate and a small plaque for outstanding journalism. She saved her recent research and unedited articles on a flash drive. If KleenBrite, or the paper for that matter, thought for one minute she would drop her investigation and series of reports, they were mistaken. She'd freelance them if she had to, but by God, she would report the misdeeds of KleenBrite.

Zeke said little as he carried the box to her car. She was glad his job was spared. She took the box from him and placed it in her trunk. Against the afternoon sun, she squinted as she looked up at him. "Zeke, now that I'm gone, you won't get into as much trouble."

He shrugged his shoulders and gave her a dismal look. "Yeah, but I won't have as much fun." Before he went back inside, he pulled something from his pocket and handed it to her. "Here, a little going-away present."

"What's this?"

"You know the memory card the security guard made me take out of my camera? Well, I did a little switcheroo. What he really got were pictures of my dog catching a Frisbee in the park. Here are the photos of the tank and the bird. May he rest in peace."

CHAPTER TWENTY

Jamie knew she was in trouble the second Bren McKeever smiled at her near the entrance of The Ming Tree Restaurant. It was the eagerness in his eyes more than his smile that made her swallow hard. She wished she shared his enthusiasm, but she didn't. In fact, she almost cancelled their dinner date because of the lousy day she had. Getting fired was not her idea of fun. She'd be terrible company, but she would go through the motions and make an effort to be pleasant. Because his smile lingered, she gave him a half-hearted one in return. *Damn! Why didn't I cancel!*

Their table was in a quiet, secluded area that offered more privacy. Maybe he requested it that way when he made the reservation, she thought. He placed his palm over the silverware laid out on the white tablecloth and moved it a smidge closer to his plate. Was he just nervous or obsessive-compulsive? What did it matter? She knew his expectations were greater than hers, but to her, it was nothing more than a meeting of two people for the sole purpose of returning her earring. After dinner, she'd say a polite thank you and goodbye. Then they would be free to go about the business of their lives — separately. Adios and farewell, or so she thought.

"You're a hard person to get in touch with," he said with an easy smile.

"I've been busy, and *you* are very persistent."

He smiled. "I left you what? Three messages?"

"Six." They broke into laughter.

While his eyes stayed on her, she dropped hers to scan the menu. It was unsettling that he had similar features to Garrett. The same blue eyes and dark hair but a different body. From golf and tennis, Garrett was in prime condition, but Bren appeared more buff. He had broad shoulders, muscular arms and legs, and a narrow waist.

Why am I comparing this man to my husband? Focus, girl. The menu. Not hungry, but order something.

During the course of their meal, Bren did his best to make small talk, to engage her in conversation. She listened politely, made occasional remarks, laughed at his jokes, but remained distant, her thoughts elsewhere.

"Jamie, is something wrong? Did I say something to offend you?"

She dropped her eyes and shook her head. "No. It's not you."

"If something is bothering you, maybe I can—"

She ran her finger around the rim of her wine glass, buying time. She felt pity for him. He didn't deserve this. Although he was charming and engaging, she had nothing to give back. Her mind was on her troubles. The failed marriage, Garrett's betrayal, her arrest and her firing. He knew nothing of this, and she was determined to keep it that way.

"It was a mistake for me to come." She pushed her chair back and started to stand, but Bren's hand landed on her arm.

"Please. Stay. Whatever it is, it's okay."

"No. It's not okay." She snatched her clutch purse from the table. Before she left, she said, "Thanks for dinner, Bren. I'm so sorry, I have to go."

No further than half a block away, she stopped to stare mindlessly at a fountain in a brick courtyard. Water cascading over two tiers of sculptured marble made a soothing gurgling sound. It was enough of a distraction that Jamie did not hear footsteps stop behind her. A hand gripped her shoulder. She turned to look directly into Bren's eyes. He looked as though he wanted to take her in his arms, kiss her, stroke her hair, comfort her. She would make sure none of that happened. She stepped back.

"My life sucks right now," she explained. "I lost my job today. I'm terrible company for you, Bren, and you've been so nice. Look, I just want to go home and wallow in self-pity."

"Where's home?"

"The next block." She pointed down the street. "The condos."

He put his hand on her waist. "I'll walk you home."

"There's no need. Really."

"I'll walk you home." The forcefulness of his voice made Jamie relent with a shrug of her shoulder.

She didn't bother to make small talk and was relieved that he made no attempt either. The sound of traffic and their footfalls on pavement were the only sounds that followed them into the building. Without asking permission first, Bren stayed at her side into the elevator and up to her condo. She slipped the key into the lock and pushed the door open. He followed her inside.

She stepped out of her strappy heels and tossed her purse onto a chair. A clock in the foyer ticked loudly, filling the void of unspoken words. She didn't know what to say, and it seemed to her that Bren was debating his next move. He attempted a weak smile as his eyes studied her face.

"I wish I could do something for you," he said. "Maybe if you talked, you might feel better. I'm a good listener. A better listener than a talker," he added with a shrug.

"I'll take a hug," she said, trying to sound upbeat. "Bren, I'll be fine — I just need some alone time."

As if eager to please, he stepped closer and drew her into his arms. When she buried her face in his chest, his fingers stroked her hair, threading through her long tresses.

She stepped back and said, "It's been a bad day. I should have canceled our dinner. I thought it might cheer me up, but I think it brought us both down. Sorry."

"It's okay. We'll do this again — when you're up to it."

She shook her head. "No, I don't think so. You need to forget me, Bren."

"I don't think I can."

Their eyes locked. She did not know what to say in response.

She didn't ask what he meant because she was afraid to know.

"I made a mess of my life," she explained. "A mess of tonight. It's better if you distance yourself from me before I jinx you too."

He smiled and brushed the back of his fingers across her cheek. One finger lifted her chin. Before she could stop it, his lips pressed lightly against hers. One kiss led to another and another. She kissed him back with an eagerness that she seemed unable to reign in. His kisses were soft, tender, and full of heat. He brought her tighter into his arms, his hands groping her back and then sliding lower, resting on her buttocks. She tilted her head further back and accepted more of his kisses to her neck. This time he kissed her open mouth, wet kisses, full on and passionate. His body pressed more forcibly against hers. She became aware of her rapid heartbeat and her quick breaths. She felt helpless to diminish the arousal building inside her. Yet she knew it was wrong to lead him on, to deceive and manipulate him as Garrett had done to her. It was lust, nothing more, and it had to end.

She pushed him away. "No. I can't. Please." Her gaze concentrated on his hand that stayed on her arm. "Bren, you should go. I want you to go."

"Are you sure that's what you want?"

She knew why he asked it. It was a contradiction to her obvious pleasure in his embrace, his kisses.

"Yes. I think it's for the best. Thank you for dinner. And thanks for walking me home."

He kissed the top of her head and walked out. She pressed her back against the door and placed one hand over her lips, stunned that she had allowed him to kiss her in the manner that he had.

She'd had a lousy day and let it carry over into the night, ending what could have been a wonderful evening with a sweet man. No, she wouldn't wallow in self-pity, she'd stay strong and resilient. She would not seek revenge. From Garrett or the paper. She would seek justice. And if the lines got blurred, then so be it.

§

The eyes of the portrait seemed to stare back at Catherine. The likeness of her father captured every line, every wrinkle in his somber face. She remembered how much her father hated posing for the artist. To him it was a waste of time. He had argued that he was a doctor, a leading cardiologist, and he did not have time for such frivolity. But his wife and daughter had insisted. Catherine planned to move the portrait to the lobby of the new hospital wing with a plaque mounted below it to let everyone know that the building was dedicated to his memory.

"You'd be proud of me," she said out loud. *If Gar knew how often I talk to my deceased father through his portrait, he'd think I've lost my mind.* But she found it therapeutic, knowing that his spirit was still there watching over her.

"It's all for you, Daddy," she said as she gazed into his piercing eyes. The artist had captured just the right gray-green hue of his irises. "I wish you could have lived to see what your foundation has achieved. You'd be proud of your grandson, too. Garrett's been a big help with the project. All grown up now — married to Jamison Jackson. Wish you had lived to be present at their wedding, Daddy. What a happy day. And soon, they're going to make beautiful babies. My grandchildren. Your great grandchildren. Garrett's going to take over Gar's business and be better at it than Gar. Not that I would ever tell Gar that, but you know it's true. Garrett has a good heart like his mentor, Scott Michaels — very much like Scott. Not forceful and domineering like Gar."

Below the portrait, on the mahogany lowboy, Catherine picked up a small, framed photograph. She remembered posing with a chubby two-year-old Garrett in her arms. She smiled because it was her favorite of all the photographs that were scattered throughout the house. It was taken in Paris somewhere along the

Champs-Elysees. The toddler wore a navy sailor suit with short pants and knee socks, which she still kept tucked away in her memory drawer. Right before the picture was taken, Garrett saw a dog coming toward them. His joy was apparent with his big smile and wide-eyed look. Afterward, he giggled when the owner allowed him to pet the dog.

The memories of their trip held a special place in her heart. Every day they had spent in Paris was a happy adventure. She loved the people, their carefree attitude, the wondrous sights and the sidewalk cafes. She considered it the happiest three weeks of her life.

She had taken the trip with Garrett to recover from the loss of her father. Daniel Benjamin Bartlett died of a heart attack at home while his wife, Margaret, held him in her arms. Catherine got the news while she was with Gar on a business trip. They packed up and rushed home. After her father was laid to rest, she moped around the house for weeks until she got the idea that she needed to get away. At first, Gar said no, but finally he allowed her to take the toddler and fly overseas to her favorite place: Paris.

The memories of that time were still fresh in her mind. She often drew on them whenever she felt depressed or bored, which happened often lately. Gar was too busy to notice unless she had one too many martinis. He'd snatch the drink from her hand and order her up to her room. They had separate suites and she couldn't remember the last time Gar had slipped into her bed. But perhaps it was her fault. After all, she gave him no clear signs she wanted his affection.

"A penny for your thoughts."

Catherine jumped, startled out of her private thoughts. She turned around to face Gar and hugged the cherished photograph against her chest. "My goodness, Gar, you scared me to death! I didn't know you were there."

"Sorry, darling." He kissed the top of her head. "Catherine, you're not having one of your dark spells, are you? You know when you do, you drink too much."

"No, Gar, I was just rearranging the picture frames. Every time Marlena dusts, she puts them in a different order. I've told her a hundred times, but she doesn't seem to listen." She held out the one in her hands for him to see. "This one goes in the center, but she never places it there."

"If it's that important to you, I'll speak to her myself. Now come out on the terrace with me, Catherine. There's something I need to tell you."

"It sounds serious. What's wrong?"

"Just come out with me. Marlena's bringing some refreshments for us."

A large oak tree shaded the entire patio while a gentle breeze off the lake teased them with temporary relief from the heat of the day. Catherine sat next to her husband on a cushioned love seat that faced out toward the rose garden. He still wore his starchy dress shirt, which rubbed against her arm. She looked on while he loosened his tie and tilted his chin up to stretch his collar loose.

Once Marlena brought out a tray with two apple martinis and retreated back inside, Gar took his wife's hand. After a sip of his drink, he turned from the view of the lake to make eye contact with her.

"Catherine, I think we made a mistake encouraging Garrett to marry Jamie."

"Why in the world would you say that? Jamie is wonderful for him."

"She was arrested yesterday at the KleenBrite plant. She and some hippie photographer were trespassing on their property. The guard called the police and Jamie pitched a fit. She was charged with assaulting a police officer and resisting arrest."

"Oh my goodness!" Catherine brought her hand to her lips. "Jamie did that?"

"Yes. I found out through Bert Castleman. He called me at the office very upset over the whole business. I guess I'm partly to blame. I asked him to meet with her for an interview. Didn't have any idea just how far that girl would go to try to get a story."

"Where is she? Is she in jail?"

"No, no. Somehow the charges got dropped. But I called Garrett into my office and let him have it good. Told him he needed to get control of his wife. Guess it doesn't matter now. She lost her job."

Catherine wrung her hands in her lap. "My goodness! I had no idea."

"Confidentially, I'm partly to blame for that. I made a few phone calls on behalf of Bert. Fortunately, I still have some influence. The publisher assured me she would be terminated. That newspaper is no place for her. It's too controversial in my opinion. She needs to work for a women's magazine or something like that. Talented girl, no doubt, but too ballsy."

"I think she should stay home," Catherine said. "Garrett makes a nice living. There's no need for her to work. She could be doing so many enjoyable activities or charity work. If only she'd give it a chance. I never regretted staying at home."

"You, my darling, like to be pampered."

"Yes, I do." She shot him a playful smile and then said, "So what did Garrett say when you spoke to him about Jamie?"

"He told me to mind my own business. I don't know what it is with him lately. This morning he got into a shouting match with Bill Harris over some stupid report. He accused Bill of falsifying the numbers. I had to play referee and separate the two. I think Garrett's letting his new title of Executive VP go to his head."

"Why don't you retire and let Garrett take over, darling? You know how smart he is. He'll do just fine."

"No, Catherine. Not until he gives us a grandchild like he promised. When I'm sure there will be an heir to the business, then I'll step down. It's imperative that the company stays in the family's hands. I promised my father I would see to it and by God, I will."

CHAPTER TWENTY-ONE

As Bren lay in bed, he replayed in his mind his evening with Jamie. Her beautiful dark eyes, their kisses, her body against his, and their mutual arousal, all shut down before it went anywhere. But what he had forgotten until he awoke at two in the morning was her earring. He never returned it, but that put a smile on his face. Now she *had* to see him again, or she'd have one very expensive earring with no mate.

It took playing phone tag all morning to finally touch base with her. She called early afternoon and agreed to lunch the following day. Until then, he tried to concentrate on making changes to the drawings of the new hospital wing per the Reynolds Foundation's request. The structural engineer was on his case to have a revised plan by the end of the week. He was on a deadline, but he'd take time to have lunch with Jamie.

He grabbed a table at a sushi bar she'd suggested mostly for its proximity to his office and her condo. He watched out the window and soon spotted her removing sunglasses and setting them on top of her head. She was casual in jeans with a pink cotton shirt. Her ponytail swished back and forth as she made her way toward him. He stood up to kiss her cheek and pull out a chair for her.

"I'm better company today," she said as she sat down. "Sorry I was such a drag the other night."

"Glad you're better."

"Yes. My father taught me when you get knocked down, it's best to get right back up — if necessary, with clenched fists."

"So you're a fighter."

"I'm fighting to keep my sanity," she said with a playful smile. She dropped her gaze and studied the menu. "If you haven't been here before, I recommend the spicy tuna roll or maybe the salmon. Can't go wrong either way."

But the idea of eating raw fish did not appeal to him. He ordered a California roll and enjoyed watching Jamie capture her tuna roll in chopsticks like a real pro. He used a fork. His plan was to spend their brief time together learning all he could about the woman across from him, but the skilled reporter had a way of extracting information from him.

He found himself telling her about his mother whom he missed desperately since her death two years ago from breast cancer. Then he was on to his father, a retired firefighter who built a log home "out in the sticks." He told her he was the oldest of two boys. His brother, Joe, also single, lived near Atlanta where he worked for a software company. Bren talked about his time at North Carolina State University on a swimming scholarship, where he majored in architecture.

"You swam your way through school?" He noted the tease in her voice.

"I guess you could say that. It wasn't as easy as it sounds. I'd get up around four-thirty in order to get to the pool before the lanes were all taken. I'd swim to about seven, then go to class. Then, in the afternoon, I'd train for three hours with the team. In between, I ran six miles and lifted weights. Somehow, I found time to do class assignments and study. Weekends were spent going to meets. It was grueling. I wouldn't recommend it."

"Do you still swim?"

"Yes, but not as much. I go to the Y every morning before work. I swim for about an hour and do some weight lifting. I run at night and on weekends. Just to stay in shape. At least now I don't have to shave my body all over like I did in competition."

"Male strippers shave, too." When he arched his brow, she quickly added, "I mean, I've heard that. I wouldn't really know."

He chuckled. "Okay. We'll go with that." After a pause, he said, "Hey, you know all about me, but I know almost nothing about you, Jamie."

"I'm trouble," she said without hesitation. "If you don't

believe me, ask my former boyfriend. That was his nickname for me. I got arrested the other day, did I mention that?" He shook his head. "Yeah, well, that's what got me fired. I had another encounter with Tough Guy from the fundraiser. Fortunately it all worked out. The charges were dropped."

"You're a piece of work, Jamie," he said with a grin. "Get into an arm-twisting argument with Tough Guy, and then you get arrested."

"If you're smart, you'll keep your distance from me. Bad karma."

"If you're trying to discourage me, it's not working. As a matter of fact, I'd like to have dinner with you again."

"A do-over?"

He laughed. "How 'bout it? Tomorrow night?"

She glanced out the window and then back at him. "Let's keep it simple," she said. "Lunch. We'll do lunch again. Maybe Mediterranean next time. Okay with you?"

"Sure. I can do Mediterranean."

"Great. Call me."

Later, they walked out together into bright sunlight. Jamie removed the sunglasses from the top of her head and slipped them on. As Bren said goodbye, she turned her head sideways to accept his kiss, which he had hoped to plant on her lips. He swallowed down his disappointment and retrieved an envelope from his pants pocket.

"I almost forgot. Your earring, Jamie."

"Oh, yes. Of course," she said with a smile. "That's the reason we met for lunch."

Maybe your reason. "I'm glad it's back with its rightful owner. Thought I might get my ear pierced, but it didn't really go with anything in my closet." He gave her a wink.

Before he left, she placed her hand on his arm. "Bren," she said, but then stopped. While he waited, he kept his eyes locked on hers. "We'll do lunch. That's all. I don't want you to think that—"

"That I want you for dessert? I do, Jamie. I won't lie. If you hadn't shut it down the other night..." He didn't finish, just broke into a weak smile. "I'll take what I can get. I'll take lunch over not seeing you."

He kissed her on the forehead and turned to leave. In the front window of the restaurant, he saw her reflection, as immobile as a statue, watching him walk away. He'd love to know how long he'd have to settle for quick lunches and a kiss to her cheek. If he was a gambler, he'd bet money that she'd been hurt recently. Maybe by the ex-boyfriend that called her *Trouble*. Whoever the asshole was, he'd like to punch him, because he had apparently hurt his chances. And he didn't like that one bit.

CHAPTER TWENTY-TWO

Keep your friends close and your enemies closer. Jamie was familiar with the saying and thought it was prudent advice for a person trying to end a marriage with both finances and sanity intact. Garrett had been her friend, lover, spouse, and now an adversary. Her attorney advised her to keep things amicable if at all possible. Besides, she still needed — and wanted — Garrett's sperm. They had yet to make an appointment at a fertility clinic.

As far as Garrett was concerned, she'd let him think he had dealt himself the perfect hand. She'd bluff for a while before she played her trump card. The prenuptial agreement had been fraudulently altered and her attorney said he would find a way to prove it before they went to court. *But could he?* she wondered.

She agreed to go with Garrett to another fundraising gala for the Reynolds Foundation. He had insisted that their attendance was mandatory. Just to keep the peace, she agreed to keep up the pretense of their sham marriage. She joined him on the dance floor where he held her close. She imagined they appeared to be the happy newlyweds, so much in love. But in Jamie's opinion, it was a fairy-tale that lost its luster in a pile of shit.

The theme for the gala was *Casino Royale*. Men dressed in tuxes pretended they were James Bond with a femme fatale on their arms, the ladies with gowns slit up their thighs and coated in sequins. Jamie wore a beige gown of shimmering fabric that hugged her body and accentuated her curves.

While she danced with Garrett, she whispered in his ear, "Does Erica know you're here with me?"

"Yes, she knows. She understands."

"I once loved you so much, but now I feel like I don't even know who you are. It's difficult to be around you now, Garrett, because I miss the old you."

"I'm sorry you feel that way. But once our goals are met, we can go about our separate lives."

"Our goals?"

"Yes, the birth of our baby and my full control of Reynolds Industries."

"Ah, yes. The heir apparent of said company," she said in a tone tinged with sarcasm. "It's a game of deception. Is that what happens when you marry into the Reynolds family?"

"You have to beat them at their game. What we're doing is outfoxing the old man who thinks he's in control. Speaking of the devil, he's on his way over here. Give 'im a big smile."

In a black tuxedo, Gar Reynolds looked as debonair as Bond himself. He stood before them with a broad smile that showed dazzling white teeth. His thick crop of white hair was combed to perfection. As he stepped closer, Jamie caught a whiff of masculine scents: scotch, aftershave, and cigar.

"May I cut in, son? I want to dance with my beautiful daughter-in-law."

"Sure, Dad. Just don't monopolize her. She's mine."

Gar was a better dancer than his son. In his arms, Jamie seemed to float across the dance floor. His hold was firm, but he kept her at a respectable distance. He hummed the music played by the band.

"I don't know the song, Gar. What is it?"

He smiled down at her. "You're too young to know it, honey. It's called 'Some Enchanted Evening.' It's from a musical written by Richard Rogers and Oscar Hammerstein. Catherine and I saw all their musicals, some on Broadway. This particular song is from *South Pacific*. The lyrics are beautiful."

"I've heard of *South Pacific* but I don't know the story."

"I'll give you the DVD to watch. You and Garrett should watch it together. It's about true love, the type of love I have for Catherine and you have for Garrett." His strange smile made her pull back, but she noted that Gar chose to ignore her discomfort.

"Jamie, I'm sorry you lost your job," he said. "Garrett told me about it. Maybe it's for the best. It just shows that the story you were going to do about KleenBrite should be scratched. It would have a damaging effect. If it led to legal action, people could lose their jobs. You wouldn't want to be responsible for that. It's good that it's dead on arrival, if you know what I mean."

"Actually I haven't given up on the story. There's another person I'm hoping to meet with, but he wants some assurances that I won't use his name. I have photos that prove there was a spill. And I have an environmental magazine interested in running the article in their October issue."

He stopped dancing but continued to hold her. His eyes became dark and foreboding, like a laser beam designed to target and obliterate her autonomy. It sent a chill down her spine. He stayed silent with lips pressed tightly together. His jaw was tense and tight. He slowly moved his feet about, putting up the pretense of a dance partner.

He kept his eyes on her when he said, "You never quit, do you? Always hell-bent on some crazy cause. Think about us for a change, Jamie. Catherine and I are friends with Bert and Joan Castleman. You're putting us in an awkward position. Bert is a good man. He would never intentionally do anything unethical or harmful to another living soul. You're accusing him of a cover-up. Just think what that will do to his reputation."

"I go wherever the evidence takes me. If I'm wrong, then he has the opportunity to prove it — to salvage his reputation, his company's reputation. You know, he's lucky there are no criminal charges. My concern is for the ones hurt by his irresponsibility. They have developed all kinds of health problems caused by the contamination of the lake."

"And you know this how?"

"For one, the camp kids all had health issues after swimming in the lake, and secondly, the water was sent off for testing. Shall I name the harmful chemicals found in their samples?

Some I can't even pronounce."

"You're getting in way over your head, young lady."

"Is that a warning?"

"Forget it. You won't listen anyway."

"No, I'm serious. Is there something you know that I don't?"

Gar pulled away and stopped dancing. "I guess we didn't notice that the music has stopped."

She looked around at the empty dance floor where they stood alone, exposed to quizzical looks.

"Thank you for the dance," she said.

"My pleasure. I found it very enlightening."

His unctuous smile sent a shiver down her spine.

CHAPTER TWENTY-THREE

Afew miles from downtown Charlotte, a man with a ball cap with the Dallas Cowboys logo sat on a park bench in Freedom Park and checked his watch. His contact was late. Although they had spoken by phone, this would be their first face-to-face meeting. The voice on the other end of the line never identified himself, and he figured it was best that he not learn the man's true identity.

A slight breeze blew across the lake and threatened to remove his cap. He pushed it down tighter. He wondered if the buildup of clouds threatened rain. If a storm came, he hoped it would be later and not interfere with their meeting. Again, he checked his watch.

As he directed his gaze across the lake, a man appeared in a dark blue jogging suit. He ran out of the woods from a trail that led into the park. Although he could be any ordinary jogger, the man in the cap kept his eyes trained on him. His features matched the man's description: tall, slim, with a thin face and a beak nose.

Half way around the lake, the man took the path that led over to him. The beaked nose man stopped at the bench and put one foot up, stretching out his back leg, then repeated the action with the other leg. Never looking at the man in the ball cap, he sat down and stared straight ahead.

"You have the package?"

"Yes, right beside me," Dallas Fan replied.

Still winded from his run, Beak Nose detached a water bottle from a belt around his waist. He gulped down half its contents. His eyes shifted downward and studied the black canvas bag on the ground.

"Does it include the information requested?"

"Yes, of course. Photo, addresses, daily routine, acquaintances, family. Everything is there."

"And the money?" He looked amused at the team logo on the man's cap. "Got the money, Dallas?"

"Yes. Half now, and the rest when the job is finished. Wanna count it?"

"Not necessary. You know better than to cheat me." He gave him a hard look that made Dallas gulp. "I'll need three weeks to set it up."

Dallas furrowed his brow and frowned. "My friend wants it done sooner."

"Your friend needs to grow some patience. I gotta fly to Chicago to finish another assignment. Besides, I need time to do surveillance, get things set in place."

"But three weeks? You do understand that my friend wants the target to be terminated only as a last resort. The best scenario is for you to persuade the woman to hand over the information she has. Photos, documents, anything else that is damaging."

"Understood, but something like that can't be rushed. I need a solid approach. So three weeks is reasonable."

"But this woman is a threat *now*. There's not much time. She could release the information to another source. If so, then that person should be terminated also."

"Are you afraid of the word *killed,* Dallas?"

"Okay, have it your way," he said with a shrug. "The target is to be killed per my friend's instructions."

"Some friend," Beak Nose said sardonically. "And I imagine you are very loyal for reasons I don't even want to know. A second hit will double the price. Does your friend understand that?" The wind picked up and rippled the surface of the lake. It lifted a tuft of thinning hair straight up on Beak's head. He patted it down and took another big gulp of water. "Repeat. Does your friend understand two hits, two payouts?"

"Yes, yes. Okay," Dallas said and exhaled with exasperation. "Now there's something else we must discuss."

"What's that?"

"The weapon." From his pants pocket, he pulled out a clear plastic bag that contained a knife. "Use this."

Beak Nose gave him a hard stare and refused to take the offered bag.

"Not necessary. I use my own equipment. Sometimes my bare hands."

"Actually, it's said that you prefer that method."

A caustic grin curled the man's lips. "No bloody mess. No weapon to trace."

Dallas was not fooled by the man's slender physique. He knew under the loose jogging suit, the man was solid muscle. His strength would give him the ability to snap a target's neck with precision and quickness, bringing instantaneous death.

Dallas jiggled the plastic bag in the air. "Please take this. I will explain what we have in mind."

Beak Nose set hard eyes on the bag and grimaced. "This better be good."

CHAPTER TWENTY-FOUR

Whatever Bren was saying, Garrett didn't know and didn't care. His mind was still processing some disturbing news he had received prior to the Foundation meeting. He had arrived thirty minutes late and slipped into the only available seat at the conference table. To address his mother's questioning gaze, he gave her an apologetic shrug from across the table.

Garrett felt sure Bren had waited until he was present to announce a critical new development in the project. He pointed to a drawing projected on the whiteboard from a computer file that explained how the topography of the sloping land would require a design change. Then, with the lead architect's head-nod, Bren hit the committee with the bad news. The changes would increase the cost of construction and push back the completion date. He gave an option one and an option two scenario that Garrett pretended to comprehend.

His mother's question jarred him. "What do you think, Garrett?"

"What?"

"Didn't you hear what Brennan just said?" Catherine asked. "The changes. Which plan do you suggest we pursue?"

"Actually, I'd like a little more time to think it over." To Bren, he said, "I'll have to get back to you with a decision."

"Sure. But understand that we can't proceed until we know which way you want to go."

"Understood."

At last, the meeting concluded. Tapping the roll of drawings against his palm, Garrett walked out with Bren and said to him, "I'll let you know in the next day or so. I'd liked to look at our financial picture first."

"Sure. If your pocketbook can handle it, option one would be the way to go."

Garrett nodded. They walked toward their cars and drove off in opposite directions. Garrett headed downtown for the condo to make an unexpected visit to Jamie. As he weaved through heavy traffic, he rehearsed in his mind how he would break his news to her. Once the doctor had given him the lab results, he went into shock. It was not what he had expected to hear.

He parked in his old reserved space next to Jamie's car and made his way upstairs. The concierge greeted him as he walked to the elevator. He hadn't given his key back to Jamie, despite her repeated requests, and why should he? He owned the damn place. He let himself in and found Jamie on the balcony, staring out at the street with her elbows resting on the wrought iron railing. He focused on the way her skirt billowed out from the breeze and delayed making his presence known. A sense of dread kept him glued to the spot, organizing his thoughts.

She spun around when she caught a glimpse of him out of the corner of her eye. "Garrett! What are you doing here?"

"We need to talk."

"Without the presence of your lawyer?" she asked with a sardonic smile.

He scolded her with a look. "There's something I have to tell you. Come sit down."

"It must be bad if I have to be seated. What's wrong?"

He waited until she was comfortable in a padded patio chair and he was settled into the matching settee facing her. While he leaned forward, he rested his forearms on his knees and clasped his hands together.

"Jamie, there's not going to be a baby. Not for us."

"What do you mean? I told you I got checked and the doctor said I was fine."

"I'm sterile."

It took a minute for her to process his simple statement. Finally, she said, "What? How do you know?"

"I just got back from the urologist. I have a low sperm count, making it almost impossible to conceive. Sorry. Guess I'm less of a man than I thought."

"Don't say something so ridiculous. It has nothing to do with your masculinity, Garrett. It's nothing to be ashamed of." She glanced up at a sky that had the same intense blueness as the eyes that stared back at her. She swallowed hard and said, "Then we can proceed with a divorce. No need to stay in a sham marriage."

"Actually, I have a plan where we can get what we want. We'll have a baby, I'll get the business, and you'll have a substantial living allowance for you and the child. Remember our agreement — we'll share joint custody."

"I'm almost afraid to ask. A plan? What kind of plan?"

"A sperm donor that we pass off as mine." He quickly added, "No one will ever know."

"By in vitro fertilization?"

"No, too time consuming. Could take several tries and may not even work. I'm told that it could result in multiple births, too. Not what we want." He kept her in suspense before he said, "I'm thinking of a more natural way."

"More natural? What are you talking about?"

"I'm thinking of a sexual liaison with a man who has similar features to mine. Dark hair, blue eyes. I'd at least like the child to look enough like me to pass for a Reynolds."

"You mean close enough to fool your father," she said. "So you want me to have sex with a stranger that looks like you? Are you out of your damn mind?" She raised her brow with incredulous disbelief to what he was suggesting.

"No stranger, Jamie." After a long pause, he added, "Your boyfriend."

"I don't have a boyfriend."

"Sure you do. I saw the two of you at the Chinese restaurant and then again at the sushi bar near the condo."

"I don't know what you're talking about."

"Jamie, c'mon now. You think I don't know?" He gave her a smug smile, pleased with himself. "You're seeing Bren McKeever. Even before we separated, he was drooling over you at that fundraiser, and I bet you didn't bother to tell him you were married, did you?" He stepped up to her and lifted her chin with one finger. "I just left him at a meeting. And guess what? Bren smelled of you. The perfume I bought you on our honeymoon."

"We're just friends. We have lunch occasionally, that's all."

"Like today?"

"Yes," she admitted. "I'm not sleeping with him if that's what you think."

"Then see that you do."

§

She believed Garrett when he said Bren smelled of her. Images of her lunch with him flashed in her mind. They had eaten in the back corner of a tiny diner, sharing laughter, small talk, and an order of fries. She slapped his hand playfully when he poured ketchup over the potatoes. When he looked up with surprise, she explained that she liked hers plain. He scraped the sauce off the best he could and teased her for being so picky. His goodbye hug had been tighter than usual, pulling her plum against him. His lips kissed her cheek, then moved to her ear, where he whispered a sexual innuendo so uncharacteristic of him, it made her laugh. He followed his remark with an apologetic shrug and a wink. His hand squeezed hers affectionately as his thumb rubbed her palm in a sensual way that made her reluctant to let go. The heat she felt from his touch, and the humidity, caused beads of moisture on her skin that made the transfer of her perfume likely.

She blinked away her private reminiscences and focused on the discussion with Garrett that went on for over an hour. He brought up the prenuptial agreement whenever he wanted to emphasize the need for her to abide by the ground rules. If anyone was divorcing anyone, it was *him* divorcing *her* and not the other way around. If she pursued a divorce on her own, she'd end up with what she had now — nothing. Without a job, she was living in *his* place and on *his* generosity.

She had vehemently argued with him. "Don't try to control me with talk of money, Garrett, because I don't care about that. I'm not as helpless as you think. I've listed my wedding rings on E-bay. It should bring a fair amount. And I'm working on selling some articles to magazines."

"And when that runs out, what then, Jamie? Got a job lined up? Going to ask your daddy for a loan?" She gave him a hard stare. "Didn't think so. You've got too much pride for your own good."

"I can't use people like you do, Garrett. I won't deceive Bren."

"You already are. He doesn't know you're married to me. Wouldn't it be interesting if I mentioned it in one of our Foundation meetings? I'd loved to see his reaction to the news. He thinks you're single, unattached, doesn't he?"

"Okay, so he doesn't know I'm currently married. But using him to become pregnant is the lowest form of deception. I won't do it."

He laughed at that. "Jamie, you're so naive. He's playing you."

"What are you talking about?"

"He only wants to get in your pants. That's it! He's already accepted a position in Richmond. He leaves when his contract runs out in a month. Then he'll be gone, and you, forgotten."

"You're lying," she said through clenched teeth.

"He told me himself."

Garrett could be right. She had forgotten that Bren's six-month contract with the architectural firm would soon be up. He had mentioned it the night they met, but she had not thought about it since then.

"He's not looking for someone special, Jamie. He's looking for a good time. That's what men do."

§

Jamie would do things *her* way. If Brennan McKeever was going to be a sperm donor without his knowledge, without his consent, then it served him right. Like Garrett said, he wanted her for his own sexual gratification. He practically admitted as much when he said he wanted her for dessert. Then off he'd go to another job, another city, and never think of her again. On to the next woman, the next conquest.

Okay then. By God, she'd give him what he wanted.

But first, she'd prepare for what she was about to do by downing a few drinks. She went to her old watering hole, one block from her former office. She, Zeke, and other members of the news department would sometimes gather there after work. They had a favorite booth in the back corner, all the servers knew them by name, and their choice of beverages never changed. She ordered her standard apple martini with a twist of lime.

As she sat at the bar with her back to the room, she recognized Zeke's Alabama drawl and Stu's booming voice spewing out a string of words without stopping for a breath. If she kept her focus on the TV screen behind the bar, maybe they wouldn't notice her. She'd pretend to care about the baseball game, although she wasn't sure who was playing. But it didn't take long for Zeke to sneak up behind her and put his cold mug of beer on her arm, making her jump.

"Jamie! Stu and I were just talking about you and here you are!"

"Hi, Zeke." She swiveled around on her stool and waved at Stu.

"C'mon and join us, Jamie. I miss you like crazy," Zeke said. "It's no fun since you left. Stu thinks you're going to hire a lawyer and sue the paper for wrongful termination. Is that true?"

"No, Zeke. I have a lawyer for something else and he's not worth shit. He says he can't do what he promised to do. I might have to fire him, especially since I can't pay him."

"What are you talking about?"

"Nothing. Forget it," she said with a shrug.

Zeke helped her down and put his arm around her shoulders as they walked over to where Stu sat. Any other time, she'd enjoy the happy reunion. But now that she no longer worked with them, she felt like an outsider, not a comrade in the search for truth. She specialized in lies.

"What brings you here, JJ? Nostalgic about old times?" Stu asked.

"I'm preparing for a mission."

"What sort of mission?"

"A secret mission," she said curtly and took a big gulp of her drink. She winked at Zeke, who displayed his cynicism with a raised brow. She motioned to the server that she wanted another, a double.

"C'mon, JJ, don't play games with us," Stu said. "We're your friends, although I guess you think I threw you under the bus. I had no choice. It was either both of us or just you. Well, we gotta have somebody in the news department that keeps the insanity in check. I had to stay to be the mild-mannered reporter for a great metropolitan newspaper who fights a never-ending battle for truth, justice, and the American way."

"Superman!" Zeke shouted as he clinked his glass against Stu's for a spontaneous toast. Jamie refused to participate in their tomfoolery.

Stu studied Jamie for a minute and said, "Hey, JJ, if you're going to do some kind of covert mission, you'd better slow down on the booze."

"The drinks are helping me build up the courage to carry out the plan."

"So tell us what it is. Maybe Zeke and I can help."

She giggled, wiping where her drink had dribbled down her chin. "No, I don't think you can help out with this."

"What are you going to do, JJ?"

"I can't tell you, Stu. If I did, you'd lose all respect for me."

"Is this about losing your job, JJ? Don't make this a legal mess, okay? I made some calls on your behalf. I'm looking out for ya. 'Course no one's hiring now, at least not in our market. Maybe it's time you look into a new career. I'll bet you'd make a great English teacher. The kids could relate to you since you're so energized. Or you could work with a news station — radio or television. Go that route. They're hiring — at least, that's what I've heard. 'Member that guy we called Too Tall? Y'know, the six-five dude, sat in the cubicle near Zeke's rat's nest. I heard he's at one of those stations where they just report news, weather, traffic, that kind of shit. Want me to call 'im? He might be able to—"

She cut him off, "This has nothing to do with getting canned, Stu. This is something I have to do. I started a little project even before I married and it requires teamwork. My partner in the project quit on me, so now I'm recruiting someone else without their knowledge, which pretty much makes me a manipulative, conniving bitch." She tapped her glass against Zeke's mug and Stu's shot glass. "A toast, guys. To the new me."

While Stu frowned, Zeke gave her a cold stare. He said, "Not funny, Jamie. What is wrong with you?"

"Zeke, you don't even want to know. Let's just say my life is complicated." She glanced at her watch. "Well, guys, I gotta run. It's show time."

CHAPTER TWENTY-FIVE

Jamie waited for Bren to leave his office, hoping that she'd find him alone, no one else in sight. While she stood partially concealed beside an artificial palmetto plant in the lobby, she caught a glimpse of him as he pressed the down-button for the elevator. When the doors opened, he stepped inside the empty car. Placing her hand on the door panel, she prevented its closing until she made it into the car beside him.

Before he could process her sudden appearance, she stood on tiptoes to kiss him passionately. Instinctively, he drew her in close. Then she pulled away to meet his gaze.

"Let's do this," she said, giving him a sexy smile.

"What exactly do you have in mind, Jamie?"

"What do you think?"

He gathered her in his arms. His kiss was full-on, rough, and his hold became tighter, more forceful. He didn't release her until the elevator doors opened onto the main lobby. Two stunned women watched as they stepped out and walked hand in hand outside, where the after-hour's mad rush of pedestrians and vehicles spilled out onto the sidewalk and street.

"Your place?" he asked.

"Yes. It's close by."

As they walked into the lobby of her building, Bren said, "Are you sure about this, Jamie?"

"Yes. You're not having second thoughts, are you?"

"I can tell you've been drinking. When you sober up, you might say—"

"That you forced yourself on me when I was inebriated?"

He shrugged. "The thought occurred to me."

Suddenly, she stopped and turned to face him. "Not a chance," she said. "I want this."

She ran her finger over his shirt front in a tight circle, tilting her head up so he could see her playful smile, the longing in her eyes.

He smiled his pleasure. "I'm glad we're finally on the same page, honey."

The concierge gave her a judgmental squint when they passed his desk, but she didn't care. In the elevator going up to the condo, she kissed Bren again. She deliberately slipped her leg between his so that her thigh made soft contact with his crotch. He let out a soft moan.

Once inside the condo, he wrapped his arms around her, ready to resume the touching, the kissing, the groping, but she pulled away. Noting his baffled look, she quickly led him over to the sofa. After she kicked off her shoes, she pulled him down next to her.

She jacked up her skirt and straddled him. When she stretched up, his face pressed between her breasts. He managed to unbutton the first two buttons of her blouse and then brushed his lips across her exposed chest. While his hands squeezed her buttocks, she rocked from side to side. The slow, steady momentum built, increased his arousal. She wouldn't keep him waiting any longer. Without a word, she led him into the bedroom.

As she stood facing him, his hands worked at a frantic pace, but she cautioned him not to pop the buttons on her blouse. He reached behind her to unfasten her bra, then unzipped her skirt, letting it fall to the floor. With hands splayed across her buttocks, he worked his hands inside her panties and pulled them down. Together they tumbled onto the mattress. He managed to tear out of his own clothes, and then stretch out over her, kissing, touching, caressing. She wrapped her hand around his hardness, but he stopped her.

"Let's slow it down, baby. I'm not ready to end this yet."

He rolled off of her and reached for his pants, then shook out his wallet.

"What are you doing?" she asked.

"Getting a condom. We'd better play it safe."

"There's no need. I have an IUD. We're good to go."

"Still, to be on the safe side, we'd better use extra protection."

She sat up and clamped her hand around his wrist. "No, Bren. No."

"Why not?"

"I'm allergic to the latex in the condom. I said we're okay."

"Are you sure?"

"Yes, I'm sure."

His eyes stayed locked with hers in several moments of uncertainty. Because of his hesitation, she gave him a more pointed gaze, her lying eyes so convincing he tossed the wallet in the air and reached for her. Using both hands, he gripped her buttocks and pushed her tighter, closer, and penetrated her deep, then deeper. When she rocked her body, he either moaned or cursed, she wasn't sure. But as though he couldn't hold back any longer, he climaxed. It looked to her like his eyes were being sucked into the back of his head. His breathing intensified and every muscle in his face constricted.

When his lips took a pleasure trip from her nipples to her abdomen, she felt an electric current course through her body. But when his fingers worked their way inside her most erogenous zone, it sent a tsunami of pleasure that caused her to let out a string of moans and groans that could have alarmed the neighbors if it hadn't been for the soundproof walls.

§

Now that their romp in bed was over, it felt all wrong. She might have conceived and it should have been with a man she loved, more pointedly, her husband. But he had broken their vows, had violated the sacred trust of marriage. She was reduced to tricking a man she barely knew into inseminating her. It was more than wrong, it was treacherous, deceitful. But she had to admit that over time, their relationship probably would become intimate anyway. She rationalized her actions by admitting that there was a definite attraction, which possibly could lead to love. Therefore, she could justify the sex, but never the lie.

She didn't do tricks for money, but she *tricked* a targeted male for her own ill-gotten gains. In her mind, she was a scheming, conniving whore, worse than a prostitute. At least, hookers were honest. Their johns paid a set amount to be pleasured in an agreed-upon sexual activity. She used sex to get something in return also — not money, but a baby. And why? Because the traditional marriage route seemed out of reach. Because she let a member of the Reynolds family blackmail her into a method both deceitful and morally wrong.

Her conscience weighed so heavy with sins of transgression she felt her head would explode. Bren lifted her chin with one finger and kissed her. But it was his smile that made her do the unthinkable.

She pulled away, flipped over on her side, and bawled. To muffle her cries, she covered her head with her pillow. She felt his hand on her shoulder and heard his voice, low and soft. As he stretched over her, he lifted her pillow away.

"Jamie, what's wrong?"

She grabbed the pillow back, covered her face, and continued to cry.

"Jamie! What is it? Did I hurt you? What's wrong?"

"Nothing."

"Tell me, damn it!" he said with alarm sounding in his voice. "Please!"

She mumbled to herself, "I just want somebody to love me."

Although her pillow would have muffled her words, she knew he had heard. Awkward silence hung in the air like a foul odor. If ever there was a time she wanted a do-over, it was now. She felt movement on the mattress and knew he was pulling away. At last, she took the pillow away. She looked up and when their eyes met, he quickly diverted his away. He gathered his clothes, then came around to her side of the bed.

"Jamie, I don't know what you want from me."

She wiped tears from her cheeks and looked up at him. "I want you to leave. I want to be alone. Can you do that for me?" Although unintentional, her voice hinted at anger, directed at herself, not him. She added, "Please, just go."

"Okay. If that's what you want."

In the time it took him to dress, she stayed motionless on the bed, almost afraid to breathe or utter a sound. She heard him turn the door-knob and let himself out. After she heard the sound of the door closing firmly behind him, she cried herself to sleep.

CHAPTER TWENTY-SIX

The next morning a shaft of sunlight in her eyes awoke Jamie and reminded her of the prior night of humiliation. She assumed Bren left thinking she was a mental case. How else could she explain her uncontrollable sobs after the best sex she had had in a long time? *If a girl wants to scare away a guy, that's the way to do it,* she thought. She hoped that he got her pregnant because the chances of ever seeing him again were about zero.

Her phone rang, but she refused to pick up. Three minutes later, the incessant ringtone started again. Still, she ignored it. In less than ten minutes, there was a knock at her door. She hoped whoever was there would give up and go away. But a persistent pounding ensued. Her name was shouted repeatedly. She recognized the voice as the concierge who worked the morning shift. If she didn't respond, she knew he had a key and would enter on his own.

In her T-shirt that barely covered her butt, she answered the door. It shocked her that behind the dapper little man in a navy blazer stood Bren, holding a paper bag and a cardboard tray with two cups of coffee. He looked relieved to see that she had regained some semblance of a sane person and hadn't done something stupid like slit her wrists. She stared back at him and ran her hand through her tangle of dark curls. She was as embarrassed by her disheveled appearance as her behavior of the previous night.

"Miss Jackson, you okay?" Henry said. "We were worried. This gentleman said you were sick last night. And then you didn't answer, so we had to make sure."

"I'm fine, Henry. Just had a rough night. You can go back to your desk now." She locked eyes with Bren. "And you. You can go, too."

But he pushed the opening wider and stepped inside. "I'm staying."

Henry said to Jamie, "You want me to call security, Miss Jackson?"

"No, that's okay. I guess he can come in for a few minutes." Bren waltzed into the living room like he owned the place. He headed straight for the kitchen, where he set the bag and coffee on the countertop. After he pulled out pastries wrapped in crisp white paper, he smiled at her.

"Thought you might be hungry this morning."

"After the way I acted last night, I'm surprised you're back."

"I don't scare easily."

"And the way I look doesn't scare you?"

"I've seen worse." He chuckled. "I mean — you know what I mean. You look fine."

"I can't figure you out, Bren. You're either a hopeless romantic or you're just plain clueless."

He shrugged. "Maybe a little of both."

"Well, I'm going to wash my face and put on some decent clothes. Be right back."

She returned wearing shorts and a tank top. Her hair was tied back in a ponytail, her face scrubbed clean and free of makeup. She sat across from him at a glass-top table, sipping coffee and nibbling on one of the raspberry scones he had brought. Bren stared up at the skyscraper across the street as though making mental, analytical notes of its cantilever design.

Jamie sliced through the uncomfortable silence by saying, "What happened last night — I mean, when I was crying — well, it had nothing to do with you, so don't take it personally."

At first he seemed too stunned to speak, but then blurted out, "Are you crazy? Jamie, I just had sex with you and then you started crying and ordered me to leave. Why shouldn't I take it personally?"

"There's something I haven't told you, something you should know. I'm getting over a marriage breakup. My husband left me for his former lover. I told you I wasn't ready for a relationship. Now do you understand why?"

"I didn't know you were married."

"Separated. We're not getting back together. Ever!"

"I see," he said. After a long pause, he added, "So he broke your heart. Okay, I get it."

"Do you? Do you have any idea what it's like to find out that the person that you've loved so deeply never loved you back?"

"Hearts get broken, but hearts heal."

"You make it sound so simple. I was right, you *are* clueless."

"No, Jamie. I'm not clueless, believe me. I've been there. You're right, it *does* hurt. But it wasn't the end of my life, and it's not the end of yours. I can tell that you're strong. Nothing will keep you down for long. Look, it didn't scare me away when you said you just want someone to love you. To tell the truth, it made me respect you more. You want more than sex. You want a meaningful relationship. Well, so do I."

"But you're leaving. Moving to Richmond."

His eyes widened, displayed surprise. "How do you know that?"

She licked her lips, buying time to recover her mistake. "You told me."

"No, I don't think so. Because it's not even official yet."

"Well, you told me you have a six-month contract and it's about to end, and then you'll go somewhere else. I just said Richmond randomly. So maybe it's Chicago or Atlanta. Hell, I don't know."

"I should have told you I've been offered a position in Richmond. Good guess, by the way," he said with a smile. "We obviously like each other. Let's just see where this leads. Okay?"

He took a firm hold of her hand and pulled her around to his side of the table, letting her fall onto his lap. He kissed her, his hands groping her backside. Finally, she took a breath and stood up.

From a distance of a few feet she watched him watching her. She recorded to memory his face, his blue eyes, his dark hair, straight nose, muscular build. A clone of Garrett, except with integrity.

A sperm donor, nothing more. If I think of him that way, it'll be easier to let him go, she thought.

§

That afternoon Bren drove Jamie to his house. Before they even turned onto his street, he prepared her for the worst.

"It's just a rental, so you know it's got problems. Nothing like your place, Jamie. I just took it for the fenced-in backyard. So Quincy would have a place to run around."

With her lips pressed together, she studied the ugly brown clapboard with yellow shutters and sagging flower boxes. It had a high-pitched roof and a tiny front stoop that led up to a front door with peeling paint the color of dark chocolate. She noted that at least the lawn was mowed and the shrubbery trimmed.

"It's not so bad," she said.

"You don't have to spare my feelings. Fortunately, I spend more time in the backyard than inside. The sundeck's nice."

Once out of the car, Bren led her around to the backyard, where Quincy awaited their arrival. Ignoring Bren, he jumped up on Jamie, almost knocking her down. While he whined and drooled with unbridled excitement, she held up her arm to fend off his aggressive affection, but used her opposite hand to pat his head.

"Quince! Bad dog! Leave the lady alone. Sit!"

Quincy got off of Jamie, but he continued to nudge his nose and bump his long lean body against her. She bent over to rub behind his ears, which made him even more exuberant. He licked her face.

Finally, Bren pulled him away by the collar and made him sit down. "Sorry about that. He likes to meet new people."

"It's fine. Quincy is a beautiful dog. I love golden retrievers. How long have you had him?"

"Since he was a puppy. I think he was around three months old, not really sure. I found him alongside a road when I was driving back to Boston. It was after a big snowfall and he was shaking like crazy. I took him to the vet and they treated him for hypothermia. He wasn't micro-chipped and no one claimed him, so the vet said I could keep him. We've been best buddies ever since. Right, Quincy?"

The dog let out a deep bark as if he understood every word Bren had said. Bren sat on the top step of the deck next to Quincy and slid over to make room for Jamie.

He smiled at her and said, "This feels good. The outdoors. You. Me. Quincy."

That evening Bren grilled steaks and potato wedges on his gas grill while Jamie put together a salad. They ate outside on a wooden picnic table and shared a bottle of Pinot Noir. From speakers that Bren had wired from a CD player inside, they listened to sultry sweet jazz from his massive collection. When the song *Moonlight* began with Kenny G on saxophone, Bren brought Jamie into his arms for a slow dance.

His chin rested against her head as he held her close. She felt his hand slip underneath the hem of her top and make contact with bare skin. His touch was gentle, fingertips lightly massaging her back. She lifted her head to meet his gaze and responded to his smile with one of her own.

He cupped her face in his hands and kissed her lightly. Then his hand ran down her neck to cover her breast and squeeze firmly. When she edged closer so that there was no separation between them, he lifted her into his arms and carried her inside.

After they made love, they lay with her back pressed against his front and his arm draped over her. Quincy stretched out on the floor nearby, letting out an occasional moan every time he shifted positions. When she heard Bren's even breaths, Jamie turned onto her back and slid away from him so he could continue his deep sleep. She noticed how the illumination from the streetlight slipped through the slits in the blinds and bathed his face in pale light, so peaceful, so serene.

If he was going to be the father of her child, she hoped the baby would have his gentle, kind spirit. She had no doubt with their combined gene pool they would create an awesome child. One she would love with all her heart. Her chances of being pregnant were good — ovulation, viable sperm (she hoped), and repeat performances (twice — two nights in a row). She had used a digital reader and test sticks to determine the best time for pregnancy to occur. According to the results, she was at her peak of ovulation. Yes, she could be with child already. She smiled as she ran her hand over her abdomen.

CHAPTER TWENTY-SEVEN

Since they had first made love, time had flown by like on the tail of a comet. So fast. It was Jamie's first thought when she was awakened by Bren's touch. The days were eating away with little left before he was expected to move to Richmond to begin his new job. She spent hours wondering if it would be the end of their relationship and hoping it wasn't. She agonized over a risky possibility: dare to love again, wanting to, longing to, but cautious. Hopeful, but realistic. Her heart guarded and healing at the same time.

Who was she kidding? Did she really want to set herself up for another one-sided love affair, later to be heartbroken? Although Bren gave signs that he really cared for her, he never said the L-word. Besides, he was leaving soon for a job in another city.

As planned, she would honor the contentious agreement with Garrett in which he set the terms of their divorce. But there was one thing out of his control — pregnancy, her trump card. If she and Bren had a mutual love for one another, and if they were to conceive a child, then in her opinion, the contract with Garrett was null and void. Screw the prenups that said differently. Just like the forefathers wrote in the Declaration of Independence, the pursuit of happiness was her inalienable right. *No one* could take that away from her, not Garrett, or the entire Reynolds empire.

For once she allowed Bren to stay the night, risking that the Reynolds family would somehow find out and think she was cheating on their precious son, Garrett, when in fact, her liaison with Bren was *his* idea.

It was a sunny morning with clear skies, a day full of promise. A Friday, no different than any other. But it would progress into a series of synchronicities that would turn from a dream-come-true to a nightmare. There was no forewarning, and the fact that Bren sat down on the bed and looked at her in his tender way made her more oblivious for what was to come later that day.

The morning sun illuminated one side of his face, shadowed the other, but made visible his easy smile as he gazed at her. Jamie sat up and propped her pillow against the headboard. She raked her fingers through her long tresses. Just being in his presence, having him close, gave her a warm feeling. Memories kicked in of their night of lovemaking that started out in a nest of pillows on the living room floor and ended in her bed. By the time they had reached the bedroom, she was groggy and tipsy from two glasses of wine, yearning for his touch, begging him to come inside her, feeling his hands and then his penetration, her hips rocking with each thrust, and finally the orgasmic explosion that left them both spent. After they'd made love with his tender eyes locked onto her closing ones, Bren said something to her. She didn't know what it was because she couldn't will herself to stay awake. Her head plopped against his bare chest and she awakened in the morning to find that he had settled her into her side of the bed, pulling the sheet up to cover her.

She welcomed the cup of coffee he handed her. He had prepared it the way she liked it — strong with extra cream. *How sweet he remembered,* she thought.

"You spoil me, Bren."

"I like spoiling you."

His smile disappeared, replaced by a somber expression. It made her uneasy, but she stayed silent, not inquiring about the shift.

"Jamie, I have something to tell you."

"You look so serious, you're scaring me."

He's leaving. He's telling me goodbye. Oh God, no. Not now. Not today!

His face softened into a smile. "I think you'll like what I have to say. I've set up a meeting this morning with Miller. I'm telling him that I'm turning down the position in Richmond, and I'll see if he's willing to extend my contract in Charlotte. I want to stay. You see, there's a woman I love very much and I can't leave her." He seemed amused by her reaction. She almost choked on her coffee. "I love you, Jamie."

She stretched forward, almost tipping the coffee over as she kissed him. "I'm so glad you said that. I was hoping — wishing. I feel the same, Bren. I love you too."

"I told you last night, but then I realized you were already asleep. So I saved it until this morning." He took the cup from her hand in order to bring her into his arms. "If I didn't have to leave now, I'd make mad passionate l—"

Her phone trilled on the bedside table. She looked at the display. "Oh my gosh, it's Stu!" She held up her index finger. "Hold that thought." Her eyes stayed on him as she answered the phone. "Hi, Stu." A pause, then, "No, that's okay. I was awake." His rapid-fire words, jumbled together, making it impossible for her to understand. "Whoa, whoa, you're talking way too fast. I didn't understand a word you said."

This time, much slower, he tried a different approach. "I am not making this call. You are not talking to me, JJ. You haven't heard from me since that night I saw you at the bar. This is off the record. I did not give you this information. You got that?"

"Sure, sure. What's going on?"

"Your story, Jamie. That KleenBrite debacle. I got an anonymous call from a Deep Throat kind of guy. He said to follow the money, just like in that movie about Watergate. Same shit. So guess what? I did. I checked public records, land deeds, property tax listings, liens, judgments, stock reports. The more I dug, the more I hit pay dirt. JJ, your father-in-law owns the land. He's an equity partner in the business, financed the buy-out of the camp. He's up to his neck in this thing, and

I'm sure he's pissed off at you for pursuing the story. You put all your focus on the contamination, didn't think to look to see who was behind the money."

Jamie glanced momentarily at Bren, knowing she was projecting a strong reaction to Stu's remarks by the horror on her face. She gave him a weak smile and returned her focus to the phone call.

When she hung up, Bren said, "What was that about?"

"Stu just gave me some new information about someone's involvement in KleenBrite."

"You're talking about that asshole who tried to strong-arm you at the fundraiser? His company?"

"Yes. It seems the spill was intentional, no accident. It was done to force the camp to close and sell at below market value. Since the land was spoiled, contaminated, it was of no value to anyone except KleenBrite. They plan to drain the lake and use it as a containment pond."

"Jamie, why the long face?" Bren asked. "Isn't this good news for you? I mean, it gives strength to your story."

"I'm fine," she answered softly. "It just hits closer to home than I thought."

"What do you mean?"

"It means you never really know the culpability of a person until the truth comes out." She threw the covers back and tugged at the hem of her silk nightshirt that had gotten twisted around her hips. Bren's eyes stayed on her as if waiting for more details, but she didn't want to discuss it with him. Instead, she said, "Shouldn't you be leaving?"

He stood up and reached for his cell phone on the bedside table. "Trying to get rid of me, Miss Jackson?"

"No, it's just that I don't want you to be late for your meeting with Miller. It sounds important," she said with an impish smile.

"It is, and you're right. I'd better get going, but first a kiss."

After he bent down to kiss her, he said, "Any plans for today?"

"Yes, I have a special dinner planned for us. I have something to tell you tonight."

"Tell me now."

"You'll have to wait. Besides I want to make sure about the accuracy of my information first. You know how we reporters are."

"Yeah, they're a strange bunch," he joked. "You sound mysterious, babe. Can I have a hint?"

Think blue or pink, she was tempted to say, but she didn't. Until he was gone, she wouldn't know for sure if she was even pregnant. The EPT kit was under the bathroom sink. The directions said "for best results use after rising in the morning." Now, if only he would leave, she could get up and pee on the stick and find out.

"Well, I'm off," Bren said.

Hallelujah!

§

Jamie had no reason to suspect she was being followed except that the dark sedan matched the description of a car she had seen parked across the street from her condomium building the prior morning. While most men gave her an appreciative glance, the man with thin hair and a beak nose had seemed to make a point of not looking her way. As he had sat behind the steering wheel, he sipped coffee from a Styrofoam cup and stared straight ahead as she walked past on her way to the Farmer's Market. Because he gave her an eerie feeling, she made a point of memorizing the license plate.

The car — a Hyundai same as yesterday she noted — stayed suspiciously with her in traffic, making her concerned enough to call Chris.

He answered right away. "Hi, Jamie. How are you?"

"Right now, I'm a little worried. I think I'm being followed, Chris. Can you check out a license number for me?"

"Whoa, slow down. Tell me what's going on."

"I'm on Tryon near the Observer building and I'm on my way to Garrett's office. It seems that a dark sedan is following me. I took a crazy detour and he stayed with me. I think it's the same car that was in front of my building yesterday. Can you check the license plate and see what comes back?"

In five minutes, he called her back. "It's a rental, Jamie. Can't give you a name. I'm headed in your direction. I'll make up some excuse to pull the guy over and find out who he is and what he's up to."

"Never mind. He's gone. He turned down a side street. Maybe it was just my imagination."

"Still, we need to talk. The guy in the car must have something to do with that company where you got arrested — I'd bet money on it. Didn't I tell you to leave it alone? Still working on it?"

"A little. I've checked out a few leads. I got a major break this morning, but I haven't had time to follow up on it. It's one of the reasons I'm on my way to see Garrett."

"What's he got to do with it?"

"I hope nothing, but his father is involved."

"Damn, Jamie. Pull over and wait for me. Tell me what you've learned. I think maybe you're too close to this."

"I can't talk now. Like I said, I'm on my way to see Garrett, and I've got to get to his office before he leaves. He promised to wait for me, but I can't trust him to stay until — never mind — Look, Chris, I can't talk now."

"Wait a minute, don't leave me hanging," he said.

"Forget what I said. I've heard that cops don't like it if you drive and use your cell phone at the same time, so I'd better hang up before I get in trouble with one."

His brusque laughter was tinged with irritation. "I'll cut you some slack. Pull over and I'll catch up to you. I'm not far behind you."

"Sorry, Chris. I can't."

There was one thing she remembered about Chris. He was as persistent as she was stubborn. She hung up while he was still trying to persuade her to wait for him.

A quick glance at the dashboard clock told her it was three o'clock, but already the traffic was heavy. She worked out in her head what she would say to Garrett, how she would back out of their agreement. So focused on her thoughts, she didn't spot a vehicle riding her bumper until she saw the blue lights flashing. Police. Unmarked car.

When she looked in her rearview mirror and caught Chris's familiar scowl she cursed out loud. She eased the car to a stop along the curb, put it in park and waited for him. Removing his Ray-Bans, he stared down at her. She hit the button to lower the window and greeted him with a sardonic smile.

He said deadpan, "Turn off the ignition and step out of the vehicle, ma'am."

"Aren't you overstepping your authority, officer?"

"Just trying to keep the citizens safe, ma'am."

She exhaled an exasperated breath, but did as he instructed. She couldn't help but notice how dressed up he was in a starched dress shirt, gray slacks, striped tie, and black tasseled loafers.

"You look nice," she said.

"Thanks. I was in court all morning. I had to testify." He gave her a once-over and didn't bother to conceal his playful smile. "You look pretty good yourself."

She ignored his remark and leaned her backside against the car door. With arms crossed, she said, "You shouldn't have pulled me over, Chris. I said I was in a hurry."

"Do you think your husband is connected to that company you were investigating?"

"Please don't say 'husband.' Garrett and I are separated."

"Damn, that didn't take long."

"I married a cheater. The night I called you he was with his former lover. They have reunited," she said with a frown.

"Damn! Do you want me to break his knee caps or just his nose? Of course, I could do both. That should send a message."

She rolled her eyes.

"I see he didn't heed the warning I gave him at your wedding reception. I'm sorry, Jamie. You deserve better. Are you okay, sweetie?"

"Do you want the truth?"

"No, lie to me," he said. "Of course, I want the truth. You okay?"

"I'm pregnant, Chris. I just found out this morning."

"Wow! Bad timing. At least Garrett has the money to support his kid."

"It's not his, Chris."

"WHAT?"

"I know it sounds crazy, but....Look, we're slowing down traffic."

"I don't give a shit." He placed his hand on her elbow and steered her over to the curb, away from the traffic. "They can use the other lane, go around us. So tell me, Jamie. Who's the daddy? Do you even know?"

With the back of her hand, she hit his chest and pushed him backwards. "How dare you! You son of a bitch! How can you ask me that?"

"Sorry, Jamie. I-I don't know what made me say that. Forgive me? Don't keep looking at me like that. I said I was sorry."

"I forgive you, but only because I know that sometimes your mouth gets ahead of your brain."

"Yeah, yeah. So tell me. Who is the father?"

Before she told him about Bren, she gave him a summation of her agreement with Garrett to delay a divorce until after the baby was born so he could claim it as his own. She admitted her deception, using Bren as a sperm donor. While traffic went around their vehicles, horns sounded, brakes screeched, a siren wailed, and Chris seemed to be digesting all that she had told him.

When she finished, she took a deep breath and waited for his condemnation of her actions, but instead he stayed silent. She watched him, biting on his lower lip like he always did whenever he was in serious mode. She remembered the look.

As an afterthought, she said, "I regret all of it, except my relationship with Bren. We're in love, Chris. That's why I'm on my way to see Garrett. To make him understand."

"Good luck with that."

"Unfortunately, Garrett has changed, but I hope he still has a heart. Maybe I can reason with him."

"I doubt it. He's a Reynolds, isn't he? They can be ruthless, so I've heard."

"I guess I'll find out soon enough."

"Does this guy — does he know you're married to Garrett? Didn't you say they work together? How could he not know?"

"I've been very careful not to mention Garrett's name. And I doubt he would ever talk about his private life with Garrett. They just have a business relationship." She ignored the uncertainty in his eyes and focused on the collage of buildings, cars, and the tree-lined sidewalk. Then she let her eyes meet his gaze. "It's getting late, Chris. I'd better go."

Chris caught her arm before she walked back to the driver's side. "Jamie, I'm worried about the guy following you. I think there may be something to it. It sounds like this company is guilty of criminal charges, and it shouldn't be you exposing them. I know it's a sticky issue for you, with your father-in-law involved, but I know you, and that won't stop you. You're hell-bent on seeing this through. Look, I've got a contact at the state attorney general's office. I could make a call. In the meantime, I want you to lay low. Promise you will."

"If you can make that happen, then yes, by all means, I'll lay low. The attorney general's office should be involved in this. They harmed children. So please reach out to your contact." She smiled. "Besides, I have other things to deal with now."

"Have you told this guy — what's his name? Brett?"

"Bren."

"Bren. Have you told him about the baby?"

"No, I'm telling him tonight. I'm going to tell him everything. I hope he'll forgive me for not being honest. I couldn't bear it if he hates me."

"If he's got any sense, he won't. What you did was wrong, but hell, who am I to judge you? The king of fuck-ups."

"No, you're not," she said. "I'm glad you pulled me over. It feels good to tell someone what I've been going through."

Chris glanced back at his car as if just realizing his emergency lights were still flashing. Before he put his sunglasses back on, he gave her a stern look. "Okay, ma'am, guess I'll let you go this time with just a warning."

Jamie clasped her hands together over her chest and said with a syrupy Southern belle inflection, "Why thank you, officer. You are too kind."

He grinned. "Bye, Jamie. Be careful, sweetie." He put his arms around her and kissed her cheek. "Call me if you see that asshole following you again."

"I will."

As he stepped back, he said, "Congrats on the baby news. You'll make a great mom. I always thought so." He gave her a poignant look that spoke to her more than his words.

CHAPTER TWENTY-EIGHT

Jamie had never seen Garrett so angry. His face turned as red as his mother's prize hybrid Americana roses. He paced in front of his desk with his hands in his pockets. She kept a safe distance on the other side. If he expected his rage to scare her into submission, he was wrong.

"I thought I could reason with you, Garrett. Obviously my happiness means nothing to you. It's all about *you*—what you want and to hell with what *I* want!" she said. "Please, Garrett, let's put an end to this farce. Let's get the divorce. I don't give a damn about your money, and it's not going to work for you to try to control me by cutting me off financially. My lawyer said that I'm entitled to half by state law. If we go to court, I might win that battle regardless of how you've altered the prenuptial agreement."

"You want have a prayer in court. My lawyers will eat you alive."

Despite the angry tone of his voice, she didn't back down. "The baby is Bren's, and I'm going to tell him. You can't stop me."

"Oh yeah? How's that going to play out? He'll know you set him up, that you got pregnant on purpose. How are you going to explain your marriage to me? He has no idea! You fucking lied to him, Jamie! You think he's going to trust you when he knows the truth? You think he'll just forgive you like that?" Garrett snapped his fingers. "*Sorry* is not going to cut it, sweetheart."

"I think when I explain how I was manipulated into making a very bad choice, he'll forgive me. At least I have to try. He deserves to know the truth."

"You are screwed, Jamie, and you don't even know it. I will fight you in court for years if I have to! I'll get sole custody of the child. My family's power and influence will make sure of it. I can *bury* you if I want to."

"No, you can't. The facts speak for themselves. The DNA, Garrett. It'll prove you're not the father."

"Don't count on it, Jamie. Again, I'll remind you of my family's influence. Divorce me now? No, I think not," he said with a smirk. "You'll do as I say, so get over your little moony-eyed romance with this guy and face the damn facts! You agreed to pretend we're still together until I get control of the company. As discussed, you'll accept that the baby is mine and then after a reasonable time, you can have your damn divorce. And all the money you ever dreamed of for you and the baby. Just sit tight and play this out, Jamie. How hard can that be?"

"Your parents will find out you have a mistress, Garrett. I'll make sure they know and the court, too, when I sue you for divorce."

"My father already knows. Your shocking announcement won't raise eyebrows, sweetheart. Trust me. My father has had flings off and on for years. My mother turns a blind eye. It's just part of being rich and powerful. You can't hurt me, Jamie, so don't even try."

"You can't stop me, Garrett. I'm going to tell Bren the truth. He loves me, and I love him."

"Well, if you really do, then you'll do as I say, or I'll take him down with you."

"You can't do anything to hurt—"

She stopped at the sound of a voice on the other side of the closed door. In a flash, it swung open. Jamie stared at the figure in stunned silence.

§

The Jackson woman had spotted him in traffic and made a call. To whom, he didn't know. But Beak Nose was forced to abort the tail on her vehicle. Thirty minutes later, he backed his rental car into a parking space that faced a brick building. A vehicle was near the front door, blocking his view, but it was of little concern to him. In the small round port in his cell phone, he inserted the cable for his ear buds and then crammed them in each ear. When he dialed and the transmitter picked up interior sounds, a smile curled on his lips. It was so sensitive that it could detect anything that created sound waves, such as the flushing of a toilet, a water faucet turning on, clinking of glasses, and a woman's screams at orgasm. He remembered a previous episode of the latter with fondness. But the nude woman had screamed a different scream right before he strangled her. She had witnessed him shooting her lover to death with a .45 equipped with a silencer.

He glanced up at the sun, still high in the sky. He adjusted his car seat back to get comfortable and settled in for what could be a long wait. The right timing was key to the execution of his plan. For now he would sit tight. Patience and perseverance were qualities required for his job. Without them he would go insane.

The car at the door was in bad need of a wash, he noted. It bothered him that the owner let it get so dirty. The entire driver's side was streaked with brownish-red mud. The windshield and hood had splats of whitish-gray bird droppings. *Disgusting*, he thought. *How much trouble would it be for the owner to run it through a car wash?* In his opinion, such indifference was unacceptable.

His work was dirty, but he never left a mess. Never!

§

Jamie noted that Catherine Reynolds waltzed into the room as if she was the queen of some damn kingdom. She acted liked she expected a curtsey and a bow from her son and daughter-in-law. From Garrett, she got a light peck on the cheek. Then she turned to Jamie to gather her to her bosoms. Jamie winced but submitted to the tight squeeze.

In a cream linen jacket and matching skirt, Catherine was dressed to impress. Her strong perfume almost made Jamie dizzy. Her red lipstick left an imprint, which Jamie discreetly wiped off her cheek.

"What was all the ruckus about?" Catherine said. "Y'all having a little lover's quarrel? My goodness, I heard it from the reception desk. Jamie, in my day, we would never raise our voice to our husband like that. Not lady-like. Of course, times are different. No etiquette or social graces whatsoever."

Garrett hung his head and gave an exasperated breath. "Mom, Jamie and I weren't arguing. We were having a very spirited discussion because we're so excited."

Jamie locked suspicious eyes with Garrett. She gave him a warning with a slight shake of her head. To her dismay, Catherine took note and egged him on with a playful smile. "Excited? About what, dear?"

"Jamie's pregnant. We're having a baby!"

Catherine brought both hands up to her lips and let out a little scream. "A baby? A baby! Oh my goodness! Oh, I'm so happy! That is the most wonderful news I think I've ever heard. Wait 'til I tell Gar. He'll be so pleased. I'll go get him now."

As Catherine opened the door, she almost collided with Bren. She put her hand on his arm and let out a girlish squeal. "Oh, Brennan, I'm so sorry. I didn't realize you and Garrett were meeting today. Don't mind me, I'm just so excited. I'm going to be a grandmother! My daughter-in-law, Jamie, is pregnant!" She waved her arm in Jamie's direction as she stood helpless, watching Bren's expression change from inquisitive to a brutal stare. "Can you believe Garrett's going to be a father? Oh, I'm so happy! I'm going to get my husband down the hall to tell him. Come on in, Brennan, my dear. Extend your congratulations to the happy couple. I'll be right back. Oh, this calls for a drink. Garrett, isn't there a bottle of champagne in the cabinet over there? Be right back, y'all."

Once she was gone, the threesome stared at each other in a veil of awkward silence. Jamie felt queasy, almost dizzy. She wanted to reach out to Bren, to utter a full explanation, but his glare kept her silent. It was Garrett who spoke first.

"Well, this is *awkward*. So Bren, now you know Jamie is my wife. Sorry no one bothered to tell you. Thought we'd have a little fun with you. Joke's on us, I guess. Now that she's having my baby, I guess our little game is over. Oh well. It was fun while it lasted. Jamie said she had a good time, didn't you, sweetheart?"

Jamie went pale. She walked up to Bren even as he backed away. "Bren, Bren, don't listen to him. He's lying. We're separated. Two months ago. Before I met you. The baby is not his. It's yours. You've gotta believe me. I was going to tell you, I swear. Tonight. I was going to tell you tonight. Remember this morning? I told you I had something to tell you."

When she put her hand on his arm, he jerked it away. "Don't touch me! Stay away from me. You lying, cheating—"

Garrett said, "Oh, go ahead and say it." Then he turned to Jamie, sporting a sardonic smile. "You lying, cheating *whore!* You'll feel better once you get the words out, Bren."

With eyes on Jamie, Bren said, "You've been a busy lady. Slipping between the sheets with me — *and* your husband."

"Bren, I told you, Garrett and I are separated. I was going to explain everything tonight. It is your baby. I know this is a shock. I never meant for you to find out this way."

"Did you mean for me to find out at all?"

Bren did not give Jamie a chance to answer. He bolted from the room, ignoring Jamie's tears and pleas, calling out to him. She followed him to the elevator, where he repeatedly punched the button to go down. She placed her hand on his arm.

"Bren, listen to me. I love you! Marrying Garrett was a mistake. His family tried to control me. *He* tried to control me, but I wouldn't let that happen. I want to be with you — only you. You've got to believe me." With his gaze still fixed on the elevator doors, he removed her hand from his arm dispassionately. "Please, Bren. Talk to me."

He turned to peer down at her, narrowing the distance between them and forcing her to walk backwards. His hard look and cold eyes made her swallow hard. He said, "I trusted you! My mistake. It's over, Jamie. Goodbye."

He watched the tears spill down her cheeks and then stepped into the elevator car. His eyes stayed on her as the doors closed, bringing an end to the drama like a curtain being drawn on a stage.

CHAPTER TWENTY-NINE

Chris got the call when he was driving to a Mexican restaurant in the Southeastern part of the city for a first date with a blonde named Jessica. He had met her at the shooting range, of all places, and it scared him a little that she was so familiar with firearms. But in all honesty, he'd be more scared if she was a bad shot like Jamie, who couldn't hit an elephant standing two feet in front of her. Because of her lack of experience, or lack of forethought — hell, maybe both — Jamie had once pointed a loaded gun right at him. Now *that* was scary. He never took her for target practice again.

"Whatcha got, Nick?" he asked as he pulled up to a red stoplight.

"We've picked up a homicide. Female, appears to be late twenties, early thirties. That's all I know. It's at 1408 Stoneybrook Drive. I'll meet you there."

"Got it. Be there in say, fifteen minutes. Y'know, this job is ruining my love life. 'Member the blonde I was telling you about? Tonight was going to be the night. She finally agreed to go out with me."

"You should know better than make big plans when we're the lead investigators on the next call. Not smart, Chris."

"Well, I'm a gambler, and I was betting the damn call would come much later. No such luck."

With apologies, Chris called Jessica and canceled their date. He felt especially bad since she was already at the restaurant, having just parked her car. Although she seemed gracious, he sensed some annoyance in her tone. *Maybe it's a sign,* he thought. *Sharp-shooter girl is not a good candidate for a workaholic homicide cop.*

By the time Chris arrived, four units had blocked the two entrances to the apartment complex and yellow tape had cordoned off a partial section of the building, while residents milled around outside with stunned expressions. Chris greeted the patrol officer stationed out front and signed the log-book. He found Nick already in the kitchen area where the body was being examined by the medical examiner and crime scene investigators. Chris hitched his chin at Sergeant Holden and two detectives as an acknowledgement. Lined up against the cabinets like wooden soldiers, they bore pragmatic stares, waiting for the ME and crime scene guys to finish doing their thing.

"What do we know?" Chris asked the question to Nick, standing next to a man he recognized from the district attorney's office. They both hovered a few feet behind the ME.

Nick flipped his notepad and read from his notes. "Female, age thirty, Hispanic. We have a positive ID of Erica Romero. She resides here."

"Have we started canvassing?"

"Yep, we got two teams knocking on doors. No working surveillance cameras."

"Figures," Chris said. "Who called it in?"

"Her boyfriend. He's in the living room, pretty broken up. We haven't got much from him yet. He's a mess."

On the balls of his feet, Chris squatted down and examined the wounds to the torso. The victim was on her back, head turned sideways, eyes open. Chris was certain of one thing: when she was alive, she was a real beauty.

"How many stab wounds, doc?"

"About ten to the torso according to the punctures in her clothing. I'll know more when we do the autopsy. The one to the heart did her in, lots of blood there. Lots of force. Whoever did this ended up covered in blood. The other wounds appear to be post-mortem. And then, see that tear across her pants? One long slash across her genital area and her thighs. Looks like a crime of passion. I found blunt force trauma to the back of her head. In all probability she was knocked unconscious with an object and then stabbed. The murderer stood over her and did this," the ME said, gesturing with a wave of his hand at the butchered corpse.

"A real psycho," Chris said with a frown. "Any estimate on time of death?"

"According to the core temperature, I'd say about one to two hours ago." He glanced at his watch that registered a quarter past seven, then he wiped sweat from his forehead with the wrist of his gloved hand. "That puts the time of death between five and six o'clock."

When Chris stood up, the police officer, first to arrive on the scene, briefed both detectives with more details, referencing his notes. He began by saying, "No forced entry. Looks like she knew her attacker."

Nick said to Chris, "Look at her hands. No defensive wounds. No scratches, no bruising, no sign of a struggle. She never saw it coming."

Chris frowned. "Nope. Like doc said. Probably knocked out, then stabbed. No blood trail either. No bloody footprints. Clean. Too clean. Looks professional."

The crime scene investigator brought over two wineglasses already bagged for evidence. "We should get good prints off these. Lipstick print on one glass but not from the victim. She wasn't wearing any."

"So the attacker could be a woman," Nick said.

"Looks that way."

Chris scratched his nose with his latex covered finger, then asked, "Find what the suspect hit her with?"

"Nope. Believe me we've looked. Still checking, but can't find it."

Sergeant Holden eased away from the cabinet and stepped over to Nick and Chris. "Okay, guys, we've got enough in here. Let's get outta the way and let the ME finish up. Crime scene needs to mark it up and get some pics. Go see if the boyfriend has anything more to say, something we can move on."

As they walked through the dining area and toward the living room, an investigator, called Einstein for his out-of-the box thinking on forensic evidence, came up holding an object. "We found her cell phone in the bedroom. She had a voicemail, one she never listened to. You guys need to hear this."

Chris and Nick strained to hear the message with all the activity behind them. It was a woman's voice, surly and loud. "Erica, we need to talk. *Now!* I will not let Garrett — *or you* — destroy my life! You created this mess, so it's up to you to fix it. You've wrecked my marriage, and now Garrett is being unreasonable. Because of you! I *hate* you for what you've done! No, hate is too mild a word. I'd like to get my hands on you and...I don't know what I'd like to do. I'm coming over! Be there in a few."

With one swift stroke, Chris snatched the cell phone from the open palm of the investigator. With an incredulous stare, Einstein said, "What are you doing, Lagoni? We have to ask that man in the next room if he can ID the caller. Then I'm bagging it for evidence. Give it back."

"No need. I'll tell you who it is. Jamison Jackson, that's who. And we're not playing it for that guy. Nick and I will handle this."

"Whatever you say. Just give it back to me."

Chris stared down at the carpet and handed it over with reluctance. He felt as if he was simultaneously sealing the fate and betraying the trust of a person for whom he cared deeply.

Nick's mouth fell open and his eyes widened as he stared at Chris. "Oh my God. What the—"

"The guy in the room will be Garrett Reynolds," Chris said solemnly.

Nick locked eyes with him and paused long enough to process the information. "Holy shit! That's Jamie's husband!"

"Yep." Chris leaned into Nick and whispered, "I recognized Jamie's voice. There has to be some explanation. Forget what this looks like, Nick, because there's no way. We need to find out what Reynolds knows. Jamie and I had a little chat today, and I'm sure he doesn't know that she confided in me. She told me some things."

"What things?" Nick asked.

"Later. Not now."

"Did she tell you that he was screwing around on her?"

"Yeah. I know more than he thinks I know. Let's keep it that way."

"Chris, you sure you can handle this?"

Chris admonished him with a hard stare. "Don't worry about me. I'll be doing my job."

"We need to tell Holden. Now!"

"Not yet. Besides, Holden just left with what's-his-name — the dude from the DA's office. C'mon, let's go talk to Reynolds."

§

They found Garrett seated on the sofa, bent forward with his face buried in his hands. He looked up when Chris spoke his name. From the agony on his face, Chris had no doubt that Erica's death had hit him hard.

"Hi, Garrett. I have Detective Nick Pulaski with me. I'm sorry for your loss. We'd like to ask you some questions."

Garrett nodded and wiped tears from his eyes with a tissue. He picked up a glass of water from the coffee table and took a sip. Then he sat up straight to brace himself for another round of questions.

"What time did you find Miss Romero?"

"Like I told the officers, Erica invited me over for dinner." Garrett paused and studied Chris's expression, which Chris intentionally kept blank. "I should explain. Jamie and I are separated. Only recently, understand. Erica and I started seeing each other. Anyway, as I was saying, she had me over for dinner."

Jesus! Is he ever going to answer my question? "What time did you arrive?"

"It was around six-thirty. We were going to cook together, something we liked to do. I knocked first, but when she didn't come to the door, I used my key and found her. Like that. Oh God!"

Garrett broke down, sobbing loudly into his hands. Nick and Chris exchanged a look and waited until Garrett got control of his emotions. He wiped at his eyes and took a deep breath. "Sorry. It's just so hard. I can't believe this happened."

"Take your time," Chris said. "Besides finding her, did you notice anything out of the ordinary?"

"No, no. She told me she was going to spend her day cleaning. She was off today after finishing three days of twelve-hour shifts. When I walked in, the apartment looked spotless, but that's Erica. A neat freak. Very clean, nothing out of place."

"When was the last time you heard from her?"

"Around noon. I called her when I went out for lunch."

From Nick, "And when was the last time you saw her?"

"This morning. I spent the night here. We had a quick breakfast. Then I showered and dressed and left for work."

Chris said, "And people can vouch for you being at work?"

Garrett let the question hang before he answered with a clipped tone, "Of course. I work in an office, surrounded by people. Am I a suspect?"

Chris ignored the question. "What time did you leave work?"

"Around five."

"Then where did you go?"

"Home. What is this? Surely you don't think—"

"Just standard questions," Chris said. Although he knew the answer to his next question, he asked it anyway. "Did your wife know about your relationship with Miss Romero?"

"Yes, she knew. I told you, Jamie and I are separated now. We've kept that a secret. Please, I'd like to keep it that way."

"Have you spoken to Jamie lately?" Chris asked.

"No, not lately."

"You didn't see her this afternoon?"

Garrett and Chris became locked in a staring contest, both men hanging tough, but at last, Garrett blinked and moved his gaze to the floor.

"Okay. She came by the office, but she left upset. We had a little altercation."

Nick flipped over to a new page of his tiny notepad. "Tell us about it."

"Not much to tell."

"You know, Garrett, it would help us find the killer if you were more forthcoming. Save us some time," Chris said.

Garrett took a deep breath and said, "It was about our separation agreement. A guy came into my office, a man Jamie and I both know. That's when things got more heated. Jamie's involved with him. They're *lovers*. Anyway, Bren McKeever left and Jamie followed him out."

"You said things got heated. Was she upset with you or the man?" Nick asked.

"She demanded a divorce from me, which means she has no intention of honoring the pre-nuptial agreement."

"So she was pissed off at you," Chris said, "because you refused to grant her a divorce."

"Yes. We're married. I want to keep it that way for now." Garrett wiped at his eyes and said, "Everything has become so complicated. It's been crazy."

"Did you know Jamie came to see Erica after she left your office?"

Garrett furrowed his brow at Chris's question, drawing out deep lines across his forehead. "That's absurd. Under the circumstances, they're not exactly best friends."

Chris crossed his arms and looked directly at Garrett. "You don't know of a meeting between Erica and Jamie this afternoon?"

"No. What are you talking about?"

"Jamie left a voice message for Erica. She was coming over."

"What?"

"We have the recorded message, Garrett. I recognized Jamie's voice."

"I can't believe Erica would agree to see Jamie."

"I don't think she had any choice in the matter."

Nick's remark earned a hard stare from Chris who added, "Maybe Jamie wanted to get Erica's help in divorcing you. What was the plan, Garrett? Stay married to Jamie and have Erica on the sly?"

"There was no plan, detective," Garrett said tersely.

Chris and Nick exchanged knowing looks, but Chris took the questioning in another direction. "Do you know anyone who would want to hurt Erica? Any known enemies?"

"No. Everyone loved her. If she had problems with anyone, she didn't tell me. Except for one man who got her upset," he said as if recalling the incident in his mind. He looked back at Chris. "Erica got along good with everyone."

"What man?"

"Huh?"

"You said she told you something about a man. What's that about?" Chris asked as he studied a change in Garrett's body language.

Garrett began tapping his hand on top of his thigh and stared straight ahead. "Nothing really. A lawyer. He works for my father and came to see her once to deliver a message."

"What message?" Chris asked.

"Get out of my life, don't wreck my marriage. My father put him up to it."

Nick flipped over his notepad again and took out his pen. "What's the guy's name?"

"Stuart Ramsey. Look, I'm sure my father just asked this guy to speak with her and let her know that our secret affair was exposed, — that my father wasn't happy about it. That's good ol' Dad for ya, using his influence to try to get his way."

Chris hitched his chin at Nick, prompting him to stand up. "Well, thanks for your time, Garrett. Sorry for your loss. We're going to do our best to find out who did this and bring them to justice." He reached inside his coat pocket. "Here's my card. Call me if you think of anything else. Anybody we can call for you?"

"Except for Jamie, my father, and his lawyer, no one knew about Erica and me. I'm certainly not calling any of them for comfort." He wiped his eyes and sniffed. "What about Erica's mom? Has anyone told her?"

"We're going there now to tell her. The worst part of our job."

"She's sick." He answered their questioning stares by saying, "She has cancer. It was in remission, but it came back. Doesn't look good for her. I know Erica was very worried. Now you have to tell her that her only child is dead."

Garrett sobbed into his hands. The detectives let themselves out, stayed silent all the way back to Nick's sedan.

Nick got behind the wheel while Chris dropped into the passenger seat with a heaviness. He ran his hand over his grim face and said, "This sucks. No fucking way Jamie's responsible for this." Chris hit the side window hard with his fist. "Damn! What the hell took place?"

Nick had his hand on his keys but had yet to turn the ignition. "It's your call, Chris."

"I'll call Jamie and tell her to meet us downtown, but first we need to break the news to Mrs. Romero."

"Chris, you're up to your neck in this. You and Jamie...Holden's not going to like it. You need to tell him now."

"Fuck the sarge," he said with hard eyes. "Pulaski, just drive the damn car!"

CHAPTER THIRTY

Sophia Romero did not react to the news of the death of her daughter. She couldn't. When Nick and Chris arrived at her modest home in South Charlotte, the door was answered by a hospice nurse. The black lady with a moon-pie face and hair styled in tight cornrows greeted them with a warm smile. She informed them that Mrs. Romero was in the final stages of her life and on a morphine drip to make her last days, or hours, comfortable. When they delivered the tragic news about Erica's death, the lady gasped and fell against the doorframe. Nick offered to help her inside and get her a glass of water, but she said she'd be fine if she could have some quiet time to herself to pray. They left their cards with the lady with instructions that they be notified if and when Mrs. Romero was conscious enough to speak with them.

On their way back to their car, Nick said, "Maybe she's better off this way. Not even aware. It would hit her hard if she knew."

"Yeah. Besides, I doubt she can tell us anything that would help."

"Nope. My guess is that Erica shielded her mother."

§

In the darkness, Bren sat on his living room floor with Quincy. He figured the dog sensed his need for comfort because he stayed at his side and did not sprint to the front window at the sound of a car door shutting in the driveway. When there was a knock at the front door, the dog's ears perked up, but he didn't give his customary growl. Prepared to tell whomever it was to get lost, Bren greeted his visitor with a furrowed brow and grimace.

A man held out an ID with an official shield. "Brennan McKeever? Detective Chris Lagoni with CMPD."

"I'm McKeever." Bren kept suspicious eyes on him.

"May I come in?"

Bren stepped aside and ushered the officer into the living room, where Quincy sniffed the visitor, running his nose up and down his pants legs.

"Hey, Quincy, back off." Bren tugged on the dog's collar and pulled him away. "What can I do for you, detective?"

"I'm here about Jamison Jackson. When was the last time you saw her?"

Bren saw something in Lagoni's eyes that made alarm bells go off. "Has something happened to her?"

"I need to speak with her. She's not home, and she isn't answering her cell phone. Since you're in a relationship with her, I thought you might know."

"How do you know that?"

"I know her, and she told me. Look, we can get into specifics another time. Right now, I need to find her. Do you have any idea where she might be?"

"No," Bren said. "I left her around five. I don't know what this is about, but I'm probably the last person who would know her whereabouts."

"Really? Why is that?"

"I think you need to tell me what's going on. Are you worried that something has happened to her?"

"That's what I'm trying to find out. I saw Jamie this afternoon. She thought a man was following her in traffic, and now a woman is dead —murdered, — someone Jamie went to see. She might have been there when it happened. So it's imperative that I find her."

Bren swallowed hard, raked his fingers through his hair, and kept his incredulous stare on the detective. "Damn! Jamie? I don't know anything about…. We had a fight. I left, but I never saw her after that. For God's sakes, what is this about?"

"I'm going to be straight up with you, McKeever. Like I said, she called me about some guy following her in traffic. When I caught up to her, the tail was gone. She was on her way to see Garrett Reynolds. Her meeting with him had everything to do with you. Know what I'm talking about?"

"Reynolds is her husband." Bren's terse words were followed by a scowl. "She went to tell him her big news — she's pregnant. But I'm sure you already know that. Guess I'm the last person to find out."

"She was going to tell you tonight. She was going to tell you everything."

"Then I ruined her surprise," he said indignantly with a shrug.

"It's yours, you know. Jamie loves you. She was trying to speed up her divorce because she wants him out of her life and wants you in."

"And she told you all that?" Bren shot him a cynical look. "How do I know that's the truth? She's lied to me about so many things. I don't even know who she is anymore."

"I understand you're pissed, but you can believe one thing — she loves you. That's what counts." Chris put his hands on his hips, exhaled a deep breath, and stared up at the ceiling. "All this can be hashed out later. Right now, we need to find Jamie, and I need your help."

"*My* help?"

"Yeah. Would you be willing to go to her condo and wait for her, then bring her to police headquarters?" He glanced at his watch. "I have to meet with my sergeant and the crime scene investigators. They're waiting for me."

"Jamie and I are not exactly on good terms right now."

"I get that," Chris snapped. "But you still care about her, don't you? I wouldn't ask if it wasn't important. I don't want to have a patrol car go by and pick her up. Out of concern for her, I'd rather she be brought in by someone she knows."

"You make it sound like she's a suspect."

"She could be a victim. I don't know, but I do know that the woman who was murdered is Garrett's lover. We can place Jamie at the murder scene, and she has motive. You and I know Jamie didn't do this. Hell, she might be a target. She left in her own car, but it doesn't mean the murderer is not after her, too."

"You must be the ex-boyfriend Jamie mentioned."

"Yeah, we had a relationship. It's been over for a while now." Chris glanced over at a laptop computer left open on the seat of a chair. It displayed a photo of Jamie, smiling for the camera and with her arms around the dog's neck. He turned back to Bren. "Are you going to help me or not?"

§

On the way back to police headquarters, Chris stayed silent, ruminating over the case and wondering how he was going to break it to Sergeant Holden that Jamie was a person of interest. He'd rather be hit with a stun gun, as he had been in training, than tell his supervisor that his ex-girlfriend was somehow involved. Of course she was innocent. Had to be, because Jamie was not capable of murder.

Sitting next to Nick, Chris briefed Sergeant Holden on the new development in their case. Although he'd preferred to keep his superior in the dark for now, he agreed with Nick that they needed to report what they had learned. Determined to appear impartial, Chris told Holden that Jamie was the last person known to see Erica alive. He left it up to Nick to tell him about her damaging voice message and potential visit to see Erica that lined up with the time of death.

"We're bringing her in," Chris said in conclusion." I know she can clear this up for us. It's possible she was also a target or *the* target. She called me this afternoon to say some guy was following her and had staked out her building yesterday. He could have followed her to the crime scene."

Holden leaned far back in his chair and crossed his arms. "I'll be sending Waller and Landon in to interview her."

Chris took a minute to let it sink in. Waller? Landon? *Holden can't be serious,* he thought. But the sergeant displayed a face like granite that not even dynamite could bust.

After a sidelong glance at Nick, Chris jumped up from his seat. He leaned over the sergeant's desk with his palms flat on its surface. "This is our case! You can't send in those guys. She'll feel more comfortable with me. I can get her to talk. She trusts me. You think she's going to trust Waller? Like I said, maybe she was there when the murder happened. Maybe the killer is after her too. She's probably scared out of her mind. It would help to have a friendly face in the room."

"Not gonna happen, Lasagna. You're too involved with the lady. You and Kielbasa can sit this one out. Watch on the monitor."

"But, Sergeant Hol—"

Holden held his hand up, palm out signaling silence, then grunted as he lifted his heavy frame out of his chair. He ran his hand over his bald head. His lips barely moved as he said, "My mind's made up. Now get out, gentlemen, and go do your job."

CHAPTER THIRTY-ONE

Jamie lingered in the shower where her tears blended with the warm water. She stood under the showerhead, hugging her arms to her chest, until she felt drained, the flood of emotion purged from her body. As she slipped on a terrycloth robe, she felt numb, empty. She barely recognized the despondent creature that stared back at her from the mirror over the sink. She should have been wearing a broad smile, and this day should have been one of the happiest of her life. That morning Bren had told her he loved her and he was staying in Charlotte. And even better, she had learned that she was carrying his baby. She longed to share the happy news with him, but he had turned her away. In fact, she felt that he hated her, and she couldn't blame him.

Chris had pretended to be happy for her, but she'd sensed his disapproval of the method she used to become impregnated. A sperm donor by deceit. Although he kept his thoughts to himself, she knew he was disappointed in her, but not as much as she was disappointed in herself. She had let her need — no, her obsession with having a child — cloud her judgment. She had known there would be consequences, but she proceeded anyway.

Her heart pounded when she heard the doorbell chime. She wasn't expecting anyone, and even if she was, the person had to go through the concierge, who would call her to get permission to send the visitor up. Fear washed her over, remembering the man who followed her in traffic. The repeat of the door chimes sent her heart racing. Up on tiptoes, she looked through the peephole to see. It was Bren! He had come to forgive her. Yes, yes, yes! She felt a surge of relief and joy.

But the grave look he gave her when she opened the door made her heart sink. He brushed past her into the center of the room. He kept his head down and his hands in his pockets.

"How did you get up here?" she asked.

"I slipped by the front desk."

"You need a card to get in the elevator."

"I rode up with a resident. She got off on another floor."

"So much for security." As she ran her fingers through her damp hair, she gave a weak smile. She brought her hands up to pull the robe tighter around her neck. "I'm glad you came, Bren. Are you ready to forgive me?"

"Not now, Jamie. Don't." His words made her keep her distance. "I was sent here to get you."

She shot him a confused look and bit down on her lower lip. "To get me? What are you talking about?"

"You didn't check your phone messages?"

"No, I turned my phone off. Why?"

"Your ex-boyfriend, Detective Lagoni, wants me to bring you to police headquarters," he said matter-of-factly. "Where have you been? He's been trying to reach you."

"I've been driving around. Trying to get my head straight."

"Get dressed. We have to go. He's waiting."

She didn't appreciate his brusque matter, so she wouldn't apologize for the annoyed tone in her question: "What's this about?"

"I'd rather you hear it from him."

She crossed her arms over her chest, refusing to budge. "No, you tell me."

He exhaled an exasperated breath and locked eyes with her. "You're going to be questioned. Someone you know was murdered."

"What? Is this a joke?"

"This is serious, Jamie. You might be a suspect in a murder."

His hard eyes and curt words made her heart drop. "Murder? Whose murder?"

"Your husband's lover."

Jamie felt her legs go weak. She walked to the sofa and

plopped down. She brought a trembling hand up to her mouth. "Oh no! Erica? There must be some mistake! Oh my God!"

"Are you involved in this mess?"

She gave him a hard stare, affronted by his question. "How can you ask me that?"

He shrugged. "There are things I don't know about you, Jamie."

"You know me well enough to know I had nothing to do with this."

"Do I?"

She wiped tears from her eyes. "What kind of person do you think I am? You must really hate me."

"I'm trying hard not to feel anything, Jamie."

§

Chris watched on the monitor with Holden and Nick as Jamie was questioned in Interview Room One. He didn't like the smug look on Waller's face when he first walked in and introduced himself to her. He had that *I'm in charge, and you're nobody* attitude that always pissed Chris off. Many times, Chris had been tempted to restructure the bull-dog face with a series of punches. Not that it would do any good; the guy would stay a hard-ass.

On the other hand, Chris liked Landon who he considered congenial and laid back. He'd been known to get confessions out of suspects when other detectives got zilch after hours of interrogation. For reasons unknown, suspects *wanted* to admit their crimes to Landon as if he was a compassionate priest hearing a confession and absolving them of guilt. The female detectives called him a teddy bear because of his short stature, expanding waistline, and his tender brown eyes.

Landon leaned forward with a hand on his knee and said to Jamie, "We're just here to get the truth. We're talking to people who have been in contact with Miss Romero recently. So Mrs. Reynolds, when was the last time you saw Miss Romero?"

"Please, call me Jamie, or if you must, Miss Jackson. I didn't take my husband's name."

Waller grunted. "Okay, *Miss* Jackson, when was the last time you saw Miss Romero?"

"I went to her apartment around five. She was fine when I left. What happened to her?"

"We'll ask the questions," Waller said.

Chris wanted to go in there and smack the guy. He was glad Landon shot Waller a hard stare and answered Jamie's question. "She was murdered."

Jamie covered her face with both hands and said in a muffled voice. "So it *is* true. It's so hard to believe."

"The medical examiner said it happened between five and six today," Landon said. "That puts you in the time frame. You may be the last person to see her alive."

"No, I wasn't. Whoever did it was the last person."

Waller harrumphed. His eyes bored into her as he said, "Tell us why you went to see her. Maybe we should start there."

"Where's Garrett? Does he know? Of course he does. You should be talking with him. He'll be able to tell you more than I can. I hardly knew her."

"Tell us about your meeting with Erica Romero," Waller insisted. "How did the meeting come about?"

"I called her to say I was coming over."

"Why?" Waller rolled his shoulders back, looking irritated with her. "What prompted the visit?"

Jamie glossed over her contentious meeting with Garrett, omitting delicate details of Bren's surprise visit and the awkwardness and controversy that ensued. She explained to the detectives that she went to see Erica to confront her about her relationship with her husband that had destroyed their marriage.

Landon stopped her at this point. "Erica greeted you at the door and asked you to come in. Was there anyone else there?"

"No. It was just the two of us. She never got my phone message so she was surprised to see me. She had just gotten back from the store. While she put food in the fridge, we talked a little and she could see I was very upset. To help me calm down, she brought out a bottle of wine and poured two glasses. Then she led me outside to the patio and told me to sit down. She had something important to tell me."

As if salivating for the juicy details, Waller licked his lips and said, "What was it?"

"She said she was going to do what she could to expedite the divorce. She had a plan."

"What was her plan?"

Landon leaned toward her and gave her a reassuring look. She responded with a shrug and a weak smile.

"Go on, tell us. What did Erica say?"

"She had a secret, but she wouldn't tell me what it was. All she said was it held the key to get Garrett to agree to a divorce and then marry her. She said she was going to meet with an attorney the next day and after that, she'd contact me. She planned to show me something. My guess is she had something damaging on the Reynolds family. Probably on Gar Reynolds."

"Why do you say that?" Waller asked, still looking unnecessarily pissed.

"Because he's a conniving, controlling man who always has to get his way. He and his wife were very unhappy about Garrett seeing Erica. She told me they paid her off just to get rid of her, but as you know, they got back together anyway. If you're looking for a suspect, that's your guy. He has motive."

"What was the time frame that you were there?" Waller asked.

"From oh, I don't know, maybe around five to five-thirty. Then I left."

"Where did you go?"

"I drove around for a while, then went home."

"What time were you back home?"

"I don't know."

"Guess," Waller barked.

"Between nine and ten, maybe. I don't know." She covered her eyes with her hands and began to cry. "I can't really think now."

Waller exchanged a look with Landon. They both stood up at the same time. Landon patted Jamie on the shoulder. "We'll be right back. Can we bring you more tissues? Water?"

She shook her head. When they left, she rested her head on the table in the circle of her arms. It made Chris want to bust into the interview room and console her. Taking in Holden's stare like he could read his mind, he squelched his urge to do so.

§

The longer Chris watched on the monitor, the more rage built up inside him. He wanted to go to her if for no other reason than to tell her to shut the fuck up and ask for a lawyer. The DA could argue that she had motive, her visit coincided with the time of death, her prints on the glass put her there, her angry voice message was threatening, and worst, she had no alibi for the time after she left the crime scene. Chris could tell that Landon and Waller did not like that she pointed the finger at another potential suspect.

But what really stuck in Chris's craw was that Jamie had no idea how much trouble she was in. He paced in the confined space and ignored Nick's pleas to stop. He was staring at the floor with his hand on the nape of his neck when the two detectives came in.

Chris let his irritation show despite a warning look from Nick. He stepped up to block Waller's path and said, "Let her go, Waller. She told you all she knows. She didn't do this. You're wasting your time. We could all be out there finding the real killer."

Waller was two inches shorter than Chris so he had to jerk his chin up to appear taller. He stayed silent long enough for Chris to appreciate his hard stare. Then he said, "She was there, Lagoni. She's hiding something. If Erica had a secret —

something damning to show — then others would want it. If there was something so important, then why wasn't the place tossed? I mean, there wasn't one fucking thing out of place."

Landon nudged his body between the two men and they both stepped back. "Still, we need to check it out," Chris said. "We need to have a talk with Gar Reynolds. See what he can tell us."

Sergeant Holden spoke up. "We're not bringing him in. That guy is friends with the DA. I heard he gave him a big campaign contribution, so we're going to tread lightly with him. Until we have reason, he's out. In the meantime, let's follow through with Miss Jackson. Make her go through the whole story again. Press her about that phone message she left. See if anything changes. Maybe she'll add something or remember a new detail she forgot to mention."

Chris shouted, "I'm telling you guys, she's not good for this. No way. You heard her — Gar paid Erica just to leave his son alone, and then they got back together. That's the fucking motive!"

Holden reprimanded Chris with a scowl. He had spittle raining out from the side of his mouth when he shouted, "Lagoni, you can quit being pissed off at everyone in this room. We're doing our jobs and you need to get your head out of your ass and quit trying to impede our investigation. Your ex is involved and that's that! In case you've forgotten, she was recently arrested for resisting arrest and assaulting an officer. She's got a temper and a woman scorned with a fiery temper has the capability of doing some bad stuff whether you want to believe it or not. If you can't handle this, then leave the room."

"Oh, you couldn't pry me away. I'm staying."

CHAPTER THIRTY-TWO

A day that started out so promising sunk into a pit of darkness, Jamie thought. She lifted her head up when the detectives came back into the room. Waller plopped a file folder on the table as though it held damning information that would send her to prison for life. His glare almost confirmed it.

In the next go-round, the detectives asked more pointed questions. She saw in Waller's eyes a fierce determination while Landon's were softer, more compassionate, as though he felt sorry for her for making a life-defining mistake.

Landon scooted his chair closer to Jamie's as if they were at a social gathering and he wanted to chit-chat with her. He said, "How is your relationship with Garrett since you've separated?"

"It's strained. I mean, I want a divorce, but he won't even discuss it. He wants to keep up this pretense that we're still together. It's crazy."

"Tell us how you found out about his affair with Miss Romero."

Like an out of body experience, Jamie went through the details without emotion as though she was talking about someone else and not herself. By now, she was numb. From the time she faced Garrett and Bren in the same room, breathing the same damn air, everything that came afterward seemed surreal. A nightmare. She wanted to wake up and discover none of it was true.

From Waller, "Are those the clothes you wore when you visited Romero?"

"What? I'm sorry. What did you ask me?"

"Your clothing, Miss Jackson," he repeated more forcefully. "Did you wear those when you visited Romero?"

"No, not these. When I got home, I showered and changed."

Waller raised his brow while Landon frowned. "We might need to examine the clothing and shoes you had on," Waller said. He then took her hands in his, turned them over to examine. "How did you get that cut, Miss Jackson?"

She had forgotten the cut on her thumb. "I cut it this morning when I was slicing a bagel."

He continued to study it but finally released his hold.

From Landon, she was asked, "Will we find your DNA on Erica's body?"

"I guess. We hugged when I left."

Waller snorted. "Hugged? Your husband's lover and you hugged?"

"Yes, that's right. It's not so hard to believe, detective. Remember I told you we were on the same page. Both of us wanted to push for a divorce."

When they requested a cheek swab, hair sample, and fingerprints, Jamie felt like the room was closing in on her. She wanted to cry. She felt the blood drain from her face, knew she had gone pale. On the table surface, she rested her head in the curve of her arm.

Then they left *again*. When they returned, Waller insisted that she go over her story from beginning to end. She told them again, not once veering from the original version. By that time, Jamie had had enough.

Physically and emotionally drained, she said, "Should I talk with a lawyer?"

"Do you think you need a lawyer?" Waller said it with an arrogant tilt of his chin, his eyes ice cold.

"Am I being charged with anything?"

Landon cleared his throat and said, "No." Then he added, "Not at this time."

"Then actually I don't have to talk with you, you can't hold me, and I'm free to go."

Landon nodded. "Yes, you are free to go, but don't leave town."

She was escorted down a hallway where Bren waited for her. If there was a bright spot in her nightmare, it was when he put his arm around her shoulders to comfort her. She assumed he took pity on her haggard appearance, a result of being emotionally flogged. She looked up at him and connected with the concern in his eyes.

"I'm scared, Bren," she whispered.

"I know," he answered softly. "Chris said to call him. I think you should."

"Where was he? Why wasn't he there?"

"They wouldn't let him question you."

"If they had, I wouldn't be so scared."

"No reason to be scared."

But Bren's reassurance was not said with conviction. Jamie recognized the emptiness of his words and felt as if she was treading water and losing strength.

§

As Bren drove her away, she spoke with Chris on her cell phone.

"It's all circumstantial, Jamie," he said. "When all the evidence is in, they'll take the focus off of you. Don't worry, we'll catch the real killer. It's just a matter of time."

"Chris, my gut tells me that Gar Reynolds is behind this. I just know it. He would do something like this. I think Erica was murdered because of the secret she was going to tell me or show me. It's got to have something to do with Gar Reynolds. Something he wants to keep quiet."

"But whoever killed her didn't ransack the apartment looking for anything. If they did, then I've never seen a cleanup like that. Not one thing out of place. If they searched, they took their time to be meticulous. But there wasn't much time between when she was killed and when Garrett found her. We've got no prints other than yours and Erica's. Could be a professional hit."

"Chris, if they didn't find what they were looking for, then maybe they think I have it. That Erica gave it to me."

"If that's the case, then you're in danger."

"So what should I do? Sleep with one eye open?"

"Don't go back to your place. Stay at Bren's. Does he have a gun?"

"I don't know."

"If he does and knows how to use it, keep it handy. Make sure he locks up tight, and I'll see if I can get a unit to patrol the street all night."

"Thanks. You know, Chris, you don't have to do this."

"Yes, I do. I care, Jamie. Don't you know that by now?"

CHAPTER THIRTY-THREE

From threats unknown and unseen, Bren's rental home was to be Jamie's safe haven for the time being. On their way there, Bren resumed his stubborn silence. Jamie tried twice to engage him in conversation, but he pretended not to hear. Even the empathy he displayed at the police precinct slid away like melting snow.

He seemed stunned when she yelled, "Stop the car!"

He slammed on brakes and looked around for a threat, but of course, there was none. "What the hell, Jamie?"

"You can drop me off here."

"Where do you think you're going?"

"Pull over." When he didn't, she yelled, "Just do it! Over there," she said, pointing to the paved bike lane. "I can't deal with this. Your silent treatment, plus the police suspecting me of murder. It's too much." She was angry at herself for letting her emotions show. She was supposed to be tough, bullet-proof, so her eyes pooling with tears was unacceptable to her. She bit down on her lower lip and said, "Bren, I said I'm sorry. I made a mistake, okay?"

He stopped along the curb and put the car in park. When he turned to face her, his eyes stayed hard. "You tricked me, Jamie. You made me impregnate you without my knowledge. I created a child that you weren't even going to tell me about. Just dismiss me and then go on with your life. You don't treat people that way."

She opened the car door a crack and stared back at him, debating whether she was more hurt than angry. With a soft, soothing tone that masked her true emotions, she said, "You forgive someone you love." After a pause, she opened the door wider. "Don't worry about me. I'll be okay and if I'm not, well, it's nothing to you."

After she stepped out, she slammed the door. With her back to the car, she looked out at the Charlotte skyline and considered her options. She could walk back downtown, maybe check into a hotel, or she could cross the street toward the bar a half-block away where she could call a real friend like Zeke who would not be surprised that she was in a tight spot.

With her back to the street, she stood very still, one foot on the curb. It occurred to her that she hadn't moved closer to downtown or the bar. And Bren had not put his car in drive to veer back onto the street. From behind her, she heard the car door creak open and then slam shut. She heard his footfalls on the pavement, sensed him standing behind her. He stepped closer and forced her to turn around to face him.

With his hands on her shoulders, he said, "It hurt me because I love you so much. I trusted you, Jamie. It will take time to build that trust again. We'll deal with all that later. Right now, our priority is making sure you're safe. Are we clear?"

"Yes, we're clear. We'll get past this, and then we'll work on us."

"Get back in the car, Jamie."

§

Jamie awoke in Bren's bed. Yes, she was at his side, but she was not yet back in his arms. Once he slipped between the sheets, he turned on his side facing away. She had managed to fall into a fitful sleep, waking every hour or so.

The ringtone of her cell phone sent her upright in bed, her heart pounding. She flipped her hair back out of her face and held the phone to her ear. Bren rolled over and rubbed sleep from his eyes.

"Jamie!" She recognized Chris's voice. "Get outta there! They're coming to arrest you. They'll go to the condo first, then to Bren's. They're waiting for the judge to sign the search warrant, then they'll come."

"What's going on?"

"They found the knife, Jamie! Outside the dumpster near the apartment. It has Erica's blood and your prints! And they found a bloody shoeprint on the sidewalk. They think it's yours. You're being set up. Get Bren to drive you somewhere out of town. Don't tell me where. Turn off your cell phones. Buy a burner. I'm using one now. When you get somewhere safe, call me at Jake's Bar. Ask for Chuck and when they say Chuck's not there, leave a number where I can reach you, but use a different name. Use cash, no credit cards. Gotta go. Did you get all that?"

"Yes. We'll leave now. Thanks, Chris."

"And, Jamie, watch your back. We'll talk later."

§

After his warning to Jamie that would end his career if anyone found out, Chris reflected on the information he had learned shortly before he called her. Her fingerprints on the knife. Erica's blood. *No way,* Chris had thought the minute he was told. As Chris sat in his car, he made the CSI repeat it to him over the phone, but still he refused to believe Jamie had anything to do with Erica's murder. He hung up and slammed his hand on the steering wheel. He'd face them all — Holden, Waller, Landon, and even Nick. It was a plant, plain and simple, and he would tell them just that. If they couldn't see it, then they could all go straight to hell.

Jamie was not capable of murder. He knew that better than anyone. He remembered the time she had found a baby bird that had fallen out of its nest. She held it and stroked it, begging it to live while tears streamed down her face. After the bird died in her hands, she was in mourning all day. Nothing he did could bring her out of her sadness.

If only she wouldn't flirt with danger, he thought. She brought bad stuff on herself. He tried to tell her many times, but she wouldn't listen, just said that he was the one wearing the gun, taking on bad guys. But while he went head-on into dangerous situations, she skirted on the edge, pushed people's buttons, stuck her nose where it didn't belong.

"You worry too much, Christopher," she would say with that little smile and a shrug of her shoulder that made him want to make love to her rather than lecture her.

So while she ran away with Bren somewhere safe, he had to stay behind and fight for her innocence. Find the real fucking killer while the other detectives ran around in circles, trying to pin it on her. And why? Because she was the easy suspect. The one who made sense. Motive, opportunity, access, threats, yada, yada, yada. It was enough to make Chris want to scream, or better yet, punch someone.

§

Jamie was amazed at how fast and efficiently Bren went into action once she told him what Chris had said. He had gathered up what they would need for a few days and gotten a neighbor to take care of Quincy, leaving his leash and dog food set out on the kitchen counter. With Jamie settled into the passenger seat, he put his SUV in gear and tore out of the driveway.

"Where are we going?" she asked.

"Backwoods country — my dad's place. We'll be safe there."

"How long of a drive?"

"Two hours max."

Bren waited until they were out of town before he stopped at a Minute Market for gas. When he went inside to pay cash, he picked up coffee and pastries for them. He alternated sips of coffee and bites of the too-sweet honey bun while he steered in and out of morning traffic.

Jamie noted that his eyes would occasionally dart to the rearview mirror to make sure they were not followed. And from time to time, she too looked around to see if any vehicle, particularly a dark Hyundai sedan, stayed doggedly behind them. After a while, she relaxed and even took time to enjoy the passing scenery.

It was still early, only eight o'clock, and the countryside still slumbered. Dew covered pastures and lawns. Rolled-up newspapers still lay in some driveways. And a white mist lingered over soybean fields. She watched a Jersey cow lying under a tree along the highway and thought about how nice it would be to lie there without a care in the world.

"I can't believe this is happening," she said to Bren. "It hasn't sunk in. I was just with Erica and hours later she is *murdered*. I wish I could call Garrett and tell him how sorry I am. Maybe that sounds strange after our big fight, but I know he's hurting. He must suspect his father's in the middle of this. Can you imagine how that must feel?"

"No, I can't. Too horrible to think about. My guess is he's in denial. Couldn't fathom his father's involvement."

"It's sad, really," she said. "His father wants to control every aspect of Garrett's life. There were times I wanted to scream at Garrett because he seemed to allow it. And I wanted to tell Gar to butt out, sometimes say the same thing to Catherine. She had the audacity to tell me how to get pregnant."

Bren chuckled, but kept his eyes on the road. "Seriously?"

"Yes. Seriously." Jamie laughed. "She told me to elevate my hips after we — well, you know." Jamie rolled her eyes. "It was actually comical because her face turned beet red and she stared down at the floor because she was embarrassed. What a prude."

Bren glanced over and said, "And we did it so effortlessly without instructions. Do you think our first time did the trick?"

Jamie smiled at him. "Yes, I think so. I was at my peak that night. And also half-drunk to build up the courage to seduce you."

"It worked."

Jamie detected a hint of animosity in his tone, but she let it go, deciding instead to enjoy the scenery. They had reached the mountainous region of Western North Carolina. She looked out the window at a scenic overlook around a bend, revealing a panoramic view of the mountain peaks somewhat obscured in a white fog. Past the guardrail, the edge of the road dropped off sharply. Below she could see the tops of trees and further out, the valley that was dotted with roofs of different houses and buildings. Off in the distance, miles away, she made out a stream winding around like a snake and glistening white from the morning sun.

Bren glanced at the clock on the dashboard and said, "Almost there." He scratched his cheek and avoided eye contact when he added, "Jamie, do me a favor. Wait in the car until I've had a chance to go inside and talk to my dad."

"You want to prepare him for our surprise visit?"

"No, I want to ask him to mind his manners around a lady. It's been a while."

Despite their dire circumstances, she had to laugh. "Just how long has your father been living in the backwoods?"

CHAPTER THIRTY-FOUR

After Chris gulped down two cups of coffee to deal with the reality of the recovery of the murder weapon, he headed for the morgue to meet with the ME. Because the place always gave him the willies and made his stomach queasy, he skipped breakfast. It was a cold, sterile room with bright lighting and steel tables. An image of hosing down the place after all the body parts had been put back in place and the corpse stitched back to resemble a human being was burned into his memory since his training at the academy.

It was not a welcoming place to be except for the hearty handshake from Doctor Harry Mathis. He reminded Chris of Mark Twain with his curly mop of white hair and droopy mustache. Drops of coffee from his mug spilled out onto his white lab coat, but he didn't seem to care. He brushed his hand over the stain and laughed.

"Come on in, detective. I've been expecting you. Your partner's already here. You know, I thought I heard the case had been reassigned to Waller and Landon."

"You heard wrong," Chris said.

"Doesn't matter to me. After all, you boys were all at the crime scene, so I'll be happy to. Shall we?" Mathis led the way to the table where Erica's grayish-white body was laid out on a metal table covered with a sheet up to her neck. Chris observed that Nick kept his lips pressed together in a grim expression. Chris knew it wasn't his partner's favorite place to be either.

The oddly cheery ME set his coffee mug aside and pulled back the sheet. In life, Chris felt Erica would have been mortified to have three strange men staring down at her nakedness as if conducting a business meeting with her being the topic of discussion. A human being now reduced to a corpse on a metal table. It was always a shock to Chris even though he had seen it many times.

"I'll have my official report later," Dr. Mathis said, "but thought you guys would want a preliminary. There are twelve stab wounds. All are deep with a penetration of six inches, width is one half inch. Same knife used on all. The slash across her genital area as you can see is more shallow. That one was only half an inch deep. No sign of sexual assault, no semen."

"What about the head trauma?" Nick asked.

"She has a circular fracture to the skull done with a blunt, rounded object, like a paperweight or something heavy. Small enough that the killer could have carried it in his pocket. The killer was directly behind her when she was hit. The person was most likely taller, judging from the angle of the wound. She would have lost consciousness on impact.

"And as you can see, there is no bruising or signs of a struggle. No defensive wounds on her hands or arms. Like I said at the crime scene, she was hit, then stabbed. The stab to her heart came first, where we found most of the blood. The others were post-mortem. A savage act. I hope you find who's responsible for this."

Chris swallowed hard. He had to finally look away from the corpse to clear his head. He said to Dr. Mathis, "Can you tell if the attacker was a male or female?"

"No. We are examining some trace evidence we found on the clothing, but it's inconclusive at this time. Whoever did this used force. Maybe strong or maybe just full of rage. Most likely a crime of passion. Personal. Except for one thing."

Chris's brow shot up. "What's that?"

"The wound to the heart was exact, right where it would be most lethal."

"Like a professional killer would know to do," Chris said.

"Could be."

Chris and Nick looked at one another, and then Nick asked,

"What kind of knife, doc?"

"An ordinary kitchen knife. The kind used to chop and dice."

Chris tapped Nick on the arm. "Let's go to the lab and see it. I want to know about the prints on it." As they walked toward the door, he called out, "Thanks, doc. You were a lot of help. Let us know when you've got the report ready."

§

Chris and Nick examined the knife, still contained in its clear plastic evidence bag. Then they stared at the computer monitor where the fingerprints were photographed in clear detail. The technician pointed out that they were a match to the prints taken from Jamie the day before and also from the wine glass. However, Chris had a strange inkling that something was off. Then, he noticed that the prints were not in the right position for someone holding the handle to stab a person. He couldn't wait to tell the sergeant.

"Let's go, Nick. We need to discuss this with Holden. You agree, don't you? No way Jamie could have stabbed someone with this knife. So her prints are on it, but it's a plant."

However, when he told Holden, his supervisor shook his head as if doubting Chris's theory. In the hallway where Holden had just come from the break room with a cup of coffee in hand, the men stood at a stalemate.

"Whaddya mean, sir?" Chris said, his voice raised to show his ire. "Look, if the knife had been used to stab someone, the prints would be on the underside, the fingers wrapped around the handle, the thumbprint on the end. The prints we have show the index finger on top of the handle, other three on underside, the thumb on the left side, all consistent with someone slicing something. Someone took this knife with Jamie's prints and planted it at the crime scene."

"With the victim's blood?"

"Sure. Why not? All they had to do was smear some of it from the corpse. No problem. Then toss it behind the garbage bin. A professional did this. Dr. Mathis thinks it could be. You said yourself that the scene was too clean. The guy cleaned up after he murdered her. Otherwise, we'd find blood in other places, not just where we found her. The killer carefully planned it out. Wore booties or changed shoes."

"Jamie could have taken her shoes off until she got outside. The bloody shoeprint on the sidewalk with some designer's initials on the sole. An expensive women's shoe. Can't remember the brand, but it's on the search warrant."

"A shoe like she might wear, but not Jamie's."

"We have Jamie there around the time of death, Chris. She has motive. You can't ignore that."

"Look, I know Jamie. Yeah, she can get upset sometimes, but she doesn't have enough strength to do that kind of thing."

"She could if she was filled with rage, you know that." Holden locked eyes with Nick. "Can't you reason with him, Polaski?"

Before Chris could argue his case further, Waller and Landon walked in.

Waller directed his gaze at Chris and said, "Well, we just got back from Miss Jackson's condo. Nice! Fancy place. She's gone. Flew the coop. Apparently with that dude she was with last night. What's his name? McGyver, I think. We'll find them. Just a matter of time. We'll get a BOLO out pronto on his vehicle. Her vehicle is in her parking space. Running a check with the DMV as we speak. And guess what, Lagoni? A knife is missing from her cutting block, not in the dishwasher either or anywhere to be found."

Chris ignored him, looked back at Holden. "Sir, Jamie is not capable of an act this violent. Jamie talks tough, but she's really not. I know her."

Waller snorted. "According to the cop who arrested her a few weeks back, she's strong as an ox and fights like a wildcat."

Again, Chris overlooked Waller's remarks and pleaded with Holden. "Sir, she was in no condition to—"

"You still sweet on her, Lagoni?"

"Shut the fuck up, Waller."

"Lagoni, you're taking this too personal," Holden said. "Should I pull you off the case?"

Chris had hard eyes for his supervisor. He blurted out, "She's pregnant! Cut her some slack, will ya?"

Waller seized on the new information. "Knocked up?" A smile appeared and one eyebrow shot up. "How did her husband feel about that since he was banging someone else?"

"It's not his," Chris said tersely.

"Oh, then is it yours, Lagoni?"

"No, Waller, it's not," Chris said between clenched teeth. "She's in a relationship with Bren McKeever, not McGyver, you idiot. He's the father."

"Wow, busy lady. When she gets some free time, she can do me," Waller said with a chuckle as he tapped Landon on the arm with the back of his hand.

Chris was on top of Waller before he saw the attack coming. A right jab sent Waller staggering backwards, followed by a punch to the gut. Waller responded with a head butt that caught Chris in the chest and knocked his breath out. He recovered quickly and was about to pounce on Waller until Nick grabbed him, and Holden pulled Waller out of his range. While Nick continued to restrain Chris, Holden blocked Waller from charging. Although the fight was stopped, their rage was still raw, on the surface. If not held back, they would have been back at it in seconds.

Holden gave them his bulldog stare that always meant an ass-chewing was not far behind. "Enough! Lagoni, another word out of you and I'll ask for your shield and your gun. And you, Waller, keep your mouth shut and go check with DMV about that license plate."

After Waller ambled away, rubbing his jaw, Holden directed his gaze at Chris. "I want to see you in my office. Now!"

Nick went back to his work cubicle while Chris followed the sergeant into his glassed-in office. Holden waved his arm to indicate a chair and then shut the door hard enough to rattle the glass. He plopped down in his chair and kicked away from the desk with his foot.

With his arms crossed over his barrel chest, Holden leaned far back, causing a strange fart-like sound from the chair's mechanism. Both men ignored it. Holden put forth his most serious expression when he said, "Chris, I'm pulling you off this case. You're too emotionally involved. It'll end up hurting us."

"No way! Please, sir. If Jamie took off, I can lead you to her. She trusts me. Please! You know Waller. He'll take a hard line, only focus on her and ignore the other stuff. It's no secret that he and some of the others still hold a grudge against her because of that article she did."

"She embarrassed the department. Made it look like the district attorney's office and the police department were at war."

"Well, they need to get over it. Look, Jamie was set up. I'd bet my life on it. Gar Reynolds — he's responsible for this. Jamie was investigating a company that he's put millions into. She had someone following her, trying to scare her off the story. I told you that already."

Holden raised his hand to interrupt. "Until we know otherwise, we have to assume there's no connection. You're grasping at straws, Lagoni. You told me about the rental car, but it wasn't seen anywhere near the crime scene. We checked. There's no proof that would lead us down that road, so don't go there."

Just as Chris started to make a stronger case, there was a tap on the door. Irritated, Holden barked, "Yeah?"

Landon stuck his head through the narrow opening and forced a smile. "Can I see you for a minute, sir?" Then he added, "Alone."

"If it's about the case, I'm staying," Chris said. But he stood up when both men gave him hard stares. "Okay, okay, I can tell when I'm not wanted. I could use another cup of coffee anyway."

When he came back carrying a mug of coffee steaming up, Landon was on his way out. The two men brushed past each other without a word.

Holden didn't bother to look up from his desk at Chris. He stared down at his interlocked fingers, where his thumbs did a fast rotation around each other. Chris knew that his silence meant that he was stewing over some new information pertinent to the case. Just as he started to demand to know what it was, the sergeant spoke up.

"Landon just told me that Jamie's condo and McKeever's house were tossed. Jamie might be right. Somebody wants something. Maybe they think Erica gave whatever it is to Jamie. She could be in danger. In hindsight, maybe that's why Erica's place was *not* ransacked. Perhaps she told the killer she had already passed the information to another person."

"That's what I've been trying to tell you! Jamie's a target, not a suspect!" Chris blurted out. "Look, Reynolds threatened Jamie to kill the story and he threatened Erica through his lawyer. He wanted her out of his son's life. There was something Erica had on the old man that he wanted to keep quiet. She was going to see her lawyer the next day. It's simple, sir. He took care of two problems at one time. Jamie and Erica. That's what this is about."

"Maybe," Holden said with a shrug. "Okay, investigate that angle, but do it quietly. We're not bringing in Reynolds. Stay away from him, and that's an order. See if you can find out who the lawyer is that Erica was going to see. Maybe he can tell us something. We've got her cell phone, so check the log. And, Lagoni, stay away from Waller. I mean it. I don't want the captain to find out I have to keep you boys from killing each other."

CHAPTER THIRTY-FIVE

The driveway up to Mac McKeever's log house was a quarter-mile of twists and turns, nothing more than dirt and gravel with a strip of dandelions and weeds down the middle. When Bren put the car in second gear, he told Jamie to hang on. He floored the accelerator to make the climb. From the corner of his eye, he watched with amusement as she braced herself with each turn.

When his father's home came into view, he smiled. It was a welcoming sight with its row of rocking chairs on the front porch and hanging baskets of morning glories mounted along the soffit.

Bren looked over at Jamie. "Stay here. Let me speak to my father first."

The thick front door creaked open into a quiet room that was the central part of the house. He always thought it resembled a ski lodge with thick log walls, a cathedral ceiling, and a massive stone fireplace with a hearth that held a stack of firewood ready for crisp, cold days.

When Bren called out, his father emerged from the kitchen wiping his hands on a dishtowel. Both father and son had the deep blue McKeever eyes, a family trait that went back several generations. And like his son, Mac had a square jaw, but his nose was not as straight. It had been broken when he was tackled in a high school football game and never healed properly. Once Mac's hair had been as dark as Bren's, but over the years it had become salt and pepper. With too much time between haircuts, it curled up over his shirt collar.

Mac gave his son a warm smile, marking his weathered face with a few wrinkles. He said, "Well, well, I'll be damned. You finally came to see your old man, huh?"

Their hug was more a back slapping event than an embrace. Mac stepped back to study his son's expression. He frowned. "What's wrong, son? You have that same hang-dog look you had when you fucking wrecked my damn truck."

"Pop, I'll explain why I'm here later, but I've got to tell you something. I have a woman with me and I'm going to bring her inside, but first you have to promise me something."

Mac knitted his brows, brushed his thumb across the end of his nose. "Promise you what?"

"That you'll behave. No cussing, no farting, no belching, no off-color jokes."

"Huh! Might as well of stayed in bed."

"Pop, please. She's a lady. She grew up with the country club set."

"Well, la-de-da."

"You'll like her, Pop. She's not what you think. Very down to earth. She's a lot like mom. That's why I love her so much."

"The hell you say!" His eyes got big. He grinned and said, "You didn't tell me you were in loooove!"

"It happened so fast. You know how those city girls are. They get their claws in you before you know what happened." Bren displayed a mischievous smile, followed by a wink.

Mac chuckled. "Oh, yeah. I know exactly what you mean. Well, fuck. Bring her on in. Wanna see your catch. See if she's a keeper, or if you need to throw her back in the pond."

Bren rolled his eyes, said nothing in response, and walked outside. Minutes later, he came back with his hand on the small of Jamie's back and his opposite hand hooking a tote bag over his shoulder. He set his load down and then slipped his arm around Jamie's waist.

"Jamie, I'd like you to meet my dad. Pop, this is Jamie."

Mac took the hand Jamie extended. "Wow, you are a pretty little thing. By the way, you can call me Mac. My given name is Josiah, but most people can't spell it, much less say it."

"It's nice to meet you, Mac. I love your home. Very cozy."

Mac looked around with pride. "Yeah, just enough room for an old cuss like me. I built it myself. Well, Bren helped some when he wasn't off swimming laps somewhere."

The three got comfortable around the unlit fireplace. While Jamie and Bren sat on the sofa, Mac faced them in his favorite rocking recliner, holding a pipe by the bowl and clicking his teeth against the stem.

Over the course of the next half hour, Bren explained what had brought them to seek shelter at his home. His father listened intently without interrupting. When Bren finished, he took a deep breath and slapped his hands on his knees.

"So that's why we're here, Pop. We need to hide out for a while. Until the police know we're here, and then we've got to find another place until we know it's safe for Jamie to go back."

"Holy shit! This is fucked up!"

Bren frowned at his father's outburst. "Dad, what did I say? Your language."

"I'm sure Jamie has heard it before. Right, Jamie?"

"Plenty of times."

"You see," Mac said. "You kids can stay as long as you like. Might want to hide that car somewhere. They'll know you're here when they see it."

"Right. I was wondering if you could get Denny to hide it inside his garage. If we have to make a run for it, maybe he could loan me his truck."

"Sure, sure. No problem." Mac paused and puffed on his pipe. "I told you he wouldn't let us take his damn boat out without him, but he'll do this. He owes me big time. I chopped a cord of firewood for him."

§

"Done!" Mac said as he walked into the kitchen and found Jamie and Bren at the counter making turkey sandwiches. "Denny's fine with you hiding your car over there. 'Course I didn't tell him the truth. Told him you were hiding from some bad dudes that you owe money. A poker game gone bad."

Bren laughed. "Pop, you make me sound like I'm some kind of hoodlum."

Mac dismissed Bren's remark with a wave of his hand. "Naaa. He knows you're a good guy. How long do you think before the cops show up?"

"Not sure," Bren said. "We left a message for Detective Lagoni to call us back on the cell phone we bought at Wal-Mart. Hopefully, he'll call soon and let us know something."

"Hellfire, it's hard to believe the police would think a little lady like Jamie could do such a thing. It's the most fucked up thing I think I've ever heard. And don't give me that look, Bren. Jamie's not a child. She's done told you she's heard bad words before."

"I don't mind, Bren." Jamie turned to face him. "I've been cussed out before, so it's no big deal. Leave your dad alone. He's right. It *is* fucked up."

"Jamie, apparently my son is more G-rated than we are," Mac said. "His mom took him and his brother to too many Disney movies, I guess."

Bren rolled his eyes. "I give up. Go ahead, Dad. Show her who you really are."

Mac got out a can from the cabinet where packaged and canned foods were stored. He used a manual opener to tear off the top of the tin that held sardines. Jamie watched in disgust as he pulled one out with his fingers and then popped it into his mouth. She slapped a hand over her lips as she fought to suppress a wave of nausea. The pungent smell and the sight of the silvery, slimy fish sent her scurrying away.

"Be right back," she said over her shoulder as she rushed for the bathroom.

Mac looked stunned. "What's with her? Is she sick?"

Bren pressed his fingers into his eye sockets and then looked directly at his dad. "She's pregnant, Pop. I'd better go see if she's okay."

"Pregnant! As in having a baby? Holy shit!" He broke into laughter. "Dang, I'm going to be a grandpa!"

§

Jamie stretched out on the double bed in Bren's old bedroom. Emotionally and physically drained, she closed her eyes and tried to fall asleep. She kept them closed even when the door opened and she heard the creaking of the wooden floor from footsteps. The mattress dipped slightly from Bren's weight when he lay down at her side and reached for her hand. His affectionate squeeze warmed her heart and gave her reason to hope.

"You okay?" he whispered, turning his head to observe her.

"Yes, just tired."

"I told Pop about the baby. He's excited. Wants it to be a boy, of course. He's already talking about future fishing trips and camping in the woods."

Jamie smiled, still keeping her eyes closed. "Girls can do those things, too."

"I know." Bren squeezed her hand tighter. "I hope the stress of this situation doesn't jeopardize your pregnancy."

"Me too," she said. "Bren, are you ready to go back to the way we were before?"

He exhaled a deep breath and did not answer right away. Finally, he said, "Jamie, to be honest, I feel like I was setup. I deserve a full explanation of what was going on in your head that would cause you to deceive me like that. But I *do* love you and I *do* want our relationship to work."

"And the baby? You want the baby?"

With tenderness, he ran a finger down her cheek. "Yes, of course. I want the baby as much as I want you."

Jamie wiped at her eyes. "Tears again. I've been an emotional wreck ever since I found out I'm having a baby. It's a pregnancy thing, I'm sure."

"I think it's sweet," he said. "Hey, I've got the car moved to Denny's garage. His house is a half mile down the road or about a quarter of a mile through the woods. So we're good if we have to make a run for it."

"I think with Chris on our side, we should be okay. It's just a matter of time and then, I'll be cleared and we can go home." At that moment, her cell phone rang. "Speaking of Chris, that has to be him now."

"Hi, Jamie," Chris said when she answered. "Did you make it somewhere safe? Don't tell me where."

"Yes, we're fine. Glad you got our message. What's the latest?"

"Well, the police went to your condo, then Bren's place. They have a warrant for your arrest. Got a BOLO out for you and for Bren's car. They assume you're with him. I'm sure they're alerting your parents and Bren's dad that you might come seeking refuge. They'll send local law enforcement to both places, so neither is a good place to hide out."

"Oh, no!"

"Jamie, I don't even want to know. Just get out. And to give you a heads up, Sergeant Holden buys into my theory that Gar Reynolds is behind this. I'm doing a little investigation on the sly. Nothing concrete yet, but I'm working on it. And Jamie, one more thing. Before the police got there, someone ransacked your place and Bren's place, looking for something. This person may have the means to track you down, so be careful."

After she hung up, she noted the questioning look in Bren's eyes. She said, "Any minute the police, the sheriff, or the dogcatcher is going to show up here looking for us. We have to leave, Bren. It's not safe here."

"Damn! And just when I was starting to relax. Okay, let's grab our gear. I'll go tell Pop."

They said their goodbyes to Mac on the back porch. Their supplies of water, food, and a change of clothes was split up and put into Bren's old backpacks, the heavier of the two going to Bren.

Mac hugged Jamie and then held her hand in his palm, turning it over to examine. "Jamie, I noticed your cut. Let me put a fresh bandage on it."

He led her to his first aid supply in the cabinet over the washing machine. She was amazed that it was well stocked to cover any foreseeable medical emergency. He must have noted her surprised because he said, "I was a firefighter. First aid was crucial in my line of work. I've got patched up, plugged up, and stitched back together more times than I can remember. Got a couple of pieces of steel inside me from a fall after a floor collapsed." He wiped her thumb with a cotton swab soaked in alcohol then wrapped a band-aid around the cut. "Now how's that? Not bad for an old geezer, huh?"

"Thanks, Mac. And you're not an old geezer. In fact, you look pretty good for seventy."

His eyes widened. "Seventy? Is that what my son told you? Why, I'll have you know I'm not even sixty yet!"

She laughed. "I know. I was teasing."

When they returned to the porch, she found Bren was tapping his hand on his outer thigh. "We should get moving, Jamie." A quick glance at his watch and he added, "We need to get settled somewhere before dark."

Mac hugged his son and then slapped something into his palm along with the keys to Denny's truck. Bren stared down at a wad of bills contained in a rubber band. "Pop, what's this?"

"Take it, son. You might need it. May have to stay gone for a while until this thing gets cleared up." He turned to Jamie and said, "Honey-bunch, you're in good hands. Bren has his wits about him, won't let anything happen to you. Now y'all be careful and take off."

CHAPTER THIRTY-SIX

For Jamie, nothing defined despair like being charged with a crime she didn't commit and with cops, possibly a killer, hot on her trail. She reflected on her dilemma and swallowed down her anger. Yes, she was pissed. She believed someone had set her up to take the fall, most likely Gar Reynolds. She figured he'd do whatever it took to get his way, perhaps even commit murder. She felt he wouldn't get his own hands dirty, just get someone else to do it for him. He made it clear he didn't want Erica in Garrett's life, and he didn't like Jamie poking around on the illegal dumping story that would show his involvement. Obviously, she and Erica were a liability to him.

Maybe he didn't know it, but he was messing with the wrong person. Jamie was a fighter and she'd let no one knock her down. Besides, she had Bren at her side and Chris fighting for her innocence back home.

As she and Bren walked away from his father's house, Bren said, "Let's go through the woods to get Denny's truck."

Their getaway vehicle. For her, it had the ring of Bonnie and Clyde, only she and Bren didn't have machine guns, or *any* gun for that matter.

Jamie followed Bren as he led the way down a dirt path that cut through trees and brush. Their verdant surroundings included mountain laurels in full bloom, lush ferns, and thick moss. The moist air held the scent of rich earth from an early morning rain. The beauty of Mother Nature countered the nightmare that had crept into her life so quickly without warning. When she gazed up at patches of a cloudless sky through the towering trees, her pensive thoughts were halted by Bren's voice.

"I can't remember where our tree stand was," he said.

"Tree stand?"

"Yeah, Pop, Joe, and I used to hunt deer around here. We'd sit up in the tree stands just talking junk while we waited hours for a deer to show up." He paused to take in their surroundings. "It's been a long time. Everything looks different now. The same, but different. When I was a kid, I thought the trees were as tall as the Sequoias in California. And I imagined that the woods were as wide as the ocean. I guess when you're ten, you have a different perspective of everything." He pointed to a house with wood siding and a steep, sloped roof. "That's Denny's place. The truck's in the garage next to my SUV. The key ring Pop gave me has a key to the side door on the garage, so we don't need to bother Denny."

At the corner of the house, Jamie spotted movement. She tapped Bren on the arm to make him aware of it. From the rustle of the shrubbery, a man emerged. It was the beaked-nose man she had seen in the dark sedan near her condo building. Now that he was standing, she saw that he had a formidable physique. He was tall and wiry, in cargo pants and a dark green knit shirt. He stepped up onto a concrete block to peek inside a window. With his back to them, Jamie focused on the gun tucked into his pants. Judging by the look on Bren's face, she knew he saw it too.

They inched backwards and stayed hidden behind brush. With his lips at Jamie's ear, Bren whispered, "Gimme your phone. I'll call Pop."

Not questioning him, she pulled the cell phone from her pants pocket and handed it over. She watched as he walked backwards, punching the number into the phone. In less than a minute, he came back.

As he stood behind her, he planted his hands on her shoulders. "Watch this," he whispered.

A German shepherd dog charged out the back door. He pounced on the man and knocked him to the ground. They looked on as the dog growled and clamped his jaws around the man's arm, his paws on his chest. The man hollered out, flailing his arms and legs trying to get the dog off. Suddenly, the dog yelped, went stiff, and then fell limp on top of the man. Jamie didn't know how that could be. She was puzzled until she saw a knife covered in blood in the man's hand. He kicked the dog away. The dog landed on its back, exposing his belly where the knife had gone in. Blood gushed from a deep gash. The dog's head flopped to one side with his tongue hanging out.

As if he had springs on his boots, the man hopped to his feet. He brushed off dirt from his pants. With a look of disgust, he examined the blood on his arms and clothing. When she witnessed him slashing the dog's throat, Jamie clamped her hand over her mouth and gasped. She tried to step back into Bren's embrace, but lost her footing and fell against a bush, making just enough sound that the man spotted them.

"Run!" Bren said as he grabbed Jamie and scooped up their gear. He pushed her forward. "Go, go, go!"

They kept running, forging through the untamed terrain of brush and trees. Jamie tripped, but Bren caught her before she went face forward into a tangle of thorns and twigs.

"This way," he said.

They left the path and dived behind a fallen tree, lying flat on their bellies underneath a broken limb with the density of leaves for cover. Sticking to the path, the man ran past them. When he was out of sight, Bren helped Jamie stand up.

"It's him, Bren. The man who followed me in traffic. Same guy that parked near my condo."

"You're sure?"

"It's him! What he did to that dog — oh, God, it was awful."

Bren frowned and nodded. "I've seen this guy before, too."

Her eyes grew wide. "Where? How?"

"At the police station. When I walked you out to the parking garage, he was standing behind my car. We made eye contact, then he started walking away in the opposite direction."

"I don't remember seeing him."

As if a switch had been flipped in his brain, Bren said, "My car. That's got to be it!"

"What?"

"He must have put a GPS tracker on the undercarriage. That's how he found us."

"You think? This guy must believe Erica gave me something. That damn secret she was going to share. He searched my condo and your house looking for whatever it is. He thinks *I* have it now!"

"Jamie, see if you can reach Chris."

After two attempts to reach him on her cell, she exhaled an exasperated breath. "There's no signal. We're screwed."

Bren pointed straight ahead. "There's a good spot to hide out near the river. We'll go there. We can't stay out in the open, and we can't leave yet or he'll just follow us."

"This guy won't give up."

"Nope. Whatever it is he thinks you have, he wants it bad, real bad."

"Bad enough to hurt me?"

"I won't let that happen." He reached inside his backpack and pulled out a Glock 9mm and then showed her two extra clips. "My dad sneaked this in when you weren't looking."

§

When Chris arrived at the home of Sophia Romero, the death watch had begun. While friends and neighbors sat in various rooms with grim faces and whispering voices, the priest was in the bedroom administering the last rites. Chris peeked into the room. He noticed tubes going into her nostrils to supply oxygen from a tank by the bed. Her eyes remained closed and he figured she was unconscious. He knew she was in no condition to answer questions, which made him wonder if she had gained consciousness long enough to be told her daughter was dead.

A photograph of Sophia in better days hung on a wall in the living area. In an ornate frame of gold, it contrasted with the pasty, emaciated body Chris saw in the bed. The woman in the picture was a sparkle of youth with dark alluring eyes, hair that cascaded in soft curls past her shoulders, and a shy smile that spoke to her innocence. He whispered a prayer, crossed himself, and then slipped past the curious dark eyes, all on him, sitting in every available chair in the living room.

He headed toward the kitchen to seek out the hospice nurse he'd met when he came with Nick to deliver the bad news. He found the fleshy lady who had skin the color of coffee beans, facing the sink, her back to him. When she turned to smile at him, a sweetness washed over her face that made him think she was the perfect person to care for the dying and their grieving family.

"Detective, you're back," she said. "Have you found the evil person who killed Sophia's girl?"

"No, ma'am. I was hoping Mrs. Romero could help me, but I see she won't be able to."

"No, the Lord will call her home soon." She wiped her hands on a dishtowel. "Have a seat, Detective. I'll cut you a slice of apple pie that a neighbor brought by. I don't know if we've been properly introduced. My name is Becky. I've been with Mrs. Romero since they stopped her chemo and sent her home to live out her final days."

Chris was really in too big a hurry to sit down and enjoy pie, but he figured if he took her up on her offer, it might open her up to what he hoped would be a good lead in his investigation. Besides, apple was his favorite and too good to pass up. He pulled out a chair at the table. She set the plate down along with a fork and napkin and a glass of iced tea.

"Thank you, ma'am." He cut through the flaky crust for his first bite and then looked over at Becky. "Is anyone here that worked with Mrs. Romero at the Reynolds' home?"

"Yes, Marisol Lopez is here. She and Sophia shared the housekeeping duties. They're very close, as you can imagine."

"I'd to speak with Miss Lopez."

"Well, here she comes now," Becky said, smiling at the short, squat lady who walked through the open doorway.

She focused on Chris with unsmiling, suspicious eyes. He stood up and pulled out a chair for her. "Miss Lopez, I'm Detective Chris Lagoni with the Charlotte-Mecklenburg Police Department. Please, have a seat. I'd like to ask you a few questions."

With some reluctance, she sat down and folded her arms to rest on the table surface. Chris pushed the half-eaten slice of pie to the side and hoped the woman would be more cooperative than the demeanor she presented. She stayed quiet but looked up at Becky, who made herself busy wiping the countertop.

As if taking her silence as a hint, Becky said, "I'm going to check on Sophia, see if the priest is ready to go."

When she was gone, Chris said, "Becky said you and Sophia worked together at the Reynolds home."

"Yes. Sophia and I — there over twenty years."

"Ma'am, I'll get right to the point. Do you know who could have harmed her daughter, Erica?"

"No. She had no enemies. Sweet, sweet girl."

"Do you know Garrett Reynolds well?"

"Of course. Sophia and I practically raised the boy."

"Are you aware that he was in a relationship with Erica?"

"Yes, Sophia told me."

"Was Sophia okay with that?"

Marisol shrugged and then shook her head. "No, she did not like it. She and Erica had a big argument one time when Erica came to visit."

"Why did she disapprove?"

"She knew it would be trouble. Mr. and Mrs. Reynolds would be very upset — their son with her daughter. That pair,

— well, how should I say? No one good enough for their son unless the girl come from money."

"Do you know if there was some trouble between Mr. Reynolds and Erica?"

"He's a complicated man, that one."

"What do you mean?"

"Well, he paid all of Sophia's medical bills, like he really cared. An employee of his, a man — can't remember his name, — but I certainly remember his fancy big car and his nice suits. He come. Sophia didn't have health insurance. What was she going to do? But then, out of the blue, Mr. Reynolds sent that man over to collect a stack of bills and he come by every week."

"What do you make of that, Miss Lopez?"

"What I think, detective, is that Erica was forced to do business with the devil." She paused, seemed to reflect, then added, "There. I say too much."

"Please, ma'am, anything you can tell me will help."

Marisol folded her arms over her chest. She shook her head and frowned. "I don't want to talk about it."

"Please, ma'am. I think it might be important for my investigation."

"Detective, put two and two together and see what you get. You think a wealthy, powerful man like Mr. Reynolds is going to help out a former employee like that unless there's strings attached?"

"What were the strings?"

"Sophia told me he met with Erica and told her he would pay her mother's bills if she promised to break up with Garrett. Never see him again. Made her sign some legal paper about it. Of course, she ended up breaking that promise. And no one breaks their promise to that man. No one!"

"Do you think he could have killed Erica?"

"Why not? He killed Sophia's other child. Murderer!"

Chris nearly choked on a swallow of tea. He set his glass

down hard on the table and sat up straight. He cleared his throat and said, "Gar Reynolds killed someone?"

"Well, I call it murder. He forced Sophia to have an abortion. You see, after Sophia's husband went to prison, he told her he'd help her pay for another lawyer and an appeal, but he wanted something in exchange. *Her!* So when his wife went to sleep, he slip down to Sophia's room and crawled in bed with her. He did hire an attorney for her husband's case, but then he dismissed him when Sophia got pregnant. He took her out of state to have the abortion. For the rest of her life, she cried about it. She's afraid she'll burn in hell. But of course, the priest absolved her of all her sins."

"I'm sorry your friend went through that. Now I have to ask you something very important. Did Gar Reynolds father Erica?"

CHAPTER THIRTY-SEVEN

The house seemed too empty, too quiet now that Bren and Jamie had left. It made Mac a little sad that they left so quickly. He had little time to get to know Jamie, the woman who carried his grandchild. That news alone was a lot to take in. But there was that other business: she was wanted for murder, yet proclaimed innocence. He believed her because Bren did. Damn, if it wasn't a lot to chew on all at once. And his morning had started out so ordinary. Hell, the only thing exciting about it was when he spilled wet coffee grounds on the floor trying to dump them out.

His musing of his day got interrupted when he heard a car drive up. He peeked out the kitchen window to see the sheriff's official vehicle parked behind his truck. Sheriff Harley Wright climbed out, tugging his belt up, his holstered gun at his side. Before Mac opened the door to greet him, he surveyed the room, making sure there was no trace of Bren and Jamie's visit. The screen door banged shut behind him as he stepped outside before the officer had time to make it up onto the porch.

"Howdy, Sheriff. Good to see ya. What brings you up here?"

"Hi, Mac." Sheriff Wright accepted his firm handshake. "How's it going? See you got that fence post replaced."

"Yep." Mac hitched his chin in the direction of the crude wooden railing along the dirt drive. "Got two more that need to be done. Damned if it ain't always somethin' falling apart around here."

"Mac, I'll get right to it. Don't have much time. I got a call from the police department in Charlotte and they were wondering if your son and his girlfriend came here."

"What's this about?"

"Bren's girlfriend — a woman named Jamison Jackson —

she's wanted by the police. They've got a BOLO out on her. They thought maybe Bren brought her up here. They think they're together. It's dang crazy if you ask me. Your boy and some gal wanted by the police."

"Harley, how long you known my son? You think he's got some fugitive girlfriend that he's gone on the run with? That's crazy. C'mon, man. You know Bren. They've got bad information."

"I know it's crazy, but still...I promised I'd check it out. Mind if I come inside and have a quick look-see?"

"I should be offended, but what the hell? C'mon in. Knock yourself out. While you're at it, look at the new display case I built to put Bren's swimming trophies in. It's a beauty. Solid mahogany."

§

Bren and Jamie walked briskly through the forest for about thirty minutes before they stopped to catch their breath. Bren removed his backpack to get a bottle of water. He passed it over to Jamie first and then guzzled down the remainder after she handed it back. He wiped his mouth with the back of his hand as he scanned their surroundings.

"Bren, what's the plan?" she asked, huffing and puffing.

He looked out among the trees and pointed to his right. "The river's that way. We're almost there." His brows knitted as he studied the agony on Jamie's face. "Baby, are you okay? We can rest a little longer."

"No. Let's keep going."

"When we reach the river, we'll find shelter so you can rest."

Ten minutes of weaving their way around brush led them to a drop-off point. They stood on a cliff looking down at the deep water that divided the forest. The river's surface carried a green sheen, a reflection of the trees that bordered the bank. A glimpse of a house could be seen on the opposite bank, mostly hidden behind trees. Many times in the past Bren had waved at the owners as they appeared on their dock, but never had he met them. The two-story house with a wrap-around porch seemed empty, no sign of anyone's presence.

There was an eerie peace and calm as if a looming threat was nothing more than a figment of their imagination. A slight breeze stirred the tall trees, but other than that nothing moved. All was quiet.

Bren reached for Jamie's hand. "Follow me," he said. "We're going down. It's very steep, think you can handle it?"

Jamie blew air through her lips in dismissal, as if it was as easy as climbing down from monkey bars. "No problem."

He raised his brow worried about her limitations in her present condition. "Well, take your time, Jamie. Don't rush."

Bren went down backwards, feet first, grabbing roots and branches on his way down. Once he found a firm base, he raised his arms up to guide Jamie.

"Did I ever tell you I climbed a fifty foot cliff on a dare?" she said.

"Nope, but I'm not surprised. You can tell me all about it later." He held one hand up, ready to catch her if she slipped. "Easy now. Not so fast. Make sure you've got a good grip."

She kept one hand on his shoulder and used the other to grab the same branches Bren had just released. In a flash, she almost lost her footing and started to tumble backwards, but Bren grabbed her and prevented her fall. She glanced down and realized that a tumble would have sent them landing with a splat onto large jagged rocks.

"Whew! That was close," she said.

"Yeah, you almost gave me a heart attack, girl. Easy does it. Not much further."

When they reached the rocky shoreline, she exhaled a long breath. "We made it!" Jamie put her hands on her hips and looked out over the water. "Now what? You've got an escape plan, Bren?"

"Yep, I do." He tilted his chin toward the water. "The river."

"I hate to break it to you, but we don't have a boat."

"Just a small setback."

He brushed a section of her hair off her cheek and smiled down at her. "First, we'll find somewhere to hide. He won't expect us to come down here. He'll think that we went deeper into the forest." Bren looked off into the distance and then nodded. "Aha! I know the perfect place to hide. C'mon, Jamie. It's time for you to rest."

"How can you be so nonchalant with a killer after us?"

"After us? He only wants you, Jamie. I'm just along for the ride," he said with a smile, then winked.

§

Chris lost his cool when Sergeant Holden told him something that Waller had conveniently left out when he and his partner had returned from searching Jamie's condo. Standing in the doorway of Holden's office, Chris pounded his fist against the metal doorframe hard enough to make the door bang into the wall and crack the glass. Holden looked furious, but Chris was just relieved the whole glass panel hadn't shattered. Heads popped up from cubicles to take notice.

"Now calm down, Lagoni. Close that door, or what's left of it, and sit down!" Holden no longer addressed Chris by the name of his favorite Italian dish. Tension and stress caused them to abandon their usual friendly banter.

"How can I calm down?" Chris yelled. "You just said Waller told CSI not to bother with Jamie's condo and Bren's house. The killer was there! Looking for God knows what, but something that got Erica killed! The condo will have surveillance. Maybe of the killer!"

"We don't know that."

Despite Holden's scowl that warned him to proceed with caution, Chris said, "If we don't check it out, then we're fucking idiots! I just told you, Reynolds had a forced sexual relationship with Sophia Romero and made her have an abortion. He tried to buy off Erica. Doesn't all of that make you just a little suspicious of the man? Shouldn't he be the focus of our investigation? At least a person of interest, don't ya think? For Christ's sake!"

"Chris, that's enough!" The room got quiet as they locked eyes in a staring contest. "Okay," Holden said. "Go talk with Reynolds's lawyer that threatened Erica. And also, see if anyone can tell us the name of the lawyer she'd planned to see. Since there's no trace in her call-log on her cell, she must have called the person from work. Hopefully, the lawyer, whoever he is, can shed some light. Happy? We'll keep Waller and Landon out of the loop until you have something concrete. Call me when you've got something."

§

As he walked through the parking garage, Chris stewed about what Holden had told him. Behind the wheel of his car, he loosened the knot in his tie and unbuttoned the collar of his white dress shirt. He puffed up his cheeks and then blew air out, something Nick liked to tease him about, saying he looked like a blow fish that swallowed a live grenade. Which reminded Chris — Holden had Nick teamed up with the others, chasing their tails around in a circle while he went out to find the real killer. Earlier that day, Nick tried to appease Chris by saying it wasn't his call, but Chris blew him off. He directed his anger at his partner when he knew the blame should be placed on the lead investigator, that son-of-a-bitch Waller.

"Asshole," Chris muttered between clenched teeth as he put his car in reverse and headed over to the law firm of Blake and Ramsey.

He marched into the reception area like he was now in charge of the whole damn firm, flashing his shield for the scrutiny of the beautiful blonde receptionist. Her red luscious lips curled into a smile, enough to make the tough detective soften just a bit. When she leaned forward, Chris didn't miss the view down the scoop neckline of her silk blouse. If she thought her string of pearls were her real jewels, she was mistaken. He brought his stare up to meet her green eyes.

Stuart Ramsey kept him waiting for thirty minutes, an eternity for a homicide cop with the clock ticking. He was what Chris expected. An overly confident lawyer in an Armani suit with perfect white teeth that appeared through a pretentious smile. He wondered how much the guy charged by the hour. *A helluva lot more than he's worth*, Chris figured.

"Detective," the man said, extending his hand. "Stuart Ramsey at your service. Let's go into my office."

Chris wasted no time. "Mr. Ramsey, I was told that you had an encounter with Erica Romero a few weeks ago. For our investigation, I'd like to hear what it was about. And there's no client privilege here because Miss Romero was not a client."

"Detective, I sense an attitude here."

Chris shrugged, almost as an admission. "I understand that you threatened her."

"Your information is wrong. I reminded Miss Romero of a breach of a legal document she signed in good faith. And that document is protected under client confidentiality."

"Sooner or later the facts will come out. I'll have you deposed for the grand jury."

"Do what you must, detective. I believe we are wasting each other's time." Ramsey shot up from his plush leather chair. "I'll walk you out."

Chris conceded with a nod and stood up. As Ramsey reached for the handle and started to open the door, Chris said, "Are you aware of a sexual relationship that your client had with the mother of the deceased? From the details I learned, it sounded a little like rape to me. And that abortion? I thought that Mr. Reynolds was a Christian with strong moral principles, but I swear, every corner I turn, I hear things that contradict that."

"Good day, Detective Lagoni. The receptionist can stamp your parking ticket so you won't have to pay."

Your client is going to pay, asshole. Big time.

CHAPTER THIRTY-EIGHT

Bren shushed Jamie into silence the minute he heard a sound on the cliff above them. Both strained to listen. They heard the snap of a branch being stepped on and the rustle of dry leaves under feet. Bren motioned with his index finger, pointing straight up. Jamie nodded with understanding.

On the rocky beach of the river, they found a good spot to rest and hide. A makeshift cave had been hollowed out by rising water that had flooded the western corner of the state. Bren had explained that two summers ago, the area had been hit with a series of flash floods that had washed away the steep bank in some places. Above them, the remains of the cliff that had stayed intact hung over, like a cantilever, with an oak tree stubbornly remaining on top. Its roots punched through the soil and hung down like gnarled appendages directly over their hiding place.

Bren had dragged over a thick limb that had broken off a maple tree with a plethora of green leaves. To camouflage their presence further, he weaved the foliage with the small branches of a massive tree trunk that had fallen and become wedged between the rocks jutting out over the water's surface. His handiwork served as a curtain to cover the opening of their hiding spot.

Bren held the Glock, the barrel pointed up. The person trampled above them. They heard the rustling of leaves, the snapping of twigs, the crunch of branches. Then, it was quiet. But Bren's worst fears were realized when he sighted the familiar khaki cargo pants with the gun still at the man's back. Through the branches, he watched the man descend the cliff, taking the same route they had taken.

The man's foot lost traction and started into a slide. They heard his grunt, his scramble to break his fall. There was a groan as he grabbed a branch and hung suspended in the air until his boots once again found solid footing.

To their relief, the man changed his mind. He climbed back up and was out of visual range. They stayed frozen, crouching until they were sure he was gone.

With both his hands cupped around Jamie's face, Bren said, "Jamie, it's time I told you about our escape plan. Listen carefully."

§

After leaving the lawyer's office, Chris reflected on Marisol Lopez's response to his question. At first she had given him a blank stare when he asked her the question: "Tell me, is Gar Reynolds the natural father of Erica?"

She had answered with a dour look. "No, detective, Gar Reynolds is not the father of Erica. She was ten when her mother became pregnant with Mr. Reynolds' child. As far as I know, Erica never knew about the baby. Ramon, Sophia's husband, I'm sure didn't know. And Mrs. Reynolds might have suspected her husband was up to no good, but from what I could tell, she never said or did anything about it.

"Erica had her father's eyes. Very dark. Like a deer. And like her mother, she was beautiful and sweet. Don't you think for one minute that she had one drop of Reynolds' blood in her veins!"

As Chris drove away from the law office and toward police headquarters, he thought with a smile how he had gotten a rise out of Marisol Lopez. For a moment after he had asked the question, he thought she would slap him. The ringtone of his phone shifted his thoughts. He hoped it was Jamie checking in.

But it was Nick's voice that said, "Chris, glad I caught you. I'm on my way to interview a co-worker of Erica's. Actually, her closest friend. She wasn't there when Landon and Waller did the initial interviews. Thought you might want to come along. I'm headed to the hospital now."

"Sure." Chris looked at his watch. "I can meet you in — oh, I figure in about fifteen minutes."

Nick was in the lobby when Chris walked in. Before they took the elevator up to the Critical Care Unit, Chris led him over to the seating area, where he briefed him on what he had learned at Sophia's home.

Once he finished his spiel, Nick said, "So you're thinking Gar Reynolds might have motive? We should concentrate on him."

"Yeah. I'm telling you, this is not about Jamie. I like Reynolds for the murder."

"Well, let's see if the best friend can tell us anything concrete," Nick said.

They waited at the nurses' station for Ashley Taylor, Erica's close friend. At last, a young woman in blue hospital scrubs walked up to them. She had a thick mane of red hair contained in a bushy ponytail.

Chris didn't know why she eyed them with skepticism, but he felt she would need some coaxing before they obtained any useful information from her.

He said to her, "We know you want the person who did this to be caught and punished. Please try to think of anything that Erica might have said that could help our investigation."

She squirmed in the molded plastic chair in the break room. A brief clunking noise from the drink machine broke the tense silence. Her eyes stared up at the ceiling tiles while she seemed to debate her cooperation.

"Ashley," Chris said, "we know you and Erica were good friends, and friends tell each other things. Please. We just need the truth."

She licked her lips and crossed her legs. Avoiding their stares, she said softly, "Well, first you should know that Mr. Reynolds sent his lawyer to threaten her. He didn't like—"

When she stopped talking, Chris said, "Go on, Ashley. We know about Erica's relationship with Garrett."

"Then you know Mr. Reynolds was against it. He heard they got back together."

"What else did Erica tell you?" Chris asked.

"She confided in me about...I guess since she's dead I can

say." She shrugged and continued, "Erica was given something by someone — she didn't say who — but it was something damaging about the Reynolds family. At first, she was going to hand it over to Garrett's wife, but she changed her mind. She decided to consult with a lawyer first."

"Who was the lawyer?"

She looked from Chris to Nick. Again, she licked her lips and said, "What I tell you...what I say, it won't get back to Gar Reynolds, will it?"

"No, Ashley, this is just between us. We just need the name of the lawyer, that's all."

She looked down at her feet and nodded. "Someone I recommended to her. He handled my mother's divorce. His name is Reece Parks."

"So Erica didn't tell you what she had?" Nick asked.

"No, but she said she thought once Jamie saw it, she'd have no problem getting Garrett to agree to a divorce. The quicker that happened the better, Erica told me. She wanted to marry Garrett despite his family. She was optimistic. She said Garrett was thinking about it, but he wanted to wait until after the baby was born so he could claim it as his own. Then his father would retire, as promised, and let him run the business *his* way. He asked Erica to be patient, but she hated sneaking around, keeping their relationship secret."

Chris exchanged a look with Nick as if to say *I told you so* then he turned back to Ashley. "When was Erica's appointment with the lawyer?"

Ashley stared down at her hands folded in her lap. When she looked up, Chris saw that her eyes were tearing up. From the pocket of her scrubs, she pulled out a tissue to soak up the tears before they spilled down her cheeks.

"Does it matter? She was murdered before she could meet with him," she said, closing her eyes tightly to control her emotions. "It's my fault. I pushed her to do something. To hire a lawyer and not tell Garrett. If I hadn't interfered, she'd still be alive."

"No, Ashley. That's not true," Chris said. "Whoever was responsible for this was already a threat to Erica. This was not your fault." He waited a beat, gave her time to wipe away fresh tears. "Tell me something. You said she wouldn't tell you how she got the information. Are you sure about that?"

She nodded. "She wouldn't tell me. Erica told me a lot, but she was still a private person. I got the feeling she was holding back, keeping things inside. Like talking about her father in prison or her mother's illness." She folded her arms over her chest and added, "It was good she had Garrett. He made her forget her troubles. She was so happy to have him back in her life." A tear trailed down her cheek. "I can't believe she's gone."

Nick gave Ashley a sympathetic look. "You've been a big help, Ashley. Here's my card. Call us if you think of anything else." To Chris, he said, "You got anything else before we go?"

"No. Thanks, Ashley. Don't worry. We'll catch the person who did this."

On their way out, Chris said to Nick, "Wanna pay a visit to Mr. Parks now?"

"Sounds like a plan."

Chris pressed the elevator button multiple times to go down. Waiting, he tapped his hand against his side, ignoring Nick's stare.

"What, Lagoni?"

Chris locked eyes with him. "Whaddya mean *what?*"

"I can almost hear the rusty wheels creaking in your damn brain. So spill it."

"The key to this case is that secret. Once we find out what it is, it will blow this case wide open. And to hell with Jamie's prints on the knife. That's bull-shit. Pure BS."

CHAPTER THIRTY-NINE

When Bren explained his escape plan to Jamie, she looked at him with disbelief.

"No way," she said. "You can't swim across that river! It's what? The width of two football fields. And colder than the beer in your fridge. You'll never make it. Besides, it's dark. I won't be able to see you."

"Good, that's the idea. I waited until it got dark on purpose. Look, Jamie, I can do this. Swimming is my thing. I was a record holder on my swim team in college. I need to get to that row-boat on the other side. You saw it, tied to the dock. I'll bring it back. Get you aboard and then we'll take it back across and hike up to the highway. It'll work. It has to. That guy won't give up. He knows there's no way out for us, so he'll be back."

"And what if he comes while you're gone and I'm here alone?"

"You'll have the gun. You told me you went to the gun range with Chris. Just do what he taught you. Here, I'll show you." With his hand on the grip, he turned the gun over. "Pull back this slide and it's ready to fire, aim for the torso and pull the trigger slowly. Simple."

"This sucks," she said, letting her frustration show. "I stay here while you swim away into the darkness. No way to communicate and no idea if you've made it over there!"

The tenderness in his eyes conveyed understanding for her misgivings. He lifted her chin with his index finger and managed a weak smile. "I'll come back for you, Jamie. Promise."

"Well, I'll be more than pissed if you don't. You're sure there's no one there that could help us?"

"I'm sure. The house has been dark the whole time. There's not another house around either. Once we make it across, we'll walk down a gravel road to the highway and from there, it's about a mile to a convenience store.

"I gotta go, baby. It's going to be okay." But when he hugged her and kissed her goodbye, he added words that made her heart plummet. "In case something goes wrong, I love you. You know that, right?"

She nodded, but couldn't say anything in return. Her eyes stayed on him as he walked away. From the sanctuary of their hideout, she strained to see in the darkness. His silhouette was faint, but she could detect his movements. He slipped out of his clothes, down to his boxer briefs. Then he waded into the river and was out of her sight.

§

Reece Park's name was familiar to Chris and Nick the minute Ashley had said it. The rumor they'd heard was about him being a college basketball star who turned down a tryout with the Chicago Bulls to attend law school at the University of North Carolina. Once he passed the bar, he'd opened a small firm that specialized in family law.

Well after dark, and after grabbing a bite to eat, the detectives tracked him down at a sports bar on the outskirts of the inner city. Once inside, they looked for the tallest guy crowded around the bar. But hearty laughter from a deep voice turned their attention to a man seated in the back booth. He seemed to be sharing a joke with a pretty server who had greenish eyes and mahogany skin. Chris kept it to himself, but he thought she looked like Beyoncé. It seemed he was unaware of the two detectives standing in front of him while he kept his eyes on the woman's backside as she walked away.

"Reece Parks?" Chris asked.

"That would be me." As he looked up at them and then their badges, the lawyer gripped his glass by spreading his fingers over the top to swirl the liquor around. It made sense to Chris why he was so good at handling a basketball; his hands were the size of a skillet. "You must be the detectives my secretary said called about the dead girl."

"Yes. We'd like to ask you a few questions, Mr. Parks."

"It's Reece. First names okay with you guys?"

A protocol of handshakes and name exchanges got them off to an amicable start. The server came back and gave a knowing look to Reece as if still amused by their secret joke. Chris figured she was more to Reece than just his server.

Before Chris and Nick could order, Reece said, "Guys, try what I've got. Red Bull and vodka. It's supercharged." He threw his head back and shared a laugh with the server.

Chris and Nick kept straight faces and ordered club soda. Again, Reece gave the server the kind of attention her sashay warranted and then brought his attention back to the detectives sitting across from him.

"Okay, gentlemen, how can I help?"

"We were told Erica Romero was murdered the day before she was to meet with you. We think her murder might have something to do with what she was coming to see you about. Her friend said there was some information she wanted you to see. What was it?"

Reece cocked his head to one side and squinted his eyes as if searching for an answer. He waited until he swallowed down a sip of his drink before he answered. "I was hoping you could tell me."

Chris and Nick exchanged looks.

"You don't know?" Chris asked as he scratched his cheek with irritation.

"Nah, I don't know. She wouldn't say over the phone. Said she wanted to show me, but had to go get whatever it was. She didn't have it."

"Didn't have it? Are you sure?" Nick asked.

Reece shrugged and placed his hand over the glass for another swirl. "Yup, that's what she said. Claimed someone had it in safekeeping, along with a photocopy of her lover's prenuptial agreement with his current wife. I told her to bring whatever she had and then we could discuss her options. In all honesty, I don't know what she wanted from me. Maybe some kind of legal action, maybe just advice. She was vague, I couldn't get it out of her. I wanted her to come early before I had to go to court, but she said she needed more time to pick up the item. The person holding it is a female — that much I know."

"How do you know that?" Nick asked.

"She said, 'I have to get it from *her*.'" He emphasized the word *her* and gave a shoulder shrug. "She told me she could come at two o'clock and I said that was fine." He downed the last of his drink and set his glass down hard. "Damn shame a pretty young woman like that gets killed. And for what?"

Yeah, and for what, Chris concurred in private thoughts. While Nick and Reece went off track about the Tar Heel basketball program and what they thought the team needed to win more games, Chris mulled over the information obtained from Reece.

Who was the woman who held the mysterious item, he wondered. Jamie's name popped in his head. When she was questioned by Waller and Landon, she mentioned that Erica had something to show her, but she said Erica had changed her mind. Did Jamie lie to the detectives? Would she withhold information from him? He didn't think so since he was the one person working to clear her name. Then who was the woman Erica gave it to? Apparently, someone Erica trusted.

"Sophia Romero," he said out loud, more for his benefit than the two men at the table.

"What's that?" Nick asked.

"Her mother," Chris said. "Erica must have left it with her mother. Mrs. Romero lived far enough away that it would take Erica some time to drive there and get back to town. If you guys will excuse me, I'm gonna check it out. Nick, stay and have a beer. I can do this alone."

After Chris threw some money on the table to cover his tab, he walked out. As he strolled across the parking lot, he jingled his car keys and mulled over his theory. *By process of elimination it has to be Sophia,* he surmised. *But how do you unlock the mystery if the holder of the secret is at death's doorstep, unable to speak?*

CHAPTER FORTY

Bren swam away from the bank, setting his sights on the opposite bank. The cold temperature shocked his system. From plenty of practice, he knew to pace his breathing, keep his movements tight, always in sync. Mid-way, he flipped on his back to regain his momentum, but being stationary even for a few seconds made his bones ache with cold. He found the stamina to keep swimming with the same determination he had when he broke the school's record for the four-hundred freestyle. At last he reached the shore but stubbed his toe on a jagged rock just below the surface. He got out of the water, wiping water from his face with both hands. As the pain shot through his foot, he cursed, then bent over to catch his breath, his hands on his knees. He stood up and rubbed his arms up and down as if that would take away the chill.

"Aw, shit," Bren said out loud when he found that there were no oars in the flat bottom boat. But he spotted a storage shed further up the bank. He discovered it was padlocked. In frustration, he tugged on the chain and realized the bracket that it was threaded through was loose. He gave it a yank and it popped off. The flimsy wooden door creaked open. In the darkness, his hand landed on something wooden. It made a racket when the object fell over. It whacked him hard on the head. But he smiled when he realized it was an oar and its mate was still upright in the front corner.

The boat was tied to a small dock that stretched twenty feet into the water. Bren walked gingerly toward the end. Some of the boards on the dock had warped and become loose, with rusty nail heads popping up at joists. The incessant chorus of frogs and crickets seemed to harmonize with his footfalls across the creaking wood.

He stepped aboard the small craft and spread his legs wide to maintain balance. Once he untied the rope from the metal cleat on the dock, he pushed away with the tip of an oar. The boat glided out for a few feet. He got settled on the bench seat and put the oars in their locks to begin rowing back to Jamie. If not for the crisis going on and the fact that he was freezing his ass off, he would have enjoyed being out on the river. Each stroke, each forward glide tantalized him with a calming peacefulness, but that was shattered by the sound of a loud POP! For a second or two, it caused him to pause, but then it registered. Gunfire! One shot! It came from the direction where he had left Jamie.

His heart pounded. He worked the oars like a madman, willing the boat to go faster. He strained to listen for Jamie's screams, another blast, *anything,* but all was quiet except for the churning of the water with each stroke. The crack of gunfire tormented him long after its initial sounding. He didn't know what he would find when he reached Jamie, and the not knowing made him sick with worry.

He cursed himself for not paying closer attention to his surroundings before he dove into the water. He wasn't sure where to steer the boat, where he left his clothes on the bank. The world before him was like a black abyss. The sky, the water, the ground. With no moon and no light, nothing was distinguishable. He rowed in short quick strokes, his full power invested in each movement, straining to see something familiar. At last, he came close enough to make out the jagged shoreline where brush and fallen trees dipped at the water's edge. He spotted the dead tree with a hollowed out trunk where he hid his clothes, but he had overshot his landing and had to paddle parallel to the shore. He jumped into water up to his waist and pulled the boat halfway out of the water and onto the bank. While he walked toward the hideout where he left Jamie, he dressed, stopping only once to pull up his pants.

He was startled to find the hideout empty. No sign of Jamie anywhere.

§

In frustration, Chris threw his cell phone onto the passenger seat. He made a dozen attempts to reach Jamie, but his calls went straight to voice-mail. He didn't know where she was or if she was in danger. Law enforcement was still looking for her, not as someone victimized by a hired killer, but as the prime suspect of murdering Erica Romero in cold blood.

He yelled out as he drove toward the home of Sophia Romero, "Jamie, just call me! Where in the hell are you?"

When he pulled into the driveway of Sophia's modest home, he parked behind a funeral hearse. On his way up the front walk, he stepped aside so that two men could guide a gurney toward the back of the vehicle where its rear door was open, awaiting its cargo. As the body of Sophia Romero rolled past him, he respectfully bowed his head.

Inside he found Becky with eyes puffy from crying. While she dabbed at her eyes, he placed his hand on her arm in a show of comfort. He couldn't think of anything to say, so he stayed quiet and hoped she knew he empathized with her sorrow.

One thing was for sure, if he was going to proceed with his investigation, he needed her cooperation, and her approval. Although he thought it might be awkward, he couldn't wait until a respectful mourning period had passed. He placed his hand on her elbow and led her down the hallway to the back bedroom, which he assumed had once been Erica's.

In a low voice, he said to her, "I believe Erica put something in this house for safe keeping. Did Sophia ever mention it?"

Her eyes widened. "No, not that I remember."

"Did you ever see Erica bring something here and put it away somewhere, like a hiding place?"

Becky bit her lower lip and shook her head. "No. Never. Maybe when I wasn't here. Now that's possible. Sometimes I would leave and Erica would stay with her mother. She was a nurse, you know. My goodness, she knew how to care for the terminally ill the same as me." She crossed her arms over her chest. "What do you think you're looking for, detective?"

"I'll know it when I see it."

Chris was moved by Becky's sad eyes taking in their surroundings as if she was imagining a young Erica in the bedroom. It was a girl's room with touches of pink and lavender. Becky stepped over to the dressing table and picked up a photograph. She held it up for Chris to see. He smiled at a photo of Erica in her graduation cap and gown, one arm around her mother's shoulders. Mother and daughter smiled proudly for the camera. As she set it back down, Becky's eyes pooled with fresh tears.

Chris cleared his throat, ending the uncomfortable silence. He said to her, "There's something here. I don't know where, but it's here and it might tell us who killed her. I have to look, ma'am." He walked Becky to the door. "I'll be discreet, but I have to do this. I'll start with this room."

"Do what you have to, detective. I'll be in the kitchen if you need me. Folks are gonna start coming by, so I best straighten up the house. I don't think we should mention anything to Sophia's kinfolk. They're a nosey bunch of busybodies, if you know what I mean."

"Yes, I think it's best that we don't discuss this with anyone."

Before he began the search, Chris tried to imagine himself in Erica's position. Where would she hide something important? And what exactly was it? An envelope? A document? A flash drive? Damned if he knew, but he would turn the room upside down if necessary until he found what it was.

An hour later, he decided that the room held no secrets. He walked into the kitchen feeling exasperated but still determined to find whatever it was and damn sure it was in the house.

Becky turned from the counter to meet his gaze, giving him a weak smile as if she sensed his frustration. "No luck, huh?" she said.

"No. It must be somewhere else."

"Well, you sit yourself down and I'll get you something cold to drink. Take a break. You've got maybe an hour before the chaos begins. I heard that Sophia's aunt and cousins are on their way. They all talk at once, and Lord knows I don't have a clue what they're saying. My Spanish is limited to *hello* and *thank you*. That's about it." Becky handed him a glass of iced tea. "Here you go. That should hit the spot. Well, guess I'd better get some more glasses down for all those folks."

"Can I help?"

"Nah, you stay right there. I'll just get this rickety old stepstool and then I can reach that top shelf just fine."

She pulled it over and put her right foot on the first step. It rocked from side to side. "Told ya it was rickety. One day, I saw Erica standing on the very top step and it started wobbling around. I thought she was gonna fall and break her neck. Don't know what she was after. Never would say."

Chris reflected on what Becky said. "Where was the stool when Erica stood up on it?"

"Where I have it now. Maybe she wanted a special glass from the top shelf. 'Course there's lots of glasses on the lower two. She seemed upset with me that I fussed at her for being so careless. Just didn't want her to get hurt, that's all."

With his palm open to help Becky down, he said, "Be careful." When she stepped aside, he started up the stepstool and said, "Let me check something."

The metal stool rocked from the force of his weight. Chris stepped up on the top step and stretched his arm up to reach the space between the top of the cabinet and the ceiling. With his palm flat, he felt around for what he could not see. His hand brushed across something flat. He grabbed hold of the side of the cabinet with one hand and stretched the opposite arm as high as it would go.

Becky said, "Now you be careful there."

"Got it," he said.

He didn't come down the steps, but jumped, landing solid on his feet. He held up the large envelope for Becky to see.

"This might be the answer we're looking for."

He took it to the table and unclasped the opening. Old photographs and letters spilled out across the surface. But before Becky had time to inspect the parcel, he stuffed everything back into the envelope. For now, the only person he would share the contents with was Sergeant Holden back at police headquarters.

CHAPTER FORTY-ONE

With disbelief, Bren stared long and hard at the spot where he'd left Jamie. He had spread leaves and pieces of wood over the dirt for her to sit on. Now everything was scattered about. Although their backpacks remained on the ground, his father's gun was missing.

Scared out of his mind, he walked along the shoreline looking for any sign of her. When he knocked brush out of his way at a frantic pace, a bird flew out, stunning him, causing him to reel backwards, his heart racing. He tried to calm down, but his imagination went wild with thoughts of finding Jamie injured or dead.

He heard a rustling of leaves and saw movement ahead. He stopped in his tracks. The silhouette of two figures emerged from the overgrown brush at the water's edge. It was Jamie, thank God, but the other figure...The killer who stood behind her, shoving her forward in his direction. When they were no more than six feet away, Bren saw the barrel of a gun pressed against her head.

The man gave him a hard look, but then smiled. "I'm pleased to make your acquaintance, McKeever. We've been expecting you." Bren shifted his gaze from Jamie's terrified eyes to the sight of the gun barrel. The killer smiled as he said, "Fortunately for me, your girlfriend is a lousy shot. I was standing five feet in front of her when she fired and she still missed. She couldn't even get off a second shot because the damn thing jammed." He chuckled. "It wasn't exactly the greeting I expected."

"Let her go."

"Don't think so. You see, Miss Jackson and I made a deal. I wouldn't kill you when you showed up if she hands over the packet she got from Erica. Oh, at first, she denied it, but you see, before I killed Erica she told me she gave it to your girlfriend for safekeeping. Lying about it is just a waste of my time, know what I mean?" He paused to sneer back and forth between them. "So here's what we're gonna do. We're going to go back to your little hiding place and get some rest, and then at daylight, we're hiking back to your car. Then we'll drive back to Charlotte, pick up the package from the safe deposit box where Jamie said she put it, and then everyone can go their merry way. Sound like a plan?"

"Who are you?"

"To you, I'm someone you don't want to piss off. 'Cause when I get pissed off, I lose my temper. You don't want to be around for that. Trust me."

Bren locked eyes with Jamie. He wanted to bring her into his arms to comfort her, but he couldn't. One wrong move and they'd both be dead.

He said to her, "Jamie, did he hurt you?"

"No, I'm fine."

Her words brought him no comfort. Bren said to the man, "You don't have to keep that gun pointed at her head. I think she gets the message. We're not going to fight you. We'll do as you say. Just drop the damn gun."

"Don't think so. Now let's get moving, back to your little hideout. We have a long hike in a few hours. Know what? I'm hungry. Got any goodies to eat?"

Once they arrived at the hiding place, the killer made Jamie put her hands behind her back. He ordered Bren to put plastic restraints on her wrists and bind her legs together with rope. Once Bren was done, the man inspected it to make sure it was secure. Then he bound Bren up, forcing him to sit on the ground with his back up against Jamie's.

With his back to the opening of the cave, the man kept the gun pointed at them. He dragged the backpack over with his foot and used his free hand to fish out a pack of crackers that he tore open with his teeth.

"Isn't this cozy? All we need now is a campfire to roast marshmallows. We could tell ghost stories. I bet Bren is a former boy scout. Am I right?"

Bren stayed silent. He gave him a hard stare. The killer jumped up and jabbed the gun barrel under Bren's chin. He clicked the safety off.

"Answer me, asshole!"

"Yes, I was a scout."

"There, now was that so hard? No sense in us not being friendly. Jamie and I might get *real* friendly in a little while. Know what I mean?" He leered at her and winked.

"You touch her and I'll —"

"Do what, McKeever? I'll tell ya what you'll do. You'll watch. 'Member what I said about pissing me off?"

§

A few precious moments alone, Jamie thought as the man stepped out "to take a piss," as he put it, warning them if they were to move more than an inch, there would be hell to pay. She sighed with relief when he was out of sight and whispered Bren's name.

"Shh," he cautioned. "He can still hear us."

Of course. They could hear his stream hit against the bushes and puddle in the dirt. She had to choose her words carefully, so she whispered, "I lied. No safety deposit box. I don't have it."

"I know."

"Buy some time," she said, then added, "Chris."

"I know."

The killer was back, zipping up his fly. He gave Jamie a salacious grin, a reminder of his remark about getting friendly. She vowed if it happened, she would fight like a wildcat. Scratch and claw to leave his DNA underneath her fingernails. That way if he killed her, her body would leave plenty of proof of his evil deed. His sleazy stare infuriated her more than scared her. He had refused to tell them his name, therefore Jamie privately nicknamed him Beak Nose. She thought it was fitting since his features resembled a vulture.

He squatted facing them and then plopped down to sit cross-legged in front of the opening of their hide-out to prevent their escape. Despite Jamie's efforts to stay awake, her eyes closed. When she opened them again, she realized the sun was up. The color of the sky, a blush of peach.

"Rise and shine," Beak Nose said. "Time to go."

He prodded Bren up by jabbing the gun in his side, then turned back to her. "You too, princess. Get up."

"How can I when my feet are tied?"

Beak Nose pulled a hunting knife from his belt and reached forward to cut the rope from her ankles. The process was repeated to free Bren, although he left their wrists bound. He said huskily, "Better? Let's get going, lovebirds."

"I feel sick," Jamie said. "I might have to puke."

He only snickered at her remark.

"For God's sake, let her have a few crackers and some water," Bren said, then added, "She's pregnant!"

"Knocked up, heh? Well, I'll be damned. Sure you're the daddy? With her looks, it could be anyone. Know what I mean?"

"Just give her something to eat."

"No one tells me what to do, asshole, but if it'll get her ass in gear, sure, she can have a little snack."

Beak Nose unwrapped a package of crackers that he held to Jamie's lips for her to bite into. He followed that with a few sips of water.

Bren and Jamie looked on when he retrieved thick nylon rope from his backpack and wrapped it around his elbow and open hand. He worked slowly making a tight coil. When he finished, he attached it to a clamp at his waist and let it dangle at his side. Jamie's eyes met Bren's as if to ask the question, *What is he up to?*

Jamie felt her heart thumping when Beak Nose inserted a loaded magazine into his gun and stuck it down into the waistband of his cargo pants. Then he slapped his hands together and said, "Okay, troops, time to get moving."

Bren followed Jamie out with the gun pressed against the back of his head. Following the same route that brought them to the area, they walked in single file past flowering mountain laurel and dogwood and over rich earth adorned with a scattering of green moss and lush ferns. The morning dew made their shoes damp and splashed moisture as they brushed past the foliage.

Thirty minutes into their hike, the killer ordered them to stop. He clamped his hand around Jamie's arm and pulled her over to a tree, pushing her hard enough against the trunk to cause her head to hit the rough bark with a thud.

Bren charged forward. "Leave her alone!"

"Stay back or she gets a bullet to the head!"

"What are you doing?" Jamie asked.

"Tying you up while I take care of some business." The killer unclamped the coil of rope from his belt and used it to tie her to the tree trunk. Around and around he walked the circumference of the tree, each time positioning a section of rope underneath her breasts, brushing across them with the back of his hand. His audacity drew a reaction from Bren. Jamie noted the tightness of his jaw, the fury in his eyes. Although he had his hands restrained behind his back, he charged forward, trying to ram hard enough against Beak Nose to knock him to the ground.

What a fool thing to do, she thought. *He'll get us both killed!*

Beak Nose saw the attack coming. With no free movement of his arms, Bren was himself knocked to the ground. He landed face first, spitting out dirt. The killer grabbed the back of his collar and yanked him up.

"Stay right there, asshole! On your knees!"

"Now what?" Bren asked.

"Now it's the end of the line for you, McKeever. I've got no use for you. Jamie and I will be just fine on our own."

"So you're going to kill me?"

"Yeah, and I want her to watch so she'll know she'll end up the same way if she doesn't come through with those documents."

"No!" Jamie screamed as she looked on. "Don't kill him! You promised me!"

The killer turned to her. "I lied, sweetheart. He's extra baggage."

CHAPTER FORTY-TWO

Beak Nose stepped back from Bren and pointed the gun at his forehead from a distance of about four feet. While the very core of her body shook with fear, Jamie closed her eyes. She would not witness Bren's death.

The blast was powerful and explosive, echoing through the forest and making her temporarily deaf. *But the shot...didn't it come from...*When she opened her eyes, she saw it was Beak Nose, and not Bren, who lay on the ground. The back of his skull had been shattered by the impact of the gunshot. Pieces of brain landed in pools of blood, making her queasy.

A plume of gunpowder lingered in the air. Bren looked as stunned as Jamie. They both turned from the horrific sight of the body when they heard a rustling of bushes and then voices coming from behind them.

Men outfitted as though ready for battle rushed forward. In bold letters, across their Kevlar vests, the word SHERIFF was printed. One officer pulled back on a leash to rein in the eagerness of his K-9 partner, a bloodhound.

As an officer untied Jamie, he said, "Are you okay, ma'am?" He did a quick once-over, looking for any visible injuries.

"I'm fine," she lied. Her heart still pounded, and she was shaking all over.

Among the men that surrounded the area, Jamie saw a familiar face. Bren's father pushed through the group to step forward. After she nodded to him that she was okay, he rushed over to Bren and put a hand on his son's shoulder.

"Nothing like starting the day off with a bang." Although his remark was flippant, his voice and his face were tinged with emotion. He elbowed a deputy out the way and drew a knife from a leather case on his belt to cut through the plastic handcuffs. "Damn that was close," he said. "Another minute and — well, hell, I'd hate to think about that."

Bren rubbed the soreness from his wrists. "Thanks, Pop," he said and brushed past him in order to get to Jamie. He gathered her in his arms, kissed the top of her head. "Thank God you're okay."

Jamie was separated from Bren by deputies assigned to escort them to the EMS van. She looked over her shoulder at him as she felt the powerful arms of two men keeping her upright when the impact of the ordeal forced her to succumb to a weakened state. Bren broke away from the guy charged with overseeing his welfare to come to Jamie's aid and assist her up into the medical van, but the muscled guys had already hoisted her up inside the vehicle.

"Are you okay, baby?" he asked her.

"I'm fine, considering what we've been through."

While their vitals were checked, Bren asked his father to explain how the SWAT team knew to come.

Mac sniffed and ran his hand over his face. "Well, it's like this — I called Denny after he released his dog from the house. Wanted to make sure you and Jamie got away. He told me everything was fine. That you two got away in his truck after the dogs scared the man off and the dude hightailed it out of there. I didn't think anything more about it until I went to bed, and I thought about something Denny had said. He said, 'Scout really tore into that guy.' But his dog's name is Beast. Scout died last year from a bear attack. When he said it, I thought he got confused, but then I thought — wonder if that's a code. You know, like a distress signal. I couldn't sleep 'cause I kept worrying about that. So even before the sun came up, I hustled over to Denny's place."

Mac looked down at the ground and shook his head. When he looked up again, he said with moist eyes, "He's dead, Bren. The guy must have held a gun to his head to make him say what he said to me. I found him on the floor. The sheriff said it looked like his neck had been broken. The dog's dead, too. His belly cut open something awful. He was underneath a piece of tarp next to the woodpile." Mac wiped his eyes with the back of his hand and sniffed. "Damn! Denny was my friend. And this had to happen to..."

His last words trailed off into a whispered breath that Bren couldn't understand. He put his hand on his father's arm. "Dad, I'm so sorry."

When the sheriff came over, Bren asked him, "Do we know who this guy is?"

"Funny, I was going to ask you the same question. He had no ID."

Jamie looked at Bren and said, "I wanted that guy to tell us that Gar Reynolds hired him. That's what I really wanted to hear."

§

Chris and Nick had a meeting behind closed doors with Sergeant Holden, Captain Spratt over the Violent Crime Division, and the district attorney. Papers and photos were scattered across Holden's desk like pieces of a puzzle. Through the glassed-in partition, Chris spotted Waller and Landon at a distance, looking chagrined because they were not invited to the party. Chris made eye contact with Waller and hitched his chin with a smile on his lips. Waller quickly turned away.

Holden looked over all the contents of the envelope Chris had taken from the Romero home and let out a low whistle. He re-read with interest one of the five handwritten letters included in the packet. The postmark on the envelope was dated over thirty years ago. Holden dragged his finger under one particular sentence that he showed to the DA.

District Attorney Caldwell frowned and said, "This is a shock. Maybe related to the murder, but pure speculation. Nothing concrete."

Chris felt his blood boil but kept his temper in check. He wanted to grab the DA by the collar and tell him to grow some balls. But before he could say anything, civil or crude, his burn phone started ringing. Only one person had the number. Jamie. He brushed past Nick, hitting against his shoulder, but took no time to apologize.

Out in the hallway, he said, "Jamie! Thank God! Are you all right?"

"I'm fine. Bren and I were taken hostage at gunpoint by the hired killer. Chris, he killed a man and his dog. And now he's dead. SWAT came to our rescue. The sheriff is going to call you."

"Where are you?"

"We're in the woods surrounded by officers. The sheriff is going to drive us back to Mac's house."

"Who's Mac?"

"Bren's father. He has a home in the mountains. That's where we were when you called us yesterday."

"I thought so. Jamie, that rental car that was following you — I got the name of the person who rented it. Robert Fuller. Ever heard of him?"

"No, it doesn't sound familiar."

"Well, we'll find out," Chris said. "Gotta go. We're in the middle of this and I need to get back. We'll talk later. You sure you're okay?"

"I'm fine," she said. "Chris?"

"Yeah?"

"I'm not considered a suspect any longer, am I?"

"No, you're good. I can't wait to throw this in Waller's face."

§

In an interview room at police headquarters, Robert Fuller kept his head down and seemed determined to make Chris and Nick work for every piece of information they pulled from him. They learned that it was he who had rented the vehicle driven by the killer and left abandoned on an isolated stretch of land near the McKeever property in the mountains.

"Just give it up, Fuller," Chris said. "It was your credit card used at Hertz, and we have you on camera at their service desk." The last part was a lie, but Chris figured it could be true. He learned from a customer representative that the car had been reserved by a walk-in customer at their office near the airport. They danced around the rental car issue for about an hour until Fuller admitted it.

"The car wasn't for me. For a business associate. The Reynolds family. There, you have it. Now can I go?"

But that was just the beginning. They soon learned his connection to the Reynolds family. He did landscaping for them and boasted about the award-winning roses he had planted and tended on their grounds. Chris remembered seeing the rose garden at Jamie's wedding reception.

Once Fuller started on the rose garden, the bragging rights spouted from his mouth with no end in sight, but they let him talk and pretended to be interested. Two hours in, he knew he was sunk once he let it slip about his very close working relationship with a certain member of the Reynolds family. But his allegiance to that person began to unravel like yarn once they told him he could spend the rest of his life in prison unless he cooperated. The detectives felt they had enough to charge him and keep him locked up while they went after the real mastermind behind the murder of Erica Romero. They wasted no time making their way to the Reynolds estate. Like the game of Clue, all the players would be present, only it wasn't Professor Plum in the library with the candlestick. The real question was: *who knew what and when?*

Chris parked the unmarked sedan in the circular drive in front of the Reynolds' home. Along with Nick and Holden, he was ushered inside by a woman who identified herself as Marlena. She led them into the front sitting room and told them that Mr. and Mrs. Reynolds would be with them shortly. She offered to bring refreshments but got no takers. The tension in the room kept the detectives staring down at their feet, seated but not comfortable in the plush surroundings. Chris stood up to pace, hands in his pockets, jiggling his car keys.

"Sit down, Lagoni," Holden said. "You're getting on my nerves. When they show up, let me do the talking."

Chris was about to respond when the front door opened. Garrett slipped inside and directed his gaze at the three men. His jaw was set tight, his eyes intense as he searched their faces for the meaning of their urgent call.

He went around the room, shaking hands with the detectives. Dapper in a black Armani suit, he explained that he came directly from the Romero home, where he had been helping with the funeral arrangements for Sophia and Erica, although Erica's body had yet to be released by the coroner. When Chris had called him with news of a break in the case, he had demanded to know details, but Chris had refused to say over the phone. Now that they were face to face, Garrett said, "If you know who did this to Erica, then tell me."

Holden stood up and walked over. "We'll wait for your parents, Garrett."

Dressed for an evening out, Catherine and Gar Reynolds walked hand in hand into the room. Her strong perfume lent its fragrance to the air. The plunging neckline of her cocktail dress put her breasts on full display. *She has to know it's distracting as hell,* Chris thought, but no matter, he would stay focused. He locked eyes with Catherine and wondered how she would react to the news. Her perfect world was about to implode, that much was certain.Catherine's diamond earrings swung gently as she was escorted to an upholstered chair by her husband. Gar took the one at her side and reached over to take her hand in his. He said, "Gentlemen, as you can see, Catherine and I are on our way to an event. I hope this won't take long. I wish it could have been postponed until tomorrow. What is so urgent, sergeant?"

"As I said on the phone," Holden began, "we have some questions related to our investigation. I'd have preferred that you and your family come downtown, but as a courtesy, we agreed to come here."

"Then ask away."

Holden nodded in response to Gar's remark. He cleared his throat and said, "Do either of you know a man named Bob Fuller?"

"No, never heard of him," Gar said.

Holden moved his gaze to Catherine. "Ma'am?"

"Mr. Fuller does landscaping. He planted our rose garden."

Gar looked at this wife and furrowed his brow. "That guy? The man you call Bobby Lee?"

"Yes," she answered in a weak voice.

Holden shot her a knowing look and said, "Mrs. Reynolds, wasn't he more than a gardener to you?"

Gar turned on Holden. "Exactly what are you trying to imply, sergeant?"

"Please answer the question, Mrs. Reynolds."

She paused to lick her lips. "Strictly business, I assure you. We met a few times to discuss the design of the flower garden. I went with him to see some public gardens so he would have an idea of how I wanted the rose garden laid out. How dare you insinuate some impropriety with that man."

"Go on," Holden prompted.

"What more can I say? Unless you need to know that he was in charge of the flowers for Jamie and Garrett's wedding. He did a fabulous job, too."

Holden exchanged a look with Chris. He scratched his cheek and said, "Mrs. Reynolds, Fuller told Detective Lagoni that he was in love with you. He said he would walk through fire for you. That's more than a business relationship."

Catherine glanced at her husband whose eyes stayed fixed on her with intensity. She gave him a weak smile, then turned back to Holden. "Yes, he had a little crush on me. Trust me, it wasn't reciprocated. How dare you, Detective Lagoni, believing that man. He was my gardener, nothing more."

"He said you asked for his help," Holden said. "What was he talking about?"

"I have no idea." Catherine patted her husband's arm. "Darling, shouldn't we be leaving? We don't want to be late."

"My wife has answered your questions, Holden. She has nothing more to add."

"We're not done."

Catherine had started to rise from her chair, but sat back down.

Gar said, "Look, Catherine is being honored tonight for charity work. The organizers of the event will be disappointed if we're not there for the cocktail hour."

Holden signaled to Nick to hand over the large manila envelope. Before he unclasped the flap and pulled out the contents, he said, "Mrs. Reynolds, do you have any idea what I'm holding?"

CHAPTER FORTY-THREE

All eyes were on Catherine Reynolds. In Chris's mind, her cool demeanor could have earned her an Academy Award. Stunning in a black dress that accentuated her curves, she tried to work her magic on Holden. While she had eyes only for him, she let her lush red lips curl into a smile, batted her lashes.

"Sergeant, you must be holding a package of lies. Has someone been spying on me? Am I a victim of blackmail? The curse of someone with money. Vultures everywhere."

Holden did not address her accusations. He pulled a photograph from the envelope and handed it to her. "Tell us about this photograph."

She gave a nervous laugh and looked over at Garrett. "Why it's just a photograph of me and Garrett taken on a trip to Paris. I have a similar one on the credenza in the foyer. Garrett was maybe two at the time. I was much younger as you can see. Where did you get this?"

Holden didn't respond. He handed her another photograph, this time showing herself, Garrett and a handsome man with his arm around her shoulders and his lips pressed against her temple.

It took her only a few seconds to view before she flipped it over in her lap. "Please, sergeant. Don't."

"Tell us about the man in the photo, Mrs. Reynolds."

She placed her hand on Gar's arm. "Darling, we really should be going. These men are wasting our time."

Gar snatched the photograph and stared at it. "Scott Michaels? What's he doing in this picture? Catherine, what is this?"

"Remember, darling? I told you, I ran into him in France." She gave Holden a hard stare and said tersely, "Are you happy, sergeant? Now my husband thinks I was having an affair."

"Because you were, Mrs. Reynolds." He handed her a handwritten letter.

The color drained from her face as she recognized the handwriting. She handed it back and stayed silent.

"Like the others, ma'am, that is your handwriting. Do you want to tell Garrett and Gar the truth or do you want me to tell them?"

"Please, don't do this." Her eyes filled with tears. "What I did was to protect my family. I couldn't bear for them to be hurt."

Holden was not deterred by her plea. He said to her, more for the benefit of Garrett and Gar, "During your stay in Paris, you told Michaels that you would tell your husband the truth. That Michaels is Garrett's father. You promised him that you would ask Garr for a divorce and marry him, but once home, you had a change of heart." Holden held up another letter from the stack. "This letter, dated a month later, says that you wanted Gar to keep thinking the child was his and you had no intention of leaving him for Michaels. Scott Michaels was the love of your life. Your words, not mine. But you wanted your son to grow up with the Reynolds name and inherit the Reynolds fortune. Wonder how Michaels felt when you told him he could never provide for you and his child in the manner you were accustomed. So you ended the affair."

In the tracks of her tears, black mascara ran down her cheeks. She dabbed at her eyes and said, "Stop it! Just stop it!"

But Holden continued, "Mrs. Reynolds, let me tell you what Michaels wrote on the outside of the envelope before he gave it to Erica. As you know, she was his nurse in his final days. He said that she was to keep this package somewhere safe and then share it with Garrett after your death. He was explicit about that. He was willing to take the secret to his grave — and yours — if he knew that one day Garrett would know the truth."

The agony on Garrett's face seemed to make everyone in the room uncomfortable. So wrought with emotional pain, Chris wondered if he would keel over. Tears collected in his eyes and then spilled out when he closed them. He raked his hand through his hair harshly as if he wanted to yank it out by its roots. Never once did he make eye contact with his mother even though she pleaded for him to look at her.

"Garrett, what I did was to protect you," she said. "So you could inherit everything. Not just the money held in the trust, but your father's business. It had to go to an heir. You remember how he went on and on about that. I did what I thought was best. Erica wanted to spoil everything. She came to see me and told me that she was going to tell Jamie the truth, and then Jamie would tell you so she could get a divorce. I had to stop her."

Holden leaned forward, his fingers interlaced as his forearms rested on his knees. "Mrs. Reynolds, you told all of this to Fuller. You used flirtation and empty promises to get him to help you. You got him to spy on Erica and Jamie, to study their habits. You took a knife from Jamie's kitchen counter that had her prints on it, put it in your purse, and handed it over to Fuller to give to the killer. You bought shoes identical to Jamie's to leave prints at the crime scene. You instructed the killer to make it look like Jamie murdered Erica."

Catherine turned in her chair to face Gar. He had gone rigid, no longer held her hand. She tried to reach out to him, but he shook her hand off his arm.

"I did it for you, Gar," she said through sobs. "You had money invested in the KleenBrite project. I wasn't going to let Jamie expose your involvement. Goodness, I just wanted Jamie to be a stay-at-home wife, have a baby, run the household for her husband. That's what wives do. When she lost her job at the paper, I thought that was the end of it. But she still planned to do the article. I had to stop her! You understand, don't you?"

Holden continued, "You asked Fuller to find someone to kill Erica and make it look like Jamie had done it. For ten grand, Leo Creighton was hired to do the deed."

"I've never heard of the man."

"That's right. You haven't, but your friend, Bobby Lee, was your go-to guy. He agreed to find a contract killer. To carry out your instructions to a T."

Catherine said, "Jamie cared more about her precious job than making Garrett happy. And Erica was Mexican trash, the daughter of a servant and a convicted felon. Not suitable material for our son. No way! And then to have the gall to threaten me with her secret information. She said if Gar and I would give Garrett our blessing to their union, she wouldn't tell him what she knew, but I couldn't agree to that! That's blackmail, plain and simple."

All eyes fell on Gar, who had slumped forward. He placed his hand over his heart and moaned.

Holden said, "Mr. Reynolds, are you alright?"

Gar pulled himself up out of the chair and walked to the window. With hands in his pockets, he stared out at nothing in particular. The room fell silent except for the muffled sound of Garrett's sobs that made the charged atmosphere insufferable. As Catherine rose from her chair, she regarded her husband and son and paused as if debating what she should do.

"Gar. Garrett," she muttered with a voice that trembled. Both men ignored her. She lifted her chin, rolled her shoulders back, then addressed Holden. "If you'll excuse me, I need to use the bathroom. I might be sick."

"Mrs. Reynolds, before you go, let me tell you that we have Robert Fuller in custody and he's talking. Leo Creighton, your hired killer, strangled an innocent man and killed his dog. An innocent bystander who had nothing to do with this. Think about that while you're gone."

After she pirouetted in her stiletto heels, she walked out with a tilt to her chin. *Arrogant broad,* Chris thought.

Chris got up and walked over to Gar Reynolds. "Mr. Reynolds, are you okay?" Heads turned to observe the man still standing at the window. With his back to them, he nodded.

Chris touched his arm, led him back to his chair. "You need anything? Water?"

He hung his head low and muttered, "No."

Minutes stretched by with no return of Catherine. Finally, Chris said, "I'm going to check on Mrs. Reynolds." But when he saw the door to the bathroom was already wide open, he raced back to the sitting room. "She's gone! Nick take the front. I'll get the back."

Chris sprinted out the back door and headed in the direction of the detached garage. The door was raised. A black Mercedes sedan braked as it cleared the automatic door. A police cruiser with blue lights flashing blocked it in the driveway. Chris frowned and shook his head as he strolled over to open the driver's side door.

"Going somewhere, Mrs. Reynolds?"

"I won't survive if I go to jail, detective."

"Mrs. Reynolds, you are responsible for the murder of Erica Romero, the kidnapping and attempted murder of Brennan McKeever and Jamison Jackson, and the murder of someone you don't even know *and* his dog."

"I did it all for my family! I did what I had to do for Garrett, for Gar!" Catherine looked past Chris at the approaching figures that included the police as well as her husband and son. She got out of the car and placed the keys in Chris's open palm. Her stare stayed on Gar as she said to him, "Darling, please! Say you understand. Forgive me like I've forgiven you for all your little indiscretions."

She turned to her son who stood nearby and looked as though he was locked in a nightmare from which he'd never awaken. Catherine reached for her son, but he backed away. "Garrett, sweetheart, I love you. I wanted what was best for you. Those women were all wrong for you. If it's any comfort to you, I made sure that Erica didn't suffer. I gave explicit instructions that it be quick."

Garrett let out a howl as haunting as a banshee as he lunged forward to pounce on his mother. Just before he could land a powerful punch, Chris blocked him and took the brunt of the blow. Chris pulled him away, but Garrett fought the restraint, trying desperately to break free and attack his mother. Through clenched teeth, he cursed Chris, thrashing his arms about while still being held back not just by Chris but by Nick as well who ran over to assist.

Gar looked on with a frown and then stepped close to Holden. "Get her out of here. Out of my sight."

Holden nodded and said, "Mrs. Reynolds, place your hands behind your back."

Her mouth fell open as if appalled by Holden's command. But at last she seemed to comprehend that no one around her would lift a finger to make the unpleasantness of the evening go away. She turned to Gar and said, "Darling, please call Stuart Ramsey and tell him to come to police headquarters. I won't spend one night in jail. Gentlemen, the DA is a close friend. Gar contributed money to his last campaign." She shot a half-smile at Holden. "He won't stand for me being mistreated this way. Sergeant, you can't be serious. You really plan to handcuff me and take me off to jail? A lady of my means carted off like a common criminal? Really, sergeant?"

Holden smiled. "Yes, Mrs. Reynolds. Really."

CHAPTER FORTY-FOUR

It had been nearly twenty-four hours since Bren's life had almost ended in front of Jamie. She was left emotionally and physically drained. She and Bren had told and retold every detail of their ordeal to law enforcement officials but refused to speak with the media. At last, they were free to shower, eat and go to bed. Jamie tried to sleep, but she couldn't stop her mind from replaying the events that had rocked her world.

At sunrise, she walked outside Mac's cabin, wearing Bren's jacket to keep warm. She stepped off the front porch and leaned over the railing at the property's edge. She looked up to admire the sky that looked as though a delicate veil of pink had been tossed up and landed in the east. Fifty yards away a low lying mist hugged the trunks of the densely populated trees. *Mother Nature at her finest,* she thought.

With her back to the house, she didn't know Bren had come out to join her until she felt his arms wrap around her. She felt his lips press against the back of her head.

"Are you okay, baby? You couldn't sleep?"

"No, I keep thinking about the phone call from Chris — what he told me. I can't believe that it was Catherine, not Gar that killed Erica. Catherine," she repeated the name as if trying to make sense of it. "The sweet Southern belle. The delicate flower. It's ironic that Scott Michaels fathered Garrett. I say that because one time Garrett confided in me that he wished Scott was his father. I remember him as a great guy, always so supportive of Garrett."

"Then maybe out of this tragedy, Garrett finds that welcome news."

"Maybe. I'm sure he's still in a lot of pain. Chris told me he was really torn up." Jamie turned around. "I want to go to him, Bren. Garrett and I practically grew up together. Despite everything, I'm still his friend. I forgive him. Maybe you think that's strange, but I see it this way — his love for Erica was something he had on his own, not forced on him by his parents. He made his way to her independently. Don't you see, Bren, his marriage to me was more their idea than his. They took from him the only thing he really loved." She paused, then added, "I've got to see him."

"Jamie, he's no different than his parents. He manipulated you. Me too. He forced you into a deceit before he would agree to a divorce."

"And I forgive him for that. It brought us together, didn't it?"

"He caused you a lot of pain. You can't forget that."

"So I'm not supposed to forgive him? You forgave me, Bren. After I lied and deceived you. Look, we're not supposed to pick and choose who we forgive. I don't want to stay angry. I don't know why, but I feel this strong pull to go to Garrett right now. I can't explain it."

Bren stared off into the distance. Jamie noted that his lips were pressed tightly together, a habit of his when he was deep in thought. She remembered she had once teased him about it. He brought his gaze back to her. While he stayed silent, he brought his hand up to her face and brushed a lock of hair from her cheek. "Okay, baby. If that's what you want. I'll go tell Pop that we're leaving."

"Is he up already?"

"Yeah, he's up. He's in the kitchen fixing breakfast. I hope you like eggs scrambled with liver mush."

Jamie made a face. "Oh my God, I think I'm going to be sick."

Bren laughed. "I'll tell him to make your eggs plain."

§

With only four hours of sleep, Chris counted on his second cup of strong coffee to keep him alert during his briefing with Holden and the district attorney on the Romero case. The DA was talking, but Chris wasn't listening. He couldn't get past the image of Catherine being handcuffed and put in the police car. Her beautiful face looked as if it would shatter like porcelain as she stared into his eyes with desperation, silently pleading with him to stop the madness.

He wondered if she had managed to keep it together when she arrived at the county jail. As required, she would have been stripped and issued an orange jumpsuit. Then she would have been given a blanket, toothbrush, roll of toilet paper, and pair of flip-flops. In sharp contrast to her humongous estate on the lake, she would have been taken to an eight-by-six-foot cell with a toilet, sink, and bunk bed. She would find the mattress thin and hard. The queen of high living now a low-life criminal. *Welcome to your new world,* Chris would relish saying to her if given the chance.

Although the sight of terror in Catherine Reynolds's eyes was ingrained in his mind, so was the sight of Erica's mutilated body. He could never forget that. Sometimes images of the deceased would flash in his mind without warning. A memory chip embedded in his brain with instant recall. Lifeless, pallid, empty eyes. Young, old, pretty, seedy, angelic, black, white. Death chose no favorites. The victims were reminders of why he did his job despite the gore, the crummy hours, and modest pay.

Chris tuned in to the discussion when the DA announced the time of Catherine's bond hearing. Three o'clock in courtroom 205 with the honorable Judge Shumaker presiding. The Hanging Judge, as he was known affectionately among police officials.

On his way out of the meeting, Chris heard his name being called from across the large, open room divided up with cubicles. Over the top edge of one, he saw Waller's head pop up. Chris halted and waited for the detective to make his way over to him.

"Lagoni," he said with a chin tilt. "Glad it wasn't Jamie. What I mean is, I'm glad it turned out to be someone else."

"Sure you are."

"No, I mean it. You know how it is, we gotta go where the evidence takes us. Nothing personal."

"Yeah, if you say so Waller. Just a job, shitty as it is."

Waller was about to say something more when Chris held up his hand to silence him. He drew his cell phone out of his pocket and answered a call. He bit down on his lip as he listened to the panic in the voice of the caller. He brushed past Waller and scanned the area, looking for his partner.

When he spotted him, Chris yelled, "Pulaski! We gotta go. Let's roll."

"What's going on?" Waller asked.

"A situation. Nothing you need to worry about." Chris grabbed his keys. "Pulaski! C'mon, man, let's go!"

"Need me to come along?"

"No, Waller, stay here and keep the city safe."

Nick kept pace with Chris's scramble to the elevator. He slipped on his jacket as Chris punched the down button. "What's going on?" he asked.

"Didn't want to say in front of Waller. Garrett Reynolds has a gun, threatening to kill himself, maybe his dad, too. I *knew* he wasn't okay when we left him last night."

"They gave him a sedative before we left, remember? He said he was going to stay at his parents' house and go to bed."

"Well, the drug apparently wore off. According to his father, he's flipped out."

CHAPTER FORTY-FIVE

An eerie feeling came over Jamie the moment she stepped out of Bren's SUV and faced the Reynolds's home where she expected to find Garrett. With a plea of urgency, she had convinced Bren to bring her, but now that she had arrived, she stood paralyzed outside the car.

She felt Bren's stare even with her back to him. He said, "Everything all right, Jamie?"

"Yes," she said in a soft voice that revealed doubt. "You coming with me?"

"If it's okay with you, I'll wait here. It's awkward for me."

"I know." She turned to kiss his cheek. "Be back soon."

As she walked around the back of the car, she noticed a car parked in front of the garage. Unmarked police sedan, like the one she had seen Chris drive. And coming up the street, she saw two police cruisers with lights flashing but no siren. It made her fearful for what she might find inside.

The front door was slightly ajar. She walked in. No one came to greet her. In a quick walk through, she found no one on the ground floor. She followed the sound of muffled voices that came from upstairs. At the top of the stair landing, she found Chris and Gar. They stood in front of the door to Garrett's old bedroom. The door was shut. When she saw the concern in their eyes, her heart plummeted.

"Chris, where's Garrett?" she called up to him.

She knew the answer even before she asked it. Chris jerked his head toward the locked door and said, "He's in there. Jamie, you shouldn't be here. He's armed. Threatening to kill himself."

She gasped, put her hands over her chest. "Oh no! Let me in there. I can talk to him."

"No! Can't risk it."

She ran up the stairs, and although Chris blocked her from getting near the door, she stepped around him. She rattled the knob and said, "Garrett, it's me. Jamie. Let me in. Please!"

Through the door, she heard him say, "Go away, Jamie. I don't want you here. Go away!"

"Let's talk, Garrett. Just you and me."

When Chris tried to pull her away, she brushed him off. She pressed her ear against the door. There was an agonizing silence inside the room that told her there was no time to waste. Even more troublesome, rock music suddenly blasted from inside the room. The sound was turned up to full volume.

Jamie was determined to do something. Anything! She needed to get in there quick. *Stop him, stop him!* But first she had to get past Chris.

"You've got to let me in there! Bust the lock!"

Jamie watched Chris adamantly shake his head. But he weakened and withdrew a small knife from his pants pocket. In seconds, he had jimmied the lock. With caution, he turned the doorknob and peeked in. But before Jamie could see in, he closed it. He placed his hand on her arm and pulled her aside.

"You're not going in there. Too risky. Go downstairs, Jamie."

"The hell I will!"

She tried to push him out of her way, but he slapped his hands on her arms and pulled her back.

"I said you're not going in there!"

She shrugged as if in surrender, but the minute he was distracted by something Gar was saying, Jamie bolted inside the room before Chris could stop her. She kept her distance and at first, Garrett hadn't the presence of mind to notice her. Chris slipped against the wall. Jamie knew his hard look was a silent reprimand to her disobedience.

With the heavy drapes pulled, she found the room dark and uninviting. His bed was unmade and there was an empty bottle of scotch on the floor. The usual dapper Garrett was almost unrecognizable. Blood shot eyes, unshaven and barefoot, he paced the floor in baggy running shorts and a tattered T-shirt. His shoulders slouched forward and his head stayed bowed. He ran the barrel of the gun across his outer thigh.

Filled with self-doubt, Jamie swallowed hard. Her heart pounded. In an effort to diffuse the charged atmosphere, she stepped over to the dresser to turn off the music.

"Garrett, please give me the gun. Don't do this," she said with a shaky voice.

He looked up, wild eyed, bringing the gun up against his temple. "Jamie, don't you see? My life is fucked up! My mother killed Erica! Can you believe it? My own fucking mother killed the love of my life. Had her killed! My mom, my flesh and blood is the devil incarnate! Pure evil."

As he continued pacing, he dropped the gun to his side, so that it pointed downward. Jamie kept her eyes on it and knew that Chris, at the barely opened door, did too. She feared that if Garrett pointed it in her direction, Chris's training would kick in and he would shoot with lethal accuracy. Although Garrett maintained a firm grip on the weapon, Jamie was relieved that his finger was not on the trigger.

"I have nothing now!" Garrett shouted. "I lost the love of my life, and my mother, and my father. All that's left is that fucking imposter out there who I believed my whole life was my dad. Thank God, I'm not descended from that bastard! That's the good news, Jamie. The only good news."

"Garrett, if you put the gun down, we can talk it through. I know you're in pain. I feel so bad about Erica. I really mean it. She was a wonderful person."

"I killed her! If I'd stayed away from her, she'd be alive today. She didn't want to get back with me. I begged her. *Begged* her, Jamie! It might as well have been me with the knife."

"No, Garrett. You're not responsible. Maybe I am. Chris

told me the killer must have seen me leave her apartment. He thought she gave me the envelope with the family secret. But I can't, and you can't, go through life blaming this tragedy on ourselves. Erica wouldn't want that. You know that's true."

Garrett ran his hand roughly through his thick hair, making it more of a mess than before. He heard a sound outside and went to the window. He pulled back the drapes and cursed under his breath. With crazed eyes, he looked at Jamie, who was now fighting to hold back tears.

"More cops! SWAT this time. Can you believe it? Damn fucking police!"

"Please don't do this, Garrett. If you do, I will lose someone I really care about. I'm not angry with you anymore. We can go back to being good friends. You can make it through this. You're stronger than you think. You have so much to live for, you'll see. People care about you."

"No, no, no." With his head bowed, he shook it repeatedly. "No one gives a damn. I have nothing to live for. I have to do this, Jamie. You know I do."

He took a step back and again pressed the barrel against his temple. Whimpering, she begged him not to. He closed his eyes, squeezing them tightly, his entire face contorting in emotional agony. He pulled the trigger. There was a click, but no gunfire. Garrett dropped to his knees and tossed the gun aside.

Jamie rushed over and took him in her arms. She cradled his head against her chest and rocked him as he sobbed. Through the blur of her own tears, she saw Chris pick up the gun and eject the clip.

Gar kept his distance in the hallway, far removed from the drama playing out in the bedroom. With one hand on the stair railing, he turned away as though the sight of Jamie and Garrett locked in a tearful embrace repulsed him. More to himself than to the people around him, he said, "I should have known he wasn't mine. If he was my son, the gun would have fired. No screw ups."

Jamie heard the remark and noticed that Chris did, too. She watched anger spread across Chris's face like fire. He charged out to Gar and punched him hard enough to knock him backwards. Gar flung his arm out to brace himself against the railing before he took a tumble down the stairs. Dumbfounded, Gar could do nothing more than rub his jaw.

Chris glared back at him and said, "No one in their right mind would want to have you as a father, you son of a bitch!"

Nick jumped between them, restraining his partner, who looked prime to take another swing. Still fuming, Chris elbowed him away but then turned to face him. "Nick, give the all-clear signal, and get medic up here." He paused, then added, "Pulaski, be careful on your way down the stairs. You might trip like Mr. Reynolds did."

Nick gave Chris a knowing look. "Yeah, I saw that. I'll watch my step."

CHAPTER FORTY-SIX

A gray morning with threatening clouds did not dampen Jamie's spirits. Bren accompanied her to her appointment so they could see the first sonogram of their baby. The doctor said the heartbeat was strong. It was too early to tell the sex, but there was definitely a little miracle growing inside her. Hand in hand, they left the clinic feeling elated.

Afterward, Bren took Jamie to the Chinese restaurant where they had their first date. "To celebrate," he said. Jamie pointed out to him that the hostess had seated them at the same table.

"To think that one dinner date would lead to this," he said as he reached across the table to clasp her hand.

"It almost led to nothing. Remember, I walked out, but you came after me."

He smiled. "I wasn't going to let you walk out of my life that easily."

"I'm glad you didn't." After taking a sip of water, she said with a playful smile, "Thanks for last night."

"The comforting or the lovemaking?"

"Both." She smiled with fond memory.

She had awakened around two in the morning, moaning and gasping for breath. Bren turned in bed and gathered her in his arms. He whispered, "It's okay, baby. You were having a bad dream."

With her face pressed against his bare chest, she had said through tears, "It was awful. I heard the rifle blast. Then I saw that man on the ground. His head was torn open. Eyes wide open. Blood everywhere."

He had squeezed her tighter and stroked her head. "I know, baby, but it was just a dream." He put his hand under her chin and tilted her head up to face him. "I'll get you some water."

As he started to pull away, she clasped his arm. "No, don't go. Just hold me."

For a time, he did just that. Then he kissed her, and the kiss turned into much more. Their lovemaking had been tender, his touch so sensual, she stayed in a state of euphoria until sleep claimed her.

At the table, staring out the window, she wallowed in happy thoughts of the previous night. Bren loved her like no man had in a very long time. Their commitment and love made intimacy even more special. At long last, she had what she had yearned for: finding true love and becoming a mother. *Mission accomplished.*

Bren said her name and brought her back to the present time. "That guy walking in — I think that's your former co-worker. The photographer you were with the first night I met you."

She turned around to see her former boss and her co-worker making their way to their table. With a big grin, Stu brought Jamie into his arms for a tight hug. She took Zeke's hand and gave him a light peck on the cheek. Bren invited them to join them.

"Well, we don't want to intrude," Stu said, plopping down in a chair. "I've been meaning to call you, JJ. First, I was gonna tease you about how you're supposed to be covering the news, not making it. Then I thought maybe that's not a good idea. Being charged with murder is nothing to joke about. Much worse than your little trespassing and resisting arrest charge, wouldn't you say? 'Course I knew you didn't do it. It was a helluva thing, you know. If I'd called you, what would I say? Couldn't think of a damn thing that would make you feel any better. But it all worked out, I hear. You can imagine my shock when I heard Catherine Reynolds was involved. Hell, that's all the talk. Her poor son. Heard he left the country. That true?"

"Yes, Garrett is touring Europe," Jamie said. "The last time we talked, he was in Italy, staying at a cottage with a vineyard. He's learning how to harvest grapes and make wine. He said he likes it so much, he might buy a winery somewhere in the States. The business, Reynolds Industries, is being bought out."

"Good for him," Stu said. "If I were him, I'd start a new life somewhere else. But back to you, JJ. Want your job back? I'm serious. I'd hire you back in a New York minute. Got the blessing of the publisher, too. We'll report that story you were working on. Love to have you back. We were good together, you know."

"Yes, we were, Stu. But I gave my research on KleenBrite to Chris. He's passing it on to the state attorney general's office. Remember my confidential source, that guy named Steve? He's willing to testify and so is the chemist who signed off on the fraudulent reports. It's just a matter of time before KleenBrite's owner and Gar Reynolds are charged.

"But to answer your question, Stu, I'm not interested in my old job. Bren and I are moving to Virginia to be near my parents. Bren has been offered a position with an architectural firm in Arlington."

Stu tapped Bren's forearm. "Congrats. You take good care of this girl, will ya? And good going on that baby-making project I heard about." He winked at Jamie.

"You know about that?" she said, eyes widened. "I was just going to tell you."

"I got an anonymous tip about the merger of Jackson-McKeever and its expansion," he said with a grin. "Aw, hell, JJ, you know I get all my info from Zeke. He told me."

She turned to face Zeke with an incredulous stare. "And how did you know?"

"I saw Detective Lagoni at the courthouse. I asked him how you were and he told me."

Bren looked over Jamie's shoulder and laughed. "Speaking of Chris, here he comes."

"No way!" Jamie said, turning around to see. She watched as Chris threaded his way around the tables to them. When he reached them, she said, "Chris, come join the party."

He acknowledged the group with a congenial smile. "What

are we celebrating?" He kissed Jamie on the cheek and pulled over a chair.

Jamie took the sonogram from her purse to show him and the others. "We're celebrating this little miracle."

Chris studied the sonogram as if he understood what he was seeing in the pattern of black and white streaks. He handed it back to Jamie and said, "I'm happy for you, Jamie." He scratched his cheek and squinted his eyes at her. "Now that you're going to be a mommy, are you going to give up risky business?"

She bobbed her head from side to side as if contemplating. "Well, let's just say I'm taking a little break from reporting."

Chris looked at Bren. "Keep her busy having babies so she won't do any more crazy stunts and land in jail."

Bren grinned. "I will certainly do my part."

All good things must come to an end, Jamie thought as their server brought over the check, which she placed next to Stu's plate. Jamie knew Stu well enough to know his offer to treat everyone to lunch was only a polite gesture. It amused her that he got no protest from anyone, only a collective thank you. The proverbial cheapskate, as Jamie called him, ended up putting the entire tab on his credit card. Jamie laughed to herself when the server had to practically pry the Visa card from his fingers.

As the group moved outside, Jamie pulled Chris aside, out of earshot.

"Chris, I never got a chance to thank you privately," she said. "I know you put your career on the line for me. How can I ever thank you enough?"

He put his hands in his pockets and shrugged. "Don't have to thank me. I wanted to help."

"I know." She paused but then felt compelled to add, "Chris, you need more than your job. I say that as someone who cares."

He stared back. She said, "Don't give me that look. You know what I'm saying."

"Jamie, I'm seeing someone."

"Really?"

He smiled as if amused by her surprise. "Yeah, really. I met her at the shooting range. She's a crack shot. She actually hits the target and doesn't point a loaded gun at me."

"Like some other chick you know."

He laughed. "I'm not naming names. There is one thing you have in common with her. I mean, besides being pretty. She's into healthy eating. Doesn't eat red meat. Damn it. No more steak."

"Good for her. I hope she deserves you, Chris."

When his phone rang, he pulled it from his pocket and stared at the display. "That's her now," he said with a smile. "Gotta take this."

She watched him walk away with the cell phone up to his ear. Bren came up behind her and put his hands on her shoulders. She felt his lips on the back of her head.

"I guess Chris is heading back to work. Off catching more bad guys."

Jamie smiled to herself. "Not at the moment." She turned to face Bren and wrapped her arms around his waist. "Let's go home, Bren. I think I might frame the sonogram. Is that silly?"

"No, Jamie. I like the idea."

ACKNOWLEDGEMENTS

It takes more than one person to put a book together. I am fortunate to have a team of people gracious enough to help me in the process.

First of all, I want to thank my husband for his love and support. Ron is my test subject. Before anyone else sees my work, he is the first to delve into my story. He believed in me before I believed in myself, and I thank him for giving me the push to become a published author.

My editor, Christie Stratos of Proof Positive, puts the extra coat of polish on the final product. Her attention to detail and her insight to make the words come more alive is like putting makeup on a plain face. I am forever grateful for her services.

A special thanks to my book designer, Mindy Kuhn, President of Blue Butterfly Creative, who makes my book stand out with her beautiful graphic design. I am also grateful to her for her eye-catching postcards, posters, and other marketing products which she has created for me.

To my writer friends in the Mystery Critique Group who gave me solid advice on the direction of my novel. I appreciate their help in shaping the story and characters. They kept me on track and from going off the deep-end. Dennis, Reita, Geoff, Cherie, and Jim, I thank you for your counsel, encouragement, and friendship.

Lastly, I want to thank my son, David, and my daughter, Christina. Both have lent their expertise in marketing and computer skills to help out with book promotions and my website/blog. They make me proud.

Coming soon from Susan Mills Wilson

MELTDOWN

CHAPTER ONE

A low fog hugged the base of the trees like a child with its arms around its mother. As if some hardy soul might be up before dawn on a holiday weekend, Jared Bolten slunk around in the cover of darkness. Loaded down with his rucksack and rifle case, he made the trek to the church bell tower, a cakewalk compared to the hikes he'd made as a sniper specialist in Iraq and Afghanistan. He was in a different war now, dressed the part in camo, his face smeared with matching paint. He wore hiking boots and his favorite baseball cap turned backwards. His duty belt held two extra mags of ammo, a hunting knife, range finder, and a flash drive. The coil of thick rope hooked to his belt swung with each step he took.

He left his cell phone and survival kit back in his truck, awaiting his return which had to be quick. So quick, he had practiced the sprint from the tower back to the isolated wooded area. According to his stop watch, he could make the trip in five minutes flat. If anyone got in his way, he had his .45 Glock locked and loaded at his side. One shot center mass should stop them cold. Once he ran back to his truck, he'd have to gun the engine to get the hell out of there and to the main highway where he hoped to blend in with traffic. Of course, he'd have to wipe all the gunk off his face and sport a different hat, his black cowboy with the wide brim. He called it his lucky hat because he'd worn it to a bar where he'd met a hot blonde, drunk and ready for him. They did it all night long.

He had long spidery legs, and like his arms, they were all muscle. He could eat junk food, drink beer, smoke an occasional joint and still stay fit. You don't get flabby being a brick mason, working from six to six every damn day. But those days were behind him. He'd never lift another crummy brick for as long as he lived. After today, his life would never be the same. His name would be plastered on every newspaper around the country. Hell, maybe overseas. His manifesto would go viral. His message would be out, and no one—no not one fucking soul—could ignore him. They'd lap up every word he'd written, and they couldn't dispute one word of it. It was the truth, as God was his witness.

www.ingramcontent.com/pod-product-compliance
Lightning Source LLC
Chambersburg PA
CBHW061949170626
46813CB00006B/2586